SONS OF THE RAVEN

By

H A Culley

Book Eight in the Kings of Northumbria Series

Published by

Orchard House Publishing

First Kindle Edition 2018

Text copyright © 2018 H A Culley

TABLE OF CONTENTS

List of Principal Characters

VIKINGS

Ivar the Boneless – Ragnar and Queen Áslaug's eldest son; leader of the Great Heathen Army
Bjorn Ironside – Their second son; King of Sweden
Sigurd Snake-in-the-Eye – Their third son. Later King of Denmark
Halfdan Ragnarsson – The youngest son of Ragnar and Áslaug. Later King of Duibhlinn and the first Viking King of Jorvik (southern half of Northumbria)
Ubba – A Danish jarl
Guthrum – A Danish jarl; later King of East Anglia
Karl – A young Norseman captured by Drefan

NORTHUMBRIANS

Kings of Northumbria

Osberht –Deposed in 862 but still recognised as king by many
Ælle – 862 – 867. Ruled in competition to his brother Osberht
Ecgberht – 867 to 872. Appointed by the Vikings as their vassal
Ricsige – 872 to 876 (as King of the North Saxons)
Halfdan Ragnarsson – 876 to 877 (as King of Jorvik)

Ealdorman of Bebbanburg's Household

Edmund – Ealdorman 841 to 870
Burwena – His wife, daughter of a former king of Northumbria
Osgern – Their daughter. b. 849. Married King Ælle in 862
Ricsige – Their elder son. b. 852. Ealdorman from 870
Egbert – Their younger son, b. July 866
Cynefrith – Commander of Edmund's fleet of longships
Uxfrea – Cynefrith's deputy

Brictric – Captain of Edmund's warband and custos of the fortress of Bebbanburg
Drefan – Ricsige's closest companion and military tutor, later Ealdorman of Islandshire
Eadgifu – Drefan's wife
Agnes – His daughter
Edgar - His son
Hrothwulf – Drefan's elder brother and Ricsige's chaplain
Godhelm – Edmund's second cousin and the Shire-Reeve of Islandshire
Beornric – His son, later a member of Drefan's warband
Ædwulf – Son of King Ælle and Queen Osgern, Edmund's grandson
Walden – Senior warrior in Edmund's warband
Wigestan – Member of Edmund's warband and friend of Drefan
Leowine, Alcred and **Hybald** - Members of Ricsige's warband

Senior Clerics

Wulfhere – Archbishop of Eoforwīc 854 to 900
Eardulf – Bishop of Lindisfarne 854 to 899

Other Northumbrians

Ordric – Thegn of Bebbanburg
Sigmund and **Lambert** – Ordric's twin sons
Wearnoth – Thegn of Hethpool

Others

Æthelred – King of Wessex. Died 871
Burghred – King of Mercia until 874 when the Vikings forced him to abdicate
Ceolwulf - The last king of Mercia, but as a vassal of the Vikings. Died in 879
Edmund – King of East Anglia

Alfred – Æthelred's brother, later King of Wessex
Edward the Elder – His son
Ethelred – Lord of the Mercians, married to Alfred's daughter
Theobald – Former Ealdorman of Selby, later Ealdorman of Dùn Èideann
Constantín mac Cináeda – King of the Picts

Place Names

(In alphabetical order)

Many place names used in this novel may be unfamiliar to the reader. Where the Old English name is known I have used it and these are listed below, together with places in Scandinavia and on the Continent that readers may not be familiar with:

Æscesdūn – Possibly Ashdown in Berkshire or alternatively somewhere on the Ridgeway between Aldworth and the Astons. The site of the Battle of Ashdown

Alba – Scotland. At this time it usually meant the Kingdom of the Picts. The other kingdoms of Scotland being Dalriada and Strathclyde (also known as Alt Clut)

Alfheim – The coastal region of south western Sweden on the Kattegat, bounded to the north by Vestfold and to the south by Halland. It corresponds roughly to the modern Swedish province of Bohuslän

Agder – Modern Sørlandet. The southernmost region of Norway, bounded by the kingdom of Vestfold (q.v) and the Skagerrak (q.v.) to the east and the German Ocean (North Sea) to the west

Arendal – Capital of Agder (q.v.)

Arx Cynuit – The site of an important battle. Possible sites include Cannington Hill in Somerset and Countisbury Hill in Devon

Beadoriceworth – Bury St. Edmund's, Suffolk, East Anglia

Bebbanburg – Bamburgh, Northumberland, North East England

Bernicia – The modern counties of Northumberland, Durham, Tyne & Wear and Cleveland in the North East of England and Lothian, now part of Scotland

Berwic – Berwick upon Tweed, Northumberland

Bohus – Capital of Alfheim in Sweden

Caer Luel – Carlisle, Cumbria

Conganis - The old Roman fort at Chester-le-Street in County Durham

Dalriada – Much of Argyll and the Inner Hebrides. By the ninth century most of the original Scots inhabitants had been forced out by Norse settlers
Deira – Most of North Yorkshire and northern Humberside
Dol Ar - Dollar, Clackmannanshire, Scotland
Duibhlinn – Dublin, Ireland
Dùn Breatainn - Literally Fortress of the Britons. Dumbarton, Scotland
Dùn Dè – Dundee, Tayside, Scotland
Dùn Èideann - Edinburgh
Eoforwīc – York, called Jorvik by the Vikings
Frankia – The territories inhabited and ruled by the Franks, a confederation of West Germanic tribes, approximating to present day France and a large part of Germany
Frisia - A coastal region in what is today part of the Netherlands
German Ocean – North Sea
Kattegat – The sea area bounded by Jutland in the west, the Skagerrak (q.v) in the north and Sweden in the east. The Baltic Sea drains into the Kattegat through the Danish Straits
Kilrymont – St. Andrews, Fife, Scotland
Lindocolina – Lincoln, Lincolnshire
Loidis – Leeds, Yorkshire
Lothian – Region which stretched from the Forth of Forth down to the River Tweed. It was part of Northumbria until the kingdom was split into two by the Vikings, after which it was ruled from Bebbanburg (Bamburgh). It remained under English rule until Edgar, King of the English, granted it to the King of Scots in 973, provided he did him homage for it. It remained a disputed territory until 1016 or 1018 when it became a part of Scotland following the Battle of Carham
Lundenwic – London
Mercia – Roughly the present day Midlands of England
Neustria – Part of Frankia, lying between Aquitaine and Burgundy to the south and the English Channel. Roughly north-eastern France, excluding Brittany
Northumbria – The north of England and south-eastern Scotland

Orkneyjar – The Norse name for the Orkney Isles

Pictland – Originally a confederation of several kingdoms including Shetland, the Orkneys, the Outer Hebrides, Skye and the Scottish Highlands north of a line running roughly from Skye to the Firth of Forth. By this period a single kingdom, but many of the outer islands had been lost to Norse colonisation

River Twaid – The river Tweed, which flows west from Berwick through northern Northumberland and the Scottish Borders

Seletun – Selby, North Yorkshire

Skagerrak – The strait running between the southeast coast of Norway, the southwest coast of Sweden, and the Jutland peninsula of Denmark, connecting the North Sea and the Kattegat (q.v.)

Strathclyde – South West Scotland, inhabited by Britons, racially the same as the people of Cumbria and Wales

Uppsala - The main pagan centre of Sweden and the capital of the kingdom of the same name, lying on the east coast between Geatland in the south and Kvenland in the north

Vestfold – The coastal kingdom on the Kattegat lying between Agder and Alfheim

Yeavering - A late-prehistoric hillfort above the River Glen in the Cheviot Hills of Northumberland. Later the Angles added a royal hall, assembly building and huts to house the court of the kings of Bernicia. The hill on which it's built is called Yeavering Bell

Glossary

ANGLO-SAXON

Ætheling – Literally 'throne-worthy. An Anglo-Saxon prince

Birlinn – A wooden ship similar to the later Scottish galleys but smaller than a Viking longship. Usually with a single mast and square rigged sail, they could also be propelled by oars with one man to each oar

Byrnie - A long (usually sleeveless) tunic of chain mail

Ceorl - Freemen who worked the land or else provided a service or trade such as metal working, carpentry, weaving etc. They ranked between thegns and slaves and provided the fyrd in time of war

Cyning – Old English for king and the term by which they were normally addressed

Earl – A rank of noble who governed one of the great divisions of England, including East Anglia, Mercia, Northumbria, and Wessex. Originally spelt eorl in Old English

Gesith – The companions of a king, prince or noble, usually acting as his bodyguard

Hereræswa – Military commander or general. The man who commanded the army of a nation under the king

Knarr - A merchant ship where the hull was wider, deeper and shorter than that of a birlinn

Seax – A bladed weapon somewhere in size between a dagger and a sword. Mainly used for close-quarter fighting where a sword would be too long and unwieldy

Thegn – The lowest rank of noble. A man who held a certain amount of land direct from the king or from a senior nobleman, ranking between an ordinary freeman and an ealdorman

Settlement – Any grouping of residential buildings, usually around the king's or lord's hall. In 8th century England the term town or village had not yet come into use

Witan – The council of an Anglo-Saxon kingdom. Its composition varied, depending on the matters to be debated. Usually it consisted of the ealdormen, the bishops and the abbots

Villein - A peasant who ranked above a bondsman or slave but who was legally tied to his vill

Vill - A thegn's holding or similar area of land in Anglo-Saxon England which might later be described as a parish or manor

VIKING

Bóndi - Farmers and craftsmen who were free men and enjoyed rights such as the ownership of weapons and membership of the Thing. They could be tenants or landowners

Byrnie - a long (usually sleeveless) tunic of chain mail

Godi – A pagan priest

Hirdman – A member of a king's or a jarl's personal bodyguard, collectively known as the hird

Hersir – A bondi who was chosen to a leader of warriors under a king or a jarl. Typically they were wealthy landowners who could recruit enough other bóndi to serve under their command

Jarl – A Norse or Danish chieftain; in Sweden they were regional governors appointed by the king

Lagman (pl. lagmän) – Literally a lawspeaker. In Scandinavia where there were few written records, if any, a lagman was a respected individual who could recite the law from memory

Mjolnir – Thor's hammer, also the pendant worn around the neck by most pagan Vikings

Nailed God – Pagan name for Christ, also called the White Christ

Norns – The three goddesses who control the fate of all beings, including humans and gods

Thing – The governing assembly made up of the free people of the community presided over by a lagman (*q.v.*). The meeting-place of a thing was called a thingstead

Thrall – A slave. A man, woman or child in bondage to his or her owner. Thralls had no rights and could be beaten or killed with impunity

Völva – A female shaman (meaning spirit medium, magician and healer) and a prophetess

NORSE GODS AND MYTHOLOGY

Asgard - Home to the Æsir tribe of gods, ruled over by Odin and Frigg

Frey – Son of Njǫrd. God of fertility

Freyja – Daughter of Njǫrd. Goddess of love, sex and sorcery

Frigg – Odin's wife

Hel – Goddess of the underworld (Helheim *q.v.*)

Helheim - One of the nine worlds where all who die from disease, old age or other causes without having accomplished something worthy go in the afterlife. Unlike the Christian Hell, it is place of icy coldness

Loki – The mischief maker, father of Hel

Midgard – The place where men live; one of the nine worlds

The Nine Worlds – Asgard (*q.v.*), Midgard (*q.v.),* Helheim(*q.v.*), Niflheim, Muspelheim, Jotunheim, Vanaheim, Ljosalfheim and Svartalfheim. The nine worlds are inhabited by different types of being (gods, mankind, giants, the dead etc)

Njǫrd – God of the sea and of wind, fire and prosperity

Norns – The three female beings who control the fates of men

Odin – The All-Father. Chief of the gods. Associated with war, wisdom and poetry

Ragnarök – A great battle sometime in the future when the gods Odin, Thor, Týr, Freyr and Loki will die. This will lead to various natural disasters and the subsequent submersion of the world by water. Afterwards, the world will be reborn

Rán – Goddess of the sea

Thor – Odin's son, god of thunder, armed with Mjolnir, a magic hammer. An emblem depicting the Mjolnir was worn around the neck by most Vikings, which they touched for luck

Tyr – Lord of battle

Valhalla – An enormous hall located in Asgard *(q.v.)*, ruled over by the god Odin. Chosen by Odin, half of those who die in combat travel to Valhalla upon death, led by valkyries *(q.v)*. Those not chosen go to the goddess Freyja's meadow, Fólkvangr

Valkyries – The choosers of the slain. They decide who dies in battle and who lives and then choose whether the dead go to Valhalla or Fólkvangr

LONGSHIPS

In order of size:

Knarr – Also called karve or karvi. The smallest type of longship. It had 6 to 16 benches and, like their English equivalents, they were mainly used for fishing and trading, but they were occasionally commissioned for military use. They were broader in the beam and had a deeper draught than other longships·

Snekkja – (Plural snekkjur). Typically the smallest longship used in warfare and was classified as a ship with at least 20 rowing benches. A typical snekkja might have a length of 17 m, a width of 2.5 m and a draught of only 0.5 m. Norse snekkjas, designed for deep fjords and Atlantic weather, typically had more draught than the Danish type, which were intended for shallow water

Drekar - (Dragon ship). Larger warships consisting of more than 30 rowing benches. Typically they could carry a crew of some 70–80 men and measured around 30 m in length. These ships were more properly called skeids; the term drekar referred to the carvings of menacing beasts, such as dragons and snakes, mounted on the prow of the ship during a sea battle or when raiding. Strictly speaking Drekar is the plural form, the singular being dreki or dreka, but these words don't appear to be accepted usage in English

Chapter One – Internal Strife and External Threat

865

As the rain hammered down outside I sat playing nine men's morris with Ricsige in his father's hall. Often the place reeked of smoke from the two fire pits down the centre aisle, but today the raging wind created a strong enough updraft to draw practically all the smoke out through the hole in the roof.

We sat near one of the hearths, not so much for the warmth it provided, but for the light. Normally the hall was illuminated by windows let into the stone walls. They were unglazed but covered in skins scraped down to a thin membrane to allow in a modicum of light whilst keeping out the wind and rain. However, such was the ferocity of the storm today that that the wooden shutters had been closed and bolted.

'I hope father's alright, out in this weather,' my opponent muttered.

I was glad that I was inside and not out riding, soaked to the skin and buffeted by the gale, but I had more sense than to say so.

Ricsige's father was Edmund, Ealdorman of Islandshire in the northern part of Northumbria. The hall where we sat was one of the few stone buildings in his fortress of Bebbanburg, which sat on the top of the sheer sided block of basalt rock on the shore of the German Ocean.

When the door to the hall banged open we looked up to see Lord Edmund enter and we both sighed in relief. Edmund threw his sopping wet cloak to a slave, who took it over to dry by the other fire. Edmund was normally a man with an equable disposition, but it was obvious that he was in a rage over something today, and it was unlikely to be the foul weather.

He was considered to be fair and honest, attributes not shared by all his fellow ealdormen. That didn't stop him from being a talented military commander and it was his tactics that had defeated Ragnar Lodbrok and his Viking horde just three years previously.

'Ricsige, come into my chamber. There's something I need to discuss with you and your mother. You can come too, Drefan,' he added, nodding towards me. 'I know that Ricsige will tell you everything anyway.'

It was true. Although there was five years between us, we were as close as brothers; in fact much closer than I was to my own brother, Hrothwulf.

I had played my own small part in the defeat of Ragnar. From my vantage point, perched high in an oak tree, I had spotted two of the Viking leaders below me. I had drawn my bow and killed one, who turned out to be the legendary shield maiden Lagertha, and then put an arrow in Ragnar's thigh. Afterwards King Ælle had thrown Ragnar into a pit of snakes.

I was lauded for killing Lagertha and wounding King Ragnar and, as a reward Lord Edmund had made me his son's companion and military tutor. It was a great honour, of course, but my brother had been jealous, not unnaturally I suppose as he was the elder, and it had driven us apart.

He had become bitter, not just because of my good fortune. He'd been bitten by a viper on the day of the battle and, although a quick thinking monk had saved his life, his left leg had withered and this prevented him from becoming a warrior. Instead he'd become a monk in the monastery on the Isle of Lindisfarne just across the sea from Bebbanburg.

Although Lindisfarne was called an island it was only cut off at high tide. When the sea receded it became a peninsula joined to the mainland by an expanse of sand.

I'd been fifteen at the time of the battle and Ricsige had been ten, so my appointment had been in name only. I had to finish my own training as a warrior first and, in any case, Ricsige was sent away to Lindisfarne to join the novices for two years to study the scriptures and complete his education. During that time he'd made friends with Hrothwulf, who was a fellow novice, and he'd tried to reconcile the two of us – to no avail.

Ricsige had returned a year ago and, apart from training with sword and shield and teaching him how to fight on horseback, I'd also begun to show him how to hunt with a bow.

My father had been one of Edmund's best scouts before he died last year and he'd passed his skills onto Hrothwulf and me when we were boys; now I did the same for Ricsige. He was an avid pupil and he had evidently inherited his father's intelligence.

I followed Edmund and his son into the screened-off family chamber at the end of the hall and waited by the door, slightly embarrassed as Burwena, Edmund's wife, hugged and kissed him, thankful for his safe return. He'd been on a visit to Alric, the Ealdorman of Berwic, who governed the shire to the north of the River Twaid, and had obviously come back agitated about something. He gently disentangled himself from Burwena's embrace, impatient to divulge what he'd found out.

'That bloody man, Ælle,' Edmund began, pacing up and down. 'I forgave his conceit when he claimed to have been the victor against Ragnar Lodbrok, when we all know he didn't turn up until the battle was over. I even accepted the way he chose to execute him; after all our enemy was a Viking and a pagan, but now he's gone too far.'

'What's he done?' Ricsige asked, his eyes wide. He'd never seen his father so angry, nor had I.

'Alric told me that Ælle captured Loidis from Osberht three weeks ago. His brother escaped, so Ælle took his revenge out on the wretched inhabitants. He hanged the ealdorman and his whole family for supporting Osbehrt, and then he did the same to one in ten of the population, men women and children, to teach them a lesson. Well, the only thing they will have learnt is what a monster he is. Quite apart from being an atrocity that was totally unwarranted, they were Northumbrians and we need every man we have to fight the Vikings.'

'The Vikings,' his wife asked puzzled. 'Surely they will stay well clear of Northumbria after Ragnar's disastrous raid?'

Edmund snorted in derision.

'You'll remember that I told you his last words were "*the squealing of the piglets will deafen you when they hear of the death of the old boar?*" Well, it seems that those same piglets are raising a vast army to come and avenge their father.'

Burwena sat down on the bed that she and Edmund shared looking stunned. What complicated matters was the fact that their daughter, Osgern, had married King Ælle three years ago, two months after the battle with the Vikings outside Jarrow. No doubt the king thought that it was shrewd move to tie the most powerful ealdorman in the north to his side and, of course, Osgern had been dazzled by the thought of becoming a queen.

Not so, Edmund; he was ambivalent about the match and had only agreed because to do otherwise would have put him firmly in Osbehrt's camp. As the Witan had deposed Osberht and put the crown on his brother's head, he would have risked falling out of favour once more. The last time that happened he'd been exiled to the Continent; he wasn't about to risk that again.

When his daughter had given birth to a son – Ædwulf - a year later, Edmund had warmed towards their union, but the atrocity at Loidis had tuned him against Ælle once more. However, the Viking menace made it imperative that he did what he could to unite the kingdom before it was too late.

'What will you do?' Burwena asked, gnawing at her lip in worry at the thought of an invasion by a pagan horde.

'My duty is to patrol the coast, not that I could do much with my few ships if the rumour about the size of the army that Ragnar's sons are recruiting are true; but the massacre of the unarmed inhabitants of Loidis will worsen the divisions within the kingdom and that leaves us very vulnerable. I shall just have to pray that they don't arrive until I've had a chance to see Ælle and convince him that the course he's embarked upon will just make him more enemies. I'll leave for Eoforwīc in the morning.'

'Can I come, father?' Ricsige asked hopefully.

'No, son. If anything happens to me you will succeed me and you must hold Bebbanburg against our enemies. I need you here. Do you understand?'

'Yes father,' he said dejectedly.

'You don't want to interrupt your training with me, do you,' I said in an attempt to cheer him up.

I realised how trite and pathetic it sounded as soon as I'd said it, and the scornful look that the boy gave me confirmed that I'd been stupid.

'Don't patronise me. I'm not a little child anymore.'

So saying, he got up and stalked out of the room.

'I was going to take you with me as a member of my gesith,' Edmund told me, 'but I can see now that would just be rubbing salt into my son's wounds.'

I nodded and went back into the hall intending to apologise to Ricsige, but he wasn't there. The board on which we'd been playing nine men's morris had been knocked onto the floor, so presumably he'd kicked it on his way out. I went to follow him, but then reconsidered. It was probably wise to let him cool down for a while.

I was worried about him though. The storm raging outside sounded as if it was getting worse and the gusts were probably strong enough to knock over a slightly built thirteen-year-old.

In the end my concern for his safety forced me to go and look for him. He was nowhere to be found at first and I began to panic. By the time I'd thought of looking in the church I was soaked to the skin and exhausted from the buffeting of the wind. He was kneeling in front of the altar praying. Having confirmed that he was safe, I went back to the hall and changed into dry clothes, putting my wet tunic and trousers alongside Edmund's cloak to dry.

-ᚹ-

Ricsige wasn't one to bear a grudge for long. He avoided me for the rest of that day, but came to find me the next morning, grinning and as cheerful as ever. If I'd offended him yesterday, he'd evidently forgotten it.

'The storm's passed, can we go riding?'

'Very well, but this afternoon we return to training with sword and shield. You've much to learn before you'll stop being a danger to yourself and others in the shield wall.'

'I know. It takes years of training; or so you keep telling me,' he said with a cheeky grin. 'But it's such a splendid morning I want to feel White Ghost under me and the wind in my hair.'

White Ghost was the name he'd given to the beautiful little grey mare that his father had given him when he'd returned from Lindisfarne. I had a feeling that the real reason he wanted to be away from Bebbanburg that morning had little to do with riding. He didn't want to be around when his father left for Eoforwīc. I realised then how badly he'd wanted to go with him.

Ricsige was an adventurous boy who desired to see more of the world, other than Bebbanburg, Lindisfarne and the very occasional journey south to Alnwic with his parents. The hall at Alnwic was where the shire-reeve, a distant cousin called Godhelm, lived with his family.

'Very well; where do you want to go this morning?' I asked him as two stable lads brought our horses up to the hall.

Evidently my pupil had already sent for them. I had no doubt that the boys were cursing us as they'd have been busy enough getting thirty riding horses and half a dozen packhorses ready for Edmund's journey down to Eoforwīc. I thanked them and we mounted and headed for the main gate.

'I've never been to Yeavering,' Ricsige replied, catching me by surprise.

I pulled my horse to a halt and looked at him in consternation.

'But that's over twenty miles away, and through the hills. It's too far and too dangerous. There's wolves, not to mention the odd outlaw. No, we'll stick to the coast: north or south?'

I saw that Ricsige had a mischievous glint in his eye and I groaned. I knew that look. It meant that he'd made up his mind. I was his tutor and theoretically that put me in charge, and he accepted that most of the time. On the odd occasion, however, he put his foot down and I knew from past experience that it was better to let him do what he wanted.

'Very well, but on two conditions. We take two of the warband with us and we take some food. It will take all day to get there and back and I don't intend to go hungry.'

'Good idea. We'll take Wigestan and Botulf.'

I nodded, they were two of my friends and more dependable in a crisis than most, not that I anticipated any trouble, but I would rather have them with me than anyone else I knew.

'I'll go and let them know.' I said, turning my horse around and heading back into the fortress. 'Tell the stable boys we need two more good mounts. I'll also tell Walden where we're going.'

Walden would be in charge of the garrison whilst Britric, the captain of Edmund's warband, was away with his lord.

The stable boys had been less than pleased when Ricsige commandeered two of the horses they'd already saddled for members of Edmund's gesith, but they would never dare to gainsay the lord's son. With a muttered curse two of them went to get another two horses ready for the warriors in the gesith. They had little to complain about really. There were two adult grooms and six boys to look after the seventy horses used by the Bebbanburg warband. It wasn't an easy existence, but there were plenty whose lot in life was far worse.

Walden looked dubious when I told him.

'You'll be lucky to get there and back before dark so don't hang about, either on the journey or when you get there. Does the lady know?'

He was referring to Burwena. I shook my head.

'Better she doesn't, she'll only worry,' I told him. 'She's overprotective of him. The boy's more likely to die in battle than in his bed these days. He'd thirteen now; if he's going to survive he's got to learn to be a man.'

Walden looked far from happy but he agreed to say nothing unless she asked. Then he'd just say that we were out riding. I hoped he didn't get into trouble; I knew I would. Ricsige wouldn't be able to contain his excitement when he returned and would tell his mother all about it. With a sigh I re-mounted my horse and the four of us rode out of the main gates just as those accompanying their lord were collecting their horses, ready to depart as soon as Edmund was ready.

We turned to the west as soon as we were out of sight and a little later joined the track that ran from Bebbanburg to Yeavering. The latter had been the summer residence of the kings of Bernicia but it had been little used since Diera and the former kingdom of Rheged joined with Bernicia to become Northumbria several centuries before.

Bebbanburg had been the winter residence in those days but, when the capital moved to Eoforwīc, Ricsige's distant ancestor, Catinus, had become the lord of Bebbanburg. Initially it had remained a royal residence but it had been ages since any king of Northumbria had spent more than a night or two there. There was a king's hall in the fortress, kept for his use, but it had stood empty for a long time now and was beginning to fall into disrepair. Edmund had even talked of tearing it down and using the building materials elsewhere.

It was a pleasant day in late summer as the four young men rode through the hills to Yeavering. They saw little sign of habitation except for the odd flock of sheep up on the hillsides with a boy or an old man and their dogs looking after them. They caught a glimpse of a few deer but they were too far away to hunt. There was a gentle breeze and a few birds flew overheard. I felt contentment stealing over me.

Suddenly we heard the flapping of wings and a strange hooting noise as a bevy of swans flew over the crest of a distant hill and continued on their flight to the north, presumably heading for the River Twaid.

Ricsige was happier than I had ever seen him, but it didn't last. When I calculated that we must be about halfway to our destination we emerged from one valley into another with a river running along it. Judging by the position of the sun, we were still heading in the right direction but I had no idea what the river was called.

As we watered the horses and grabbed a bite of bread and cheese a man came riding towards us along the river. He was dressed in a red woollen tunic, blue trousers and a brown cloak edged in wolf fur. Although he had a sword strapped to his waist, he wore no armour. However, the five men trotting behind him wore leather jerkins and helmets. Each carried a spear and shield with both a sword and a seax strapped to their waists. Evidently the man was a noble of some sort and the men were his gesith.

'Who are you and what are you doing on my land?' the man barked at us, looking down from his horse.

The men with him had taken up an aggressive stance and I held up my hand placatingly. However, Ricsige spoke before I had a chance to.

'Your land? This is my father's land. It is you who should explain what you're doing here.'

'The man, who had to be fifty years old if he was a day, looked down at the boy who had spoken so disrespectfully to him and his face reddened in anger.

'Why you cheeky little shit,' the man bellowed and his warriors lowered their spears, looking for all the world as if there was nothing they would rather do than use them on us.

Wigestan and Botulf went to draw their swords but I gestured for them to desist.

'Wait,' I commanded. 'This is the ealdorman's son, Ricsige. I don't recognise you but I assume that you're the local thegn.'

'You assume correctly. Lord Edmund might be the ealdorman but he doesn't own this land, I do. You need to teach this little runt some manners. If he were my son I'd soon beat the arrogance out of him and I'll tell Edmund so the next time I see him.'

'I'd like to see you try,' the boy said, bristling with indignation.

'Enough, Ricsige! You are just making matters worse.'

I don't think that I had ever raised my voice to the boy before and he wisely bit back whatever retort had come to his lips.

'I'm sorry, my name is Drefan. I'm a member of Lord Edmund's gesith and, for my sins, Ricsige's tutor.'

'Waernoth,' the thegn grunted at me. 'If you're the boy's tutor you're not doing a very good job of it.'

'Military tutor. It's not my job to teach him manners.'

'Perhaps it should be,' he replied grimly before turning back to Ricsige.

'I hope that your father lives to a ripe old age, boy. At the moment I'm not sure you deserve my loyalty, and an ealdorman, however high his opinion of himself, has no power or right to govern without his thegns and his people behind him.'

We watched him go on his way and then Ricsige pulled me to one side, out of earshot of the other two.

'He's right isn't he? I handled that badly. I should have ignored his boorishness and repaid his discourtesy towards me with smooth words.'

'For God's sake, Ricsige, you sound like my brother, but you're right. You'll need his support and that of others like him when the time comes. That is why your father is such a good leader of men. They can't help but like him and respect him. He is slow to anger and quick to forgive. He is rarely as irate as we saw him yesterday, or – if he is – he hides it well.'

He nodded.

'Will those two spread the word of what happened here when we return?'

'Not if you ask them nicely not to.'

He smiled ruefully and went to have a word with our two companions. As we rode onwards I reflected that, if we had achieved nothing else that day, Ricsige had learned a valuable lesson.'

Yeavering was something of a disappointment when we got there. It was evident that the side of the large hill towering above the river had once been home to a significant settlement. On the summit there was an old hillfort and on the slope below there were the remains of a grand hall and what might have been an assembly building; one large enough to have accommodated hundreds of people. Around them stood scores of huts. However, most of them were rotting away and only a few looked as if they were still occupied. In reality the summer palace of the kings of Bernicia was now little more than a large farmstead.

The inhabitants told us that the thegn, Waernoth, used to live there, but he had built himself a new hall a few miles away at Hethpool well over a decade ago.

-ᚹ-

I was right. I did get into trouble with the Lady Burwena when we got back, but that was soon forgotten when we heard the news that Edmund brought back with him.

'The Vikings have landed, but in East Anglia, not here,' he told us. 'Reports vary, but it is said that there are sixty or seventy ships of various types. If that's true, then there must be over three thousand of them.'

'Why East Anglia?' I wondered.

Edmund gave me a sharp glance. It wasn't really my place to speak when he was meeting with his senior warriors but he'd included Ricsige in the meeting and I'd gone with him.

'It's late in the season and the weather out at sea has been stormy recently so perhaps they got blown off course?' Britric suggested.

'It's more likely that they intend to over-winter there and then invade Northumbria in the spring,' Edmund replied.

'If so, they've given us a chance to prepare,' Godhelm commented.

Edmund had stopped at Alnwic on his return journey and Godhelm had accompanied him the rest of the way. As shire reeve it would be his task to muster the fyrd.

'I'm not sure that time will help us much,' Cynefrith said thoughtfully. 'Northumbria might be able to muster five thousand men, given time, but three and a half thousand of them will be members of the fyrd; they'll be no match for the Vikings. In any case, if we march south to meet them we'll leave our northern and western borders exposed.'

Everyone looked glum and nodded, acknowledging the truth of what the old warrior had just said. Strathclyde had taken advantage of the civil war between Ælle and his brother to invade Cumbria again and raids by the Picts into Lothian had increased recently as well. It was hardly surprising. The struggle between Ælle and his brother Osbehrt had left the kingdom weak, and consequently vulnerable.

'Well, we don't know that the Viking army is heading for Northumbria,' Edmund said. 'They may be intending to move into Mercia and Wessex. As Britric said, they have arrived late in the raiding season so it seems probable that they intend to stay and over-winter in East Anglia. We'll have to wait and see where they intend to make for in the spring.'

Winter came early that year. The first blizzard blew in during the third week of November, and although the weather was warmer in early December, the snow and ice came back before Christmas and stayed until late February.

Life continued at Bebbanburg but the roads were impassable and no one was foolish enough to venture out to sea, except for a few fishermen who tried their luck close inshore. The reeve was getting worried about our diminishing food stocks as the weeks merged into months.

Thankfully the store huts in the fortress had been full of grain, dried meat and smoked fish before the snows came and made hunting impossible. We were also able to buy milk, eggs and root vegetables from the inhabitants of the settlement which surrounded the stronghold; but their own supplies were getting low as the winter wore on.

The cold made everyone miserable and many elderly people died that winter. A boy had to be lowered down the well shaft each morning to break the ice so we could draw up buckets of water. However, it wasn't long before someone realised that it was easier to collect virgin snow and melt it over a fire.

Stocks of firewood ran low in late January and so a party was sent out to cut down trees in a nearby wood. Ricsige was chaffing at his enforced confinement within the fortress and asked his father if he could accompany the wood gatherers. Reluctantly Edmund agreed, despite Burwena's protests that it was too dangerous.

Much to everyone's surprise Edmund's wife had recently discovered that she was pregnant again, fourteen years after giving birth to Ricsige. Edmund was very considerate of her health and welfare, but he was equally determined that her mollycoddling of their son had to stop.

'He's fourteen now; in two short years he'll be old enough to be a warrior. It's time he was allowed to take a few risks,' he told her in a tone that brooked no argument.

However, he did take me aside before we left and told me he'd have my hide if any harm came to the boy.

The snow was piled high against the main gate and slaves with shovels had to clear a path before we could even get out of the place. The snow lay all around us, hiding any landmarks. Even the trees and shrubs were difficult to make out under their white blanket. There was a well-trodden track leading down to the settlement and this was normally kept reasonably clear, but the snow over the past few days had obliterated it again.

In places the snow was only a foot deep, but in others it came up to your waist so it took most of the morning for us to reach the settlement. Here at least the inhabitants had cleared the snow away from the main thoroughfare, leaving it in heaps taller than a man.

The closest wood lay half a mile beyond the settlement. Thankfully the thegn of the local vill, confusingly also called Bebbanburg - a man called Ordric - sent fifty men to help us and we reached the trees less than two hours later.

Both Ricsige and I had taken our turn at snow clearance. I found my arms ached after a while and ten minutes later my biceps felt as if they were on fire. I glanced across at Ricsige and saw the sweat dripping off his forehead and the tip of his nose, despite the intense cold. If he could keep going, then I was damned if I was going to give up! My admiration for him increased immeasurably that afternoon. Thankfully, a few minutes later Walden, the man in charge of the wood collectors, called a halt so that the snow shovellers could change over.

It was dark by the time we'd finished chopping the felled trees into logs and filling the four wagons that we'd brought with us, but the sky was clear and the moonlit snow made it easy to follow the track we'd previously cleared back to the stronghold. The only difficulty we encountered was the final slope up to the gates and the incline beyond them. The passage of horses, feet and wagons had packed the snow underfoot into a sheet of ice. The horses pulling the wagons kept slipping as they tried to haul their load uphill, and men on foot pushing them had the same problem.

Surprisingly it was Ricsige who came up with the solution. The roadway beyond the outer gates ran between two walls and ended at a raised portcullis. This could be lowered if the stronghold was attacked, turning the area between it and the gates into a killing zone. The portcullis was raised and lowered by means of two windlasses, one on either side. Ricsige suggested we used ropes attached to these windlasses to pull the wagons to the top of the slope.

Edmund was impressed with the boy's ingenuity, and he was even more proud of his son when I told him how hard he'd worked clearing the snow. Ricsige had never stood so high in Edmund's estimation until that day. It was a pity that he had a competitor for his father's affections five months later when his brother Egbert was born. Edmund doted on the baby, but by then we all had other things to occupy our minds.

Chapter Two – The Fall of Eoforwīc

November 866

'I cannot believe that King Edmund was so stupid as to let the Vikings spend the winter in East Anglia without a fight,' Edmund said, pacing up and down in front of his thegns.

'Not only that, lord, but your namesake has also supplied them with hundreds of horses; some say as many as a thousand.'

The messenger who had brought the news to Bebbanburg had also brought a summons from King Ælle to muster the Islandshire fyrd and to bring it, together with Edmund's considerable warband, south to defend Eoforwīc.

'What else do we know about these Vikings?' he asked the messenger.

The man began to recite what he knew, a speech he'd already made many times to various ealdormen as he rode north.

'The horde is being called the Great Heathen Army and is thought to number about three thousand. They appear to be led by three of Ragnar's sons: Ivar the Boneless, Sigurd Snake-in-the-Eye and Halfdan Ragnarsson, but there are various other chieftains with them. The ones we know about are Jarl Guthrum, a Dane and Ubba, another Dane, but he also appears to have hundreds of Frisians in his warband. The king believes that Ivar is the leader and he seems to have gathered pagans from all over Norway, Sweden and Denmark as well as Frisia.'

'Do we know where their ships are?'

'No but, as they spent the winter at Gipeswic, it may well be that they have left their ships there.'

'Gipeswic?'

Yes, it's a port in the estuary of the River Orwell, which runs into the German Ocean in the south east of the kingdom, or so I understand.'

'Um. Now what would I do if I were Ivar?' Edmund said thoughtfully, almost to himself. 'I wouldn't abandon my ships, that much is certain. If I left sufficient men to guard them it would weaken my forces. No, I would probably send a mounted force north to draw the Northumbrian army towards them, and then invade from the sea. Eoforwīc was captured before when it was lightly defended - by Ragnar as it happens. Perhaps Ivar is trying to copy his father's ploy?'

It took nearly a week for the fyrds of Lothian to muster at Berwic on the Twaid and then join the Islandshire fyrd at Alnwic. By that time Ricsige and I were at sea. Edmund wanted most of the warriors who manned Cynefrith's longships with his army on land, but he sent Uxfrea and the three largest skeids to patrol the coast between Gipeswic and the Humber estuary, which led eventually to Eoforwīc. His task wasn't to fight the Vikings at sea – that would have been suicidal – but to find out if Edmund's theory was correct.

Uxfrea reasoned that, if the Viking fleet was indeed heading north, it would stay close to unfamiliar coastline and camp ashore each night. He therefore stayed just out of sight of land and sent one skeid at a time further in, towards the coast. The crew of this longship had to row so that their sail wouldn't be seen at a distance. It was tiring work so the ships changed over every couple of hours.

The enemy were bound to be under sail as the wind was from the east, and so the boy up the mast of our inshore ship would be able to see them at a distance – perhaps four miles or so. It would be a very eagle-eyed Viking boy who could spot a hull and a bare mast at that distance.

Our own longship was hull down over the horizon when the ship that was inshore appeared on a converging course, the rowers pulling as hard as they could. It was obvious to all that they had seen something.

'The Viking fleet?' Uxfrea asked as soon as the other longship was withing hailing distance.

'Yes, perhaps fifty craft in all, though I didn't stop to count them,' the captain of the other ship bellowed back.

'It would seem that Lord Edmund was right,' Uxfrea muttered as he gave the order to turn about and hoist our sails.

I took my place at an oar and we pulled for all we were worth. Although we were also propelled by a stiff breeze which filled the sail from the east and would have propelled us along at perhaps six miles an hour on its own, we needed to reach the mouth of the River Humber before the Viking fleet did.

My back felt as if it was on fire and my arms felt as if they would drop off at any minute by the time we saw the wide mouth of the Humber estuary to the north-west of us. By this time Uxfrea had risked taking us closer inshore but there was no sign yet of the leading enemy longship.

As we turned into the estuary with the wind on our quarter Uxfrea gave the order to cease rowing. We pulled our oars back inboard before collapsing, doubled up where we sat on our sea chests, sucking in great lungfuls of air to recover. Just as we passed Ravensrodd, the settlement on Spurn Head, the boy acting as lookout called down that the first of the Viking ships had just appeared behind us. We had only just beaten them to it.

Spurn Head was a three mile long spit of sand and shingle that jutted out from the south-easternmost point of Northumbria and Ravensrodd lay on the west side of it, sheltered from the ravages of wind and tide. We didn't have much of a lead over the enemy, but nevertheless Uxfrea ordered the ship's boys to lower the sail briefly and then raise it again.

To do the latter we had to come to a halt or the boys wouldn't have been able to get the sail fully up. They raised it braced round so that it was parallel to the wind direction and then hauled on the sheets at the bottom corners of the sail until it filled and we continued on our way once more. It had allowed the Viking ships to gain over half a mile on us, but it was the signal that the men ashore had been waiting for.

As we got underway again I saw three horsemen ride out of the settlement heading for Eoforwīc.

31

After we'd entered the Humber we headed for the junction with the Ouse and followed this towards Eoforwīc. When we reached the bend in the river at Seletun we met up with the rest of Edmund's fleet under Cynefrith's command. The ealdorman wasn't there himself, having been commanded to join King Ælle's army. The king had taken some persuading to allow Edmund to use the fleet to defend the city from an attack along the Ouse and had only reluctantly agreed to its deployment.

Ælle had taken Edmund and the rest of his army to challenge the Vikings who were reported to be advancing on Eoforwīc overland. In the event the five hundred mounted Vikings fled as soon as they encountered Ælle's scouts and the king, believing that they would lead him to the main body of the Great Heathen Army, gave chase.

I was told what happened next by Edmund much later. The mounted Vikings had launched a series of lightning strikes on the fyrd as they plodded along on foot and on the vulnerable baggage train at the rear of the Northumbrian army. Being mounted on fleet horses provided by the East Anglians, the Viking horsemen fled before they could be engaged properly. In the end Ælle gave up the chase and decided to return to Eoforwīc. By then it was too late.

Uxfrea's three longships quickly joined the rest of the Northumbrian fleet near the settlement of Seletun to form a solid barrier across the Ouse, a tactic that had worked so well against Ragnar during his advance along the Seine towards Paris a decade earlier. We had only just managed to drop a stone anchor fore and aft and lash ourselves to the ships either side of us when the first of the drekar appeared around the bend.

I waited for the Viking fleet to come within range from my vantage point at the masthead of Uxfrea's longship, taking deep breaths to calm my breathing so that my aim wouldn't be spoilt. The sail and yardarm from which it hung had been stowed but a makeshift seat had been made for me from a short length of timber and this had been attached to the sail halyard in place of the yardarm.

Ricsige was similarly seated at the top of the mast on his father's ship. His excitement at the prospect of using a bow in battle was palpable, even from the next door ship. I just prayed that my training had been good enough for him to kill the enemy and not our own men!

At first confusion reigned amongst the Vikings when they saw our makeshift boom and we even had the pleasure of seeing a few ships crash into the ones in front of them before the fleet managed to come to a halt. Instead of trying to force their way through the barricade across the river, the Vikings slowly back paddled and disappeared back whence they had come. It was obvious that this unexpected tactic had puzzled Cynefrith, as it has the rest of us, and he decided to consult Uxfrea and the ships' captains.

The banks near Seletun were marshy; indeed the place was only accessible via a causeway from the north. Like many settlements in the vast area of marshland south of Eoforwīc, it was built on dry land which emerged from the peatbog in places. There was little pasture and less arable land and the inhabitants lived on the fish and eels they caught from flat bottomed boats and coracles. They traded their surplus catch for whatever else they needed.

The settlements were connected by a network of trackways known only to the locals and so Cynefrith had discounted the possibility of the Vikings being able to find their way from Seletun to Eoforwīc. Unfortunately he'd underestimated our foes.

I was sent with two other scouts to find out where the Vikings had gone and we found their fleet fairly quickly. They were four miles downstream at another settlement called Barmby in the Marsh. Barmby was built on a section of dry land adjoining the river where half a dozen longships could be beached at a time. The Vikings were busy disembarking warriors and, as each ship emptied, the ship's boys towed it out into the middle of the river using commandeered fishing boats to anchor it.

I could see a pile of bodies from halfway up the tree I'd climbed to get a better view, presumably the local inhabitants. There were a few captives, but to my surprise, these included men as well as the usual young women and children. Suddenly I realised what they wanted the men for – to guide them through the marsh.

'Right, thank you Drefan,' Cynefrith said when I'd finished briefing him. Now this is what we're going to do.'

I waited impatiently hidden in the rushes growing in the dark brown water beside the track leading north from the river. At first my feet sank slowly into the mushy peat below me, but it was only a few inches deep at that point with a gravel bottom. Although it was sticky stuff to move through, I wasn't going to disappear into the bog. However, our guide from Seletun warned us not to move forwards from that point or we would be in trouble.

The trackway we were watching was sixty yards away from us and, although there were several ways the Vikings could take to get through the marshland, the guide had said that this was the quickest and most direct route.

It was a strange experience standing there. The mud kept my feet warm but my legs were chilled to the bone by the water. Just when I had come to the conclusion that we were on a fool's errand, we heard noises coming along the track. The Vikings had no reason to expect trouble and were chatting and laughing as they followed the men from Barmby.

Cynefrith had sent eighty of us, all archers, in four separate groups to ambush the Vikings. We were spread out along the track with three on one side and one on the other. The group I was with was the most northerly and it fell to us to time the attack correctly. The other groups would wait until they heard the signal from us – three blasts on a horn.

We waited with baited breath as the Barmby guides were prodded along the winding path through the bog by the Vikings' spears. It was difficult to be patient and not attack the vanguard but we needed to do the maximum amount of damage to the enemy and so we let the first hundred or so walk past our position. Then Uxfrea nodded to the youth with the horn and the clear notes rang out as we released our first shafts.

I had taken careful aim at a giant of a man in a byrnie so well scoured with sand that it shone in the bright spring sunshine, making him look like one of his own gods. My arrow sped towards him as he came to a halt, alarmed by the sudden cacophonous noise. I had counted on him being stationary and so hadn't aimed off. The barbed point struck him in the middle of his chest as he turned towards the sound of the horn.

The gleaming chain links parted and the arrow didn't finally lose its momentum until it had driven through byrnie, leather shirt, woollen tunic and skin. It smashed into his breastbone, driving splinters into his heart and killing him. But I wasn't watching. I had sent a second arrow at another Viking and a third was on its way before the blond haired giant fell to the ground.

Our group of twenty had killed or badly wounded perhaps fifty of the enemy before they recovered and, with a roar of rage, they splashed through the water towards us. It was their undoing. A considerable number had left the causeway before those behind them realised their mistake. The area between where we stood in the reeds and the pathway appeared to be shallow water but underneath the surface the soft peat was deeper than a man's height. The Vikings struggled but slowly they disappeared below the surface. Some were lucky enough to be able to regain firm ground but most were lost.

I don't know how many went to their deaths in the bog but it must have been a hundred or more. Meanwhile we continued to pepper the remainder until they had the sense to run north along the track and out of range.

Later we found out that the other three groups had similar success, though none could claim that they had killed as many as we had. Our estimate that upwards of three hundred Vikings had been sent to their deaths probably wasn't far out but, although it was a success, it was only a tenth of their number. Perhaps five hundred more had either escaped towards the north or had retreated back towards their ships, but that left some fifteen hundred or more unaccounted for.

It was tempting to sail down to Barmby and attack the moored Viking fleet but Cynefrith was more worried about Eoforwīc; so we rowed along the Ouse towards the old Roman city. His intention had been to reinforce the garrison but we were too late. We encountered the bodies of the slain as they floated down the Ouse with the current before we came around the final bend. All our efforts had been in vain. The raven banner of the sons of Ragnar now flew from the top of the tower beside the river gate. Evidently the Vikings had split up and had taken several paths through the marsh. The city had fallen and, as I was to discover later, now had a new name – Yorvik.

Chapter Three – Blood Eagle

March 867

We sailed back along the Ouse determined to wreak vengeance on the Viking fleet at anchor off Barmby, but the longships had gone. That puzzled us for some time as we were certain that only the ships' boys and a small guard had been left aboard.

When I thought about it later I realised that Ivar and his brothers must have realised how vulnerable their fleet was to our fully manned ships. They had therefore sent them to a safer place. With the current behind them they had evidently drifted down to the tidal part of the river, using just a few oars to keep them from running into the bank, and had then waited for the ebb tide to take them out to sea. Once there they could hoist the sails and make their way along the coast until they found a sheltered bay.

Perhaps we could have found them had we tried, but Cynefrith was anxious to get back to our harbour and await further orders from Lord Edmund. We waited there, fretting because of the lack of news, for a week before Edmund and his exhausted warband joined us.

'It was a fiasco,' he told us that evening. 'Ælle was played for a fool. He was led further and further away from Eoforwīc by a few hundred mounted Vikings without ever being able to come to grips with them. Then they disappeared. We were never going to be able to catch them with an army that was mainly on foot.'

'What happens now, lord?' Cynefrith asked.

'It's nearly winter so we have all been sent home with orders to muster again next March. Meanwhile the king has sent messengers to Osbehrt asking for a meeting,' Edmund said with a grimace. 'The brothers' fight over the throne has weakened Northumbria; let's hope that they can now unite. It's our only hope of defeating the heathens.'

-ᚹ-

I sat on my horse beside Ricsige as we looked across the open ground to the north of Eoforwīc. My charge, who was now nearly sixteen, had pleaded with his father that he be allowed to accompany him and Edmund had reluctantly agreed. However, he insisted that his son stayed close to his side and where he went, I went.

Most of the original Roman walls enclosing the city had survived, but in places they had been repaired in stone. Much of this repair work was new, having been done after it had fallen to the Vikings led by Ragnar Lodbrok a few years previously. Now we could see that there were fresh breaches, some of which had been repaired using timber. However, there was one section which gaped like a rotten tooth. The assumption was that these breaches had been caused during the capture of the city last November. They had certainly been made by the Vikings, but not, as it turned out, during the city's capture.

'Our information is that Eoforwīc was captured by the pagans using scaling ladders, Cyning,' Edmund told Ælle. 'Why then would they have broached the walls? I think something about this stinks.'

'Nonsense, Edmund,' Osbehrt cut in before his brother could reply. 'Your informants must have got it wrong. If the damage to the walls wasn't there when Ælle abandoned Eoforwīc to its fate, they must have been made during the heathens' assault.'

Ælle glared at Osbehrt, furious that his brother had openly blamed him for the loss of the capital. Edmund could see another row developing and cut in firmly before any more friction was caused.

'That's in the past, my lords,' he said quickly. 'What's important now is re-capturing the city and destroying the heathen army before it can do any more damage.'

'You're right, of course, Edmund,' Ælle said with a smile of thanks.

Osbehrt grunted but said nothing further.

'I still suspect a trap. I think that breach in the walls is too good to be true.'

'Rubbish,' Osbehrt replied. 'If I didn't know better I would think you were faint-hearted, Edmund. We need to enter the city before they have a chance to barricade that gap in their defences. Once we are inside the walls, our superior numbers will soon overcome them.'

Perhaps anxious not to have another argument, Ælle sided with Osbehrt and they drew up plans for an attack through the breach at dawn the following day.

On the twenty first of March 867 the sun rose, shrouded by grey clouds, and the Northumbrian army, some five thousand strong, advanced towards the gap in the city's defences. Osbehrt led the first wave with his brother's army close behind. Edmund was left to bring up the rear with his warband and that of another ealdorman called Ecgberht.

My mood matched the dark grey of the sky. For some reason I didn't trust Ecgberht. I thought him shifty and unusually nervous. Oh, we all felt fearful before a battle; it was natural. However, the signals being given off by the other ealdorman felt odd somehow. His warband was much smaller than ours, of course. In addition to the four hundred warriors who crewed the fleet, Edmund had another thirty mounted warriors and three hundred in his fyrd. Ecgberht's warband was very much smaller – no more than twenty five warriors – but he also had a further six hundred in his fyrd.

He was the Ealdorman of Luncæstershire on the west coast. Although his shire hadn't suffered the depredations of the Britons from Strathclyde, as Cumbria had, he had been forced to grant land to Norse settlers over the past fifty years or so. Consequently many of his fyrd were Norse and, although they wore the cross around their neck, identifying them as Christians, rather than the mjölnir – Thor's hammer – that the pagan Vikings wore, I didn't trust them.

Most of the attacking Northumbrians knew Eoforwīc well enough to find their way around and quite a few knew it well. The army had been divided into sections and each section had been told to take a different route to reach the king's hall to the southwest and the monastery in the north east. That way the two leaders hoped that they would sweep up the defenders en route.

It should not have been too difficult as we had superior numbers, but the third wave led by Edmund and Ecgberht hadn't even reached the walls before men came running back through the breach yelling that it was a trap.

To our amazement Vikings appeared from nowhere and formed a shield wall three deep across the gap in the defences to prevent any more Northumbrians escaping. We didn't have time to react to this unexpected development before Ecgberht's men turned on us and began to cut us down. We had a slight numerical advantage but it soon became apparent that the so-called Luncæstershire fyrd were actually experienced Norse warriors.

I recovered from my astonishment quickly and kicked my horse forward to come between a spearman and Ricsige, who was sitting on his stationary horse looking bemused. I bent down so that I could interpose my shield between the Norseman and my charge and then brought my sword down on the man's unprotected head. Blood spurted out as my blade cut into his scalp, turning his blond hair red.

I grabbed the reins of Ricsige's horse and, kicking my heels into the sides of my stallion, I turned intending to take the lad out of harm's way. However, Ricsige had other ideas.

'We must save father,' he yelled, desperately trying to wrest control of his horse from me.

I glanced across to where Edmund, surrounded by some of his gesith, was trying to fend off two score of the Norse fyrd, many of whom were armed with battle-axes. I nodded at Ricsige and then called to a dozen or so of our mounted warband who were milling about in confusion.

'With me,' I shouted, 'save Lord Edmund.'

It was only when we had formed a wedge and were galloping towards the heart of the fight that I realised that Ricsige was riding at my right shoulder. It was too late to do anything about it and seconds later we crashed into the Norse fyrd, scattering them and cutting down those we could reach. I felt my sword arm jar as it met something solid, but I had no idea what I'd struck, perhaps a shield or a helmet?

My hand went numb and I had trouble keeping a grip on my sword, but I didn't have time to worry about it as I saw a spear point heading for my face on the other side. I frantically raised my shield to deflect it and then I was past and found myself beside Lord Edmund.

'We must get out of here,' I yelled at him and saw him nod.

We both urged our horses forward against the press of fighting men and then I saw Ricsige struggling against a Norseman who had his arms around his waist and was trying to pull him from his horse. Edmund reached his son first and stabbed Ricsige's assailant through the neck. He fell away and the three of us formed an arrowhead to force our way out of the melee.

'Disengage and head north,' Edmund called repeatedly to his men as he rode past.

As we finally broke free of the struggling mass, I glanced over my shoulder. I gave thanks to God that quite a few of our men – both on foot and on horseback – had managed to follow us. We continued to head north and finally stopped at a settlement called Earswic, some three miles north of the city.

I looked back the way we had come and was relieved to see that Ecgberht's Norsemen were too busy looting the dead to be bothered about us. It was only then that I noticed that the side of Edmund's horse was covered in dark red blood. The ealdorman had been wounded in the side and his eyes rolled white in their sockets as he tumbled sideways to the ground.

-ᚹ-

There was nothing we could do to save him and Edmund died in his sleep that night, probably from loss of blood more than anything else. Ricsige was beside himself with grief, blaming himself for his father's death.

'Ricsige,' I said, grabbing him by the shoulders. 'It's not your fault. It's that turncoat bastard Ecgberht whose treachery cost us the ealdorman's life, along with over two hundred of our men. He's the one to blame.'

'I should have done more to save him. If you hadn't tried to drag me away...' he began.

'I was doing what your father ordered and you very well know it. At least you are able to carry on his line. It's what he would have wanted.'

The boy tore himself away from my grasp and stomped off.

'Don't follow me. I want to be by myself,' he called over his shoulder.

I looked nervously around me. It was an hour after dawn and we were still only three miles from the battlefield. We needed to get moving and, after a moment's indecision, I went after him.

'Look, I know that you mourn your father. I loved him too, but the time for grieving will have to wait. You are now the ealdorman and the lives of over three hundred men depend on you. We need to get out of here, and quickly.'

He looked at me with malice in his eyes, then the malevolence faded and he nodded dumbly.

'You're right, of course. You always bloody well are; it's what makes you insufferable.'

At first I was offended, then I noticed a hint of mischief in his expression.

'You can't do without me and you damn well know it, now move yourself, my lord. Let's get out of here.'

His face softened into a brief smile before he looked mournful again, but I was pleased to note a hint of steel behind the sad eyes.

Shortly afterwards we started on the road north again, our ranks swelled by the inhabitants of Earswic who had no intention of awaiting the arrival of the victorious Vikings. One of the carts contained Edmund's body and, as it jolted along the rutted track, his servant packed herbs around the body and sewed it into the leather tent that I had brought with me, tied to my saddle. Ricsige was determined to bury his father on Lindisfarne but we all knew that, whatever precautions we took, the body would start to rot and stink long before we got there.

We headed north-west across country to Ripon where we camped for the night outside the monastery. The monks gave us food, though they had little of it themselves after the winter, and treated our wounded. They also took poor Edmund's body, washed it and put it into a coffin lined in lead. They offered to bury him but Ricsige wouldn't hear of it. The sub-prior gave me my tent back but I shook my head and he laughed at the look of horror on my face.

'Would you like me to burn it?'

'Yes please. I would rather sleep in the open.'

'Oh, I think we can find you a bed, though we are rather full with the new ealdorman and his senior warriors.'

It was only then that I realised that no longer did I hold the privileged position of Ricsige's tutor. He was now my lord and, as Cynefrith, Uxfrea and Walden had all survived the battle, I was now little more than an ordinary member of his warband – unless, of course, he invited me to join his gesith. The elderly Britric had remained at Bebbanburg to command the small garrison left there and the shire-reeve, Godhelm, had died outside the walls of Eoforwīc, along with my friend, Botulf. Thankfully Wigestan had survived, but he was seriously wounded and would have to be left behind in the infirmary. I felt very alone at that moment.

The next day we continued our journey north, trudging along Dere Street, the cobbled road the Romans had built from Eoforwīc to the wall built by the Emperor Hadrian's legionaries. We made good progress in fine weather and just north of the wall we turned off Dere Street onto another Roman road popularly known as the Devil's Causeway, although the origins of the name were unknown.

Half an hour later grey clouds scudded in from the west and an hour later it began to rain, lightly at first but then heavily and it did so with brief periods of respite until we reached the junction with the muddy track that led to Bebbanburg. Ricsige had been morose for most of the journey and that, coupled with the miserable weather, the destruction of our army and the death of Ealdorman Edmund had caused the morale of the men to sink to rock bottom.

It was getting dark by the time we reached the turn-off and so we camped for the night there, even though we were only five miles from home. I was beginning to regret having asked the sub-prior to burn my tent and I settled down for another miserable night wrapped in my sodden cloak.

Shortly after I'd dropped off I felt my shoulder being shaken.

'Piss off and let me get some sleep. I'm not on sentry duty tonight,' I mumbled without opening my eyes.

'Now, is that anyway to talk to your lord,' I heard Ricsige's voice say with a little laugh.

'Oh, I'm sorry, lord. I didn't know it was you.'

'Obviously. I'm sorry to wake you but I need to talk; and don't call me lord. You above all people have earned the right to call me by my name.'

The rain had stopped and the clouds parted now and then to allow the full moon to illuminate the wood. We walked out of the encampment for a little way and Ricsige sat on a fallen tree, patting the space beside him, and I accepted his invitation.

'I'm sorry I have been pre-occupied. My father's death and the responsibility that placed upon my shoulders over-whelmed me for a while.'

'I understand but, if I may speak plainly, men follow a leader because they want to, for one reason or another. Ever since we began this journey home you haven't displayed many leadership qualities. With no king to confirm your appointment as Ealdorman of Islandshire your position is precarious.'

'I know that's why I need your advice.'

'Why me? I'm just a common warrior; you've got Cynefrith and the others to advise you now.'

I knew that I sounded bitter but I couldn't help it. I'd been so close to Ricsige and now it was as if we were strangers.

'Don't. Self-pity doesn't suit you,' he said with a trace of anger in his voice.

Then he sighed.

'Look, I know I've ignored you but I needed to sort things out in my mind. I've reached certain conclusions but I need someone I trust completely to discuss them with.'

'I'm sorry. You're quite right. I did feel as if you'd discarded me and I'm very glad you haven't. You know I'll help in any way I can.'

'Good. First, as you pointed out, I need to establish my position. I think we can assume that Deira, at least, is lost to us.'

'And the two shires on the west coast. Ecgberht is obviously the Vikings' catspaw and so Luncæstershire is lost to us; and I think we can assume that Cumbria is too. It was partly occupied by the Vikings or the Strathclyde Britons before, now they'll take over all of it. There's nothing we can do to stop them,' I said glumly.

'As you say, most of the ealdormen were with Ælle and Osbehrt inside the city so I doubt if any of them survived. I think we can assume that all of southern Northumbria is now lost to us, but the Vikings may not come north of the River Tees. Perhaps we can keep them out of the old Kingdom of Bernicia? However, someone will need to install new ealdormen and unite them against the foe.'

'You think that should be me?'

'Who else is there? Granted, you are very young but there have been kings younger than you.'

'King? King of Bernicia? No, I think not. Those who seize a crown tend to live short lives. If I'm to keep this part of Northumbria from falling into Viking hands I need to be their leader, I accept that, but I don't want people vying for a throne.'

'Perhaps we should just call you Lord of the North?'

'Perhaps, but that can wait. We need to create a new hierarchy in Bernicia first. Without a structured system of government we are lost anyway. Don't forget the Picts in the north. They are as much a danger to us as the bloody Vikings, and we need to know what Ivar and his brothers intend to do now that they have defeated their father's killer.'

'Sounds simple enough.'

Ricsige looked at me as if I was deranged, but when he saw me grinning at him in the moonlight, he laughed and we went to find our respective beds.

-ᛈ-

We didn't hear what had happened after we fled from Eoforwīc until over a month later. Bishop Eardulf arrived one day with my brother in tow to tell Ricsige what he had recently learned. How he heard, isolated as he was on Lindisfarne, was a mystery. Ricsige asked him, of course, but he wouldn't say. He was adamant that his information was accurate, however.

Apparently Archbishop Wulfhere had remained in Eoforwīc and had been instrumental in making peace with Ivar the Boneless and his pagan army. He had crowned the faithless Ecgberht as King of Yorvik, the name that the Vikings had given to both Eoforwīc and the surrounding region.

'How the archbishop could treat with the heathens is beyond me,' Eardulf said sadly, 'especially after the barbaric way that they treated poor King Ælle.'

Eardulf had never been one of the former king's supporters but he liked Osbehrt, who he privately maintained had committed regicide, even less. His obvious distress at Ælle's death therefore came as a bit of a surprise.

'What happened to Ælle?' Ricsige asked impatiently.

He was more interested in what the Vikings were up to now, but the bishop had piqued his curiosity. Eardulf shifted uncomfortably on the bench on which he sat and looked at my brother for help.

Hrothwulf nodded and cleared his throat. He had nodded at me when he'd arrived, and I'd nodded back, but this was the first time he'd spoken.

'It seems that Ivar and his heathen brothers administered what they call the blood eagle as punishment for throwing their father into a pit of vipers.'

'Blood eagle?' Ricsige asked curiously, 'what's that?'

46

Hrothwulf's shoulders sagged and he drew a deep breath before he continued.

'I can only repeat what the bishop was told, whether it's true or not I don't know but, if it is, it's a most barbaric way of executing someone. Ælle was placed face down on the floor of the king's hall with his legs and arms outstretched and pegged to the ground. Then one of the bloody swine used an axe to sever the king's ribs from his spine. They pulled his lungs through the openings that they had carved in his back in imitation of a pair of wings. He was pulled to his feet and hung like that from a tree until he died in great agony.'

We were all silent for a long time after Hrothwulf's graphic account. I had been appalled and at first I didn't believe that anyone could be so barbarous. However, the detail of his death wasn't something that anyone was likely to make up. I shuddered at the image my brother's tale had created in my mind's eye and, try as I might, I couldn't get rid of it. I might imagine myself to be a hard-bitten warrior but the story of Ælle's torture and death gave me nightmares for days.

Chapter Four – The Rescue Mission

Summer 867

After a long silence Ricsige asked where the Vikings were now.

'I understand that they have headed south west into Mercia and have captured Nottingham,' Eardulf replied. 'King Burghred has signed a treaty with Æthelred of Wessex and the two kings, together with Æthelred's brother, Alfred, Earl of Kent, have assembled a great army and are besieging Nottingham.'

Ricsige breathed a sigh of relief. If they were bottled up in Nottingham they couldn't be planning an attack on Bernicia; not yet at any rate.

'Earl of Kent?' I queried. 'I thought that Alfred had been made sub-regulus.'

Wessex had gradually expanded over the past century, taking over the Kingdom of the South Saxons as well at the Jutish Kingdom of Kent.

'Centuries ago the rulers of regions under a king were called eorls; it comes from the old word for a hero – eorle. They became too powerful and gradually the regions were divided into smaller shires under ealdormen. Now Æthelred has reintroduced the title, although changed a little, rather than call his brother King of Kent. Perhaps he fears him and wanted to give him a lesser title. Certainly Alfred is much cleverer than his elder brother by all accounts.'

'Yes, yes, who cares what he's called,' Ricsige interrupted impatiently. 'I'm more interested in the situation in what the Vikings are now calling Jorvik.'

'I gather that Ecgberht rules with the help of his warband- a mixture of Saxons and Norsemen – and some of the Great Heathen Army that Ivar has settled in the area.'

'So they are now the thegns?'

Eardulf shook his head.

'I don't think so. They call them bondis, whether they are landowners or tenant farmers. Strangely though, most of the Anglo-Saxon villeins have been allowed to continue as before. Only the ceorls have been dispossessed.'

'Have they been forced to renounce Christ?'

'No, not from what I have heard. Strangely enough the pagans seem content to allow them to continue as Christians, and even hold services in the churches. Provided they pay their taxes, they don't seem to care.'

'And Ecgberht collects the taxes for the Vikings?'

'Yes, I suspect that the Vikings don't want continual unrest in the lands they conquer and are prepared to compromise provided they get what they want – money and land.'

Ricsige nodded. He had a few more questions but it became evident that the bishop had told him all that he knew.

When Eardulf got up to leave I was surprised that Hrothwulf made no attempt to go with him. Ricsige's next remark took me completely by surprise and I was furious that he had not seen fit to inform me beforehand.

'Oh, and thank you for agreeing to Brother Hrothwulf becoming my chaplain.'

'Father Hrothwulf, now that he has been ordained as a priest,' the bishop corrected him with a smile.

I was upset that Ricsige hadn't bothered to tell me that he was thinking of appointing my brother as his chaplain, let alone that he hadn't discussed it with me. The previous chaplain had died in February and so I knew that one would be appointed sooner or later to look after the spiritual welfare of the garrison, as well as acting as the ealdorman's adviser, but I hadn't for a moment thought that it would Hrothwulf.

We hadn't seen each other since he'd left to become a novice at Lindisfarne Monastery five years ago. Then he'd still been recovering from the snake bite he'd received on the day of Ragnar

Lodbrok's execution and he'd rebuffed me when I'd tried to say goodbye.

Perhaps naturally, he'd been jealous of my sudden fame for killing Lagertha the Shield Maiden and wounding Ragnar from my perch high up in an oak tree, but that was only partly the cause of the rift between us. Whilst he became lame and was forced to become a monk instead of the warrior he wanted to be, I was made Ricsige's military tutor. That just rubbed salt into an already open wound.

I was aware that he and Ricsige had become close friends when the latter attended the monastery as part of his education, so perhaps the choice of him as chaplain was only natural, however insensitive I thought it.

Ricsige's inner council consisted of Britric, the captain of his warband, Cynefrith, the commander of his fleet of longships, Uxfrea, Cynefrith's deputy, and Walden who commanded the garrison at Bebbenburg. I assumed that Hrothwulf would join the council as the previous chaplain had been an adviser to Lord Edmund, but I was surprised to be invited to join them as well.

The ealdorman's hall was too busy a place for a private meeting with servants and slaves going to and fro and the reeve using it to conduct business. Lord Edmund's council had met in the chapel, but Ricsige decided to use the old king's hall, despite the fact that it was half derelict. Thankfully it was a fine day and so the holes in the roof thatching didn't matter too much. The place reeked of neglect though. It wasn't just the damp thatch lying rotting in places, it smelt as if the putrid corpses of several animals were hidden somewhere in the building.

'If you're going to use this building again, my son, you had better get it cleaned and repaired,' were Burwena's first words as she came in and sat down.

If anyone was surprised to see her they were too polite to say so.

'I've asked my mother to join us because the first thing we need to discuss is the rescue of my sister Osgern and my nephew, Ædwulf,' Ricsige explained.

My interest was immediately piqued. Osgern was Ælle's widow and no-one seemed to know what had happened to her and their four-year-old son.

'A messenger arrived today in a fishing boat,' Burwena began. 'He came looking for me because no one was sure what had happened to my husband and elder son after the Battle at Eoforwīc. I'm pleased to say that both my daughter and grandson are safe, at least for the moment. They are in the monastery at Barwic.'

'But that's in Elmet, about eight miles to the north east of Loidis. The people there have no love for Ælle, or his family,' Cynefrith exclaimed.

'Quite,' Burwena said with a nod. 'They are in double jeopardy there, both from the local people and from any bands of marauding Vikings. They hate the killer of Ragnar and anyone associated with him. If caught, the best they could hope for would be to be sold into slavery.'

'We need to rescue them as soon as possible,' Ricsige said, turning to look directly at me. 'Do you think you can manage it, Drefan? Who would you want to take with you?'

The second question rather precluded a negative answer to the first. I thought quickly. I would need enough men to ensure our safety from the inevitable small bands of lawless men who would be roaming the countryside, but not too many or we would attract unwanted attention to ourselves. Normally I would have chosen Wigestan and Botulf but one was still recovering from his wounds at Ripon and the other was dead.

'Leowine, Alcred and Hybald,' I replied.

They were young, as I was, but they were probably the best fighters amongst my contemporaries. I didn't want older men, doughty warriors though they might be. If I was to be in charge I didn't need someone challenging my orders because he thought he knew better.

'I would also like to take Sigurd and Lambert with me, if their father will agree.'

'Ordric's twins? Why? They are what? Twelve, thirteen? What use would they be? They haven't even started warrior training yet.'

'They have actually. They're thirteen and they started training a week ago, not that I want them for their fighting ability.'

'They were little terrors when they were on Lindisfarne last year,' Hrothwulf added, with an apologetic look in my direction.

I realised that my brother wasn't deliberately trying to thwart me; he was just making a valid point.

'Yes, I know they're young but, as you know, lord, they've been hunting with us and they are good at tracking, at climbing trees swiftly and they are promising bowmen, given their age and build. Boys can make useful scouts and can find out information because they don't attract the attention that grown men do.'

'Well, if you think they'll be useful,' Ricsige said doubtfully. 'But you'll have to ask their father. After his wife's death they are all the family he has left.'

Berwena got up to leave and I walked outside with her.

'Good luck, Drefan. I have a feeling that, if anyone can pull this rescue off, you can. It goes without saying that it'll will earn you the external gratitude of both me and my son.'

Ordric was less of a problem than I had imagined. He didn't want to let them go but he knew that his sons were growing up and would be training to be warriors in a few months anyway. The boys were, of course, excited to have been chosen to accompany us. I always had difficulty in telling them apart. They were identical twins, slim and wiry with a mop of unruly brown hair, the only difference between them was in the choice of clothes. Sigmund was the more flamboyant one and favoured red trousers with yellow ribbons tied around his legs below the knee and a blue tunic, whilst Lambert dressed in browns and greens.

'Sigmund, the success of our mission depends on not attracting notice to ourselves. There will be times when you need to hide up trees to observe. Gaudy clothes are the last thing you need,' I told him after I'd finished briefing them.

'Oh, yes. I see that. I'll borrow something drab and boring off Lambert then,' he said with a cheeky grin at his brother. 'Provided he washes them first, of course.'

'Huh, I'm only lending them to you because Drefan wants me to. You can wash them yourself, and give them back clean as well.'

Anyone who didn't know the two brothers would think that they were always fighting but the truth was that they got on well together and their combative talk was just friendly banter. It made me morose when I saw how close they were; Hrothwulf and I used to have that kind of relationship when we were their age. I wanted to make peace with him, but I wasn't sure that my brother was of the same mind.

At least he joined the others in seeing us off the next morning. The sky overhead was grey and a chilly wind swept in off the sea, but at least it wasn't raining as the six us rode out through the main gates. We were dressed as warriors but our helmets and shields were being carried on the two pack horses with our tent, provisions and spears.

The two boys led the pack horses mounted on sturdy ponies whilst we three warriors rode our best horses. I noted thankfully that Sigmund had taken heed of what I had said and was wearing black trousers, a grey tunic and a green cloak. At least I could still tell him from Lambert as he was dressed all in brown. Of course, neither boy was armed, except for a dagger hanging from a belt and the hunting bow and quiver on their backs.

Leowine, Alcred, Hybald and I wore our mail byrnies under our cloaks and had a bow and quiver to hand. We also had swords and seaxes belted to our waists. The day was uneventful and I was thankful that, although the sky remained threatening, the rain held off.

We stayed the night in the shire reeve's hall at Alnwic. Of course, Godhelm had been killed the previous year but his wife and children still lived in the hall. Ricsige hadn't done anything yet about appointing a new shire reeve to help him rule Islandshire but he had said during a meeting of the council that he'd prefer the new shire reeve to live at Bebbanburg. It would make liaison between the two of them easier but Islandshire had once been two shires and the advantage of having the shire reeve located at Alnwic was that the southern half of the shire didn't get neglected.

Godhelm had two boys aged fifteen and ten and a girl of eight. Ricsige might have considered making the elder boy, Beornric, shire reeve had he not been so young and untested. As the ealdorman was not quite sixteen himself, he needed someone more experienced to assist him. If the new shire reeve was to be based at Bebbanburg, Godhelm's family might be able to stay on at Alnwic, although it didn't turn out that way.

I was reticent about the purpose of our journey, but the presence of two boys younger than him had excited Beornric's curiosity and he begged to be allowed to accompany us. I was placed in a difficult position. I could hardly say that he was too young as the twins were two years his junior. On the other hand, I had a use for them and I didn't have for a boy still under training as a warrior.

'Lambert and Sigmund are skilled hunters and trackers; they are also acting as our servants, Beornric. To be candid, I don't have a role for you,' I told him as gently as I could.

'Are they as good with a bow as I am?'

I looked at the boy. He was tall and broad shouldered. Although he evidently didn't need to shave as yet, he looked big for his age.

'Very well,' I said. 'At dawn tomorrow we'll hold a little competition. If you can beat the twins you can come with us.'

His mother looked as if she might protest but in the end she didn't demur. What I didn't know at the time was that she had agreed to marry Wearnoth's son, the new Thegn of Hethpool. Beornric didn't like him and had said that he wouldn't go with her and his siblings, so the idea that he accompany me was one solution to her problem. However, I was confident that the twins would win and so never for a moment thought that he would end up joining me.

Loath as I was to delay our departure, our route lay along the old Roman road to the ford across the River Tyne at Coria. Even if we left a little later than planned we should still be able to get well south of the river before dark.

As the sky lightened in the east we gathered outside in a light drizzle. I had a feeling this would be an uncomfortable day and we had no nice dry hall to look forward to tonight either.

As they had been taught, the twins kept their bowstrings dry in a waxed leather pouch until they needed them. I was pleased to see that Beornric did the same. Alcred set up the target, a log about three feet high with a face crudely painted at the top, sixty yards from a line I had drawn in the muddy earth with the point of my sword.

A fully grown archer could hit a man at one hundred paces, or most could. It was too far for the arrow to retain enough power to penetrate chain mail at that range, of course, or even a stout leather jerkin, and these boy didn't have the muscle to use a full sized bow. However, all I was interested in today was accuracy.

Sigmund went first and put his arrow where the man's neck would have been. He gave a whoop of joy, then unstrung his bow, wiped the string dry with a piece of wool and stowed it in his pouch. Lambert went next and took careful aim before releasing the arrow as he breathed out. It struck a few inches above his brother's arrow, right in the middle of the painted mouth. He tried to hide his delight but he couldn't resist punching Sigmund lightly on the shoulder.

Beornric stepped up to the line, but then walked ten paces back from it. I groaned inwardly; it looked as if the lad was a braggart – just the sort I didn't want with me. He carefully strung his bow, which was longer than the twins' bows, and wet the feathers of the arrow he'd selected between his lips. We waited with bated breath as he drew the bowstring back to his ear and let fly. It flew true and lodged in the right eye of the painted target.

I turned to congratulate him but he'd drawn a second arrow from his quiver and had taken aim again. This time the arrow hit the target just below its left eye. The boy swore softly. Evidently he'd been hoping to put the second one in the middle of the other eye.

'Why did you shoot from seventy paces when the competition was to use the sixty yard line?' I asked him, 'and why send two arrows into the target when I asked you to just use one.'

'Sigmund and Lambert are over two years younger than me and I didn't think it would be fair to use the same mark. I shot the second arrow because I was curious to know if I could repeat my first hit; I couldn't which just proves that luck was on my side,' he grinned at me.

'Hmm,' I grunted back at him. 'If you're to come with me you do what I say and when I say, no more no less. That little display looked to me as if you were showing off. I think that you had better stay here.'

The boy's face crumpled and I could see him trying desperately hard to hide his disappointment.

'It wasn't his fault, Drefan,' a treble voice piped up. 'Lambert and I bet him a silver penny that he couldn't do what he's just done. I'm sorry.'

'Then perhaps I should leave the three of you here?' I said sternly.

He and Lambert looked at each other in consternation and I left them wondering if I meant what I said.

'However, you are normally good lads, even if your archery isn't as good as Beornric's.' I added with a smile. 'Get saddled up. We've no time to break our fast here, we'll eat bread and cheese as we ride.'

'What about me, lord?' Beornric asked eagerly.

I sighed. I suppose the boy wasn't really a little show off; he just couldn't resist a dare; and there was no question that he wasn't a good archer. He was shifting from one leg to the other whilst I debated with myself.

'Provided you're prepared to do what the twins do, that is look after us, clean our mail and hunt for our supper, you're welcome to join us,' I said, smiling at the look of delight that lit up his face.

'And I'm no lord, my name is Drefan, use it,' I called after him as he scampered away to collect his horse and his gear.

I wasn't sure I'd made the right decision, after all I knew practically nothing about the lad. As I went to mount my horse I told myself that there was no point in brooding; the decision had been made.

-\/-

Thankfully the drizzle petered out by midday and we had more or less dried out by the time we splashed across the Tyne. We camped that night near the ruins of the old Roman auxiliary fort at Vindomora. The one thing I hadn't thought about was the capacity of our one and only tent. It could just about house four men, which was fine before Beornric joined us as one of the men would always be awake on sentry duty whilst the others slept. The boys might not take up as much room as a grown man, but there certainly wasn't room for five.

My solution was to make the three boys watch over the horses in turn whilst the sentry hid in the trees, watching over the camp. I thought the twins might blame Beornric for having to do their share of sentry duty, but they seemed to accept it with good grace. In fact Beornric fitted in and got on so well with the twins that I changed my mind. I was now pleased that he had joined us.

I was even more glad the third night out. We had followed the Roman road south, passing the remains of four more Roman outposts, and halting half an hour before nightfall at the junction of the road south and the one that came in from the north-west, that is to say from Caer Luel.

The hall of the Ealdorman of Catteric, near the site of the old Roman cavalry camp at Cateractonium, lay a few miles south of us and I had no idea who currently ruled there. We were only sixty miles from Eoforwīc, now called Jorvik. Although the heathens had claimed it and the rest of Deira as theirs, no one had any idea how far their writ ran. Catteric had been included in Bernicia until the union of that kingdom with Deira in the seventh century, but it was close to the old border. Perhaps the man who ruled there now owed allegiance to the traitor Ecgberht?

Puzzling over these questions I went to sleep, squashed between the side of the tent and the bulk of Hybald. If not exactly fat, he was certainly stouter than the rest of us and there always seemed more room in the tent when it was his turn on watch. It was my turn next and, as Leowine and Beornric returned to the tent, Sigmund and I took their places.

We had camped in a hollow about four hundred yards from the Roman road near a small stream. Sigmund went to stand in the shadows about ten yards from where the horses were tethered to a line that ran between two trees. I climbed out of the hollow and found a position behind a shrub from where I could see the whole camp.

The fire had died to a few glowing embers but the crescent shaped moon illuminated the hollow with a pale silvery glow, except for the period when it was hidden behind the odd cloud. It was during one of these dark periods when I sensed, rather than saw, movement down near the horse line. I had placed three arrows in front of me when I'd taken up my position and I now silently strung my bow.

When the moon reappeared I looked for where I knew Sigmund had been but somehow I knew he wasn't there anymore. It wasn't just that I couldn't see him - after all he'd been pretty well concealed - it was a sixth sense. Either he'd moved or someone had killed him.

Then I saw a man crawl towards the tree to which one end of the horse line was secured. A second man was reaching up to untie the other end. If they succeeded in releasing both ends they could run off with all our horses.

I nocked an arrow to my bowstring and took careful aim at the kneeling man untying the end nearest to me but, just as I was about to release my arrow, another one struck his neck and he collapsed onto the ground with a gurgle. I swiftly changed my aim to the second man as he stood up, startled by the sudden death of his companion. I had aimed at his head but, as he'd moved at the last moment, my shaft took him in the side of his chest and he spun around with a yelp before hitting the ground with a thump.

I was about to run down and finish him off when I saw the point of an arrow speeding towards my head. I didn't have time to duck but it flew past my ear and a split second later I heard a thwack as it sunk itself into the chest of a man who was about to decapitate me with an axe. In my concentration on killing the man by the horses, I had missed the third man creeping up behind me.

I looked towards the tent and Beornric gave me a wave, holding his bow high. I thanked my lucky stars that he needed to defecate before he went to sleep. He always took his precious bow and quiver with him wherever he went and it was pure chance that he looked my way at just the right time.

'It was a lucky shot, though,' he told me later. 'The light was poor and I didn't have the time to take proper aim. I could just as easily have put my arrow through your neck as the attacker's.'

I couldn't make my mind up whether he spoke in jest or not. If he had, he had kept a straight face, but I had an uneasy suspicion he was kidding me in return for my reluctance to take him with us. One thing was certain – if I'd left him behind I'd be dead now.

To judge by their clothes, the horse thieves weren't Vikings. It was more likely that they were fugitives from a Saxon settlement that had been pillaged by the Vikings. I did wonder if there were more of them and, having dragged the three bodies into the woods, we set three sentries – two men and a boy – for the rest of the night.

The next morning we awoke to find our camp shrouded in mist. Although it was August there was no wind and I thought it was probably low cloud, rather than the fog typical of a November morning. Whatever the cause, it enabled us to sneak past Catteric without been seen. As the morning progressed the sun slowly penetrated the mist and it cleared to become a hot, sunny day.

The Roman roads had deteriorated over the centuries without any maintenance but their broken, cobbled surface was still a much faster way of travelling than the rutted, muddy tracks that served as roads otherwise. It wasn't surprising, therefore, that they were used where possible, even if it meant that the distance covered was greater than the direct route.

However, we had encountered no one more dangerous than a group of charcoal burners, who tended to keep themselves to themselves, until Sigmund came riding back to say that there were ten men ahead of us and coming our way.

'Eight are on foot and two are riding horses. All are armed and wearing leather jerkins and helmets. They look like Anglo-Saxons though, not Vikings.'

Sigmund was fairly certain that he hadn't been seen; at any event there was no cry of alarm when he circled back off the road to warn me.

'Who do you think they are?' Leowine asked me.

'They could be Ecgberht's men I suppose, or just a local thegn and his warriors. We are now in the land they now call Jorvik, so in either case they are likely to be hostile.'

The road was lined with trees and shrubs and so we made haste to hide ourselves; just in time as the two horsemen and their escort appeared over a crest a minute later. When they were close enough to be in easy range of my archers I rode out into the middle of the road and halted facing them.

'Who are you?' I demanded in as haughty a voice as I could manage.

One of the horsemen laughed as the group came to a halt. The men on foot swung their shields around from their backs and took up a defensive stance but the two men on horseback sat there examining me.

'Who dares challenge King Ecgberht's tax collectors?' the older man replied. 'Get off your horse and put your sword on the ground.'

'And if I don't?'

'Then my men will assume that you are one of the king's enemies and they'll kill you. It won't be much of a fight, eight against one.'

'Why don't you fight me instead? After all, we're both mounted and similarly armed.'

'I don't sully my sword with the blood of traitors.'

'It's that swine Ecgberht who is the traitor,' I yelled in fury. 'His treachery has torn Northumbria asunder and surrendered Deira to the bastard pagans.'

'Your life is forfeit for that statement. You must be a fool to challenge us single handed.'

He went to wave his men forward but I held up my hand.

'Who said I was alone?'

I chopped my hand down and seven arrows flew out of the undergrowth, killing or wounding five of the warriors and both horses. I smiled grimly, pleased that my companions had the sense to pick a specific target each. The two horsemen scrambled clear of their dead or dying mounts and looked about them in dismay. The other three warriors turned and ran, but they didn't get far. Each fell with an arrow in the back.

A few seconds later Alcred and Hybald appeared from the undergrowth on either side of the road leading their horses, with the others close behind them.

'Now I asked you who you were,' I said grimly to the two remaining men. 'No, never mind. It doesn't much matter. You will die anyway as a warning to others who support the Viking's lackey who calls himself King of Jorvik.

When we rode on we left behind the ten men hanging from trees beside the road and I had a bulky pouch of silver strapped to my saddle. The two leaders, who it turned out were father and son, were still kicking and choking as we disappeared down the road to Ripon.

Thanks to the delay we didn't reach the monastery at Ripon until after dark and the porter refused to open the gate to us. I don't suppose my description of what I planned to do to him once I got my hands on the obdurate fellow helped, but the commotion did at least attract the attention of others.

'Is that you Drefan, you misbegotten son of a whore?' someone called out.

'Wigestan? Is that you? How did you cheat death, you ugly bastard? I thought you'd be roasting in the fires of Hell by now.'

'It's good to hear your voice too. Brother porter, be good enough to open the gate, would you? I'll make sure Drefan doesn't cut off your manhood, though I don't suppose you've much use for it in here.'

We spent a pleasant night in dry beds, even if the monks were fasting and so we didn't get as much to eat and drink as we would have liked. The monks kept giving me disapproving looks but the abbot seemed affable enough. He was relieved that his monastery had been left alone but said that the surrounding countryside had been pillaged by the Great Heathen Army before they had headed into Mercia.

All he'd heard since was that the pagans had sacked Nottingham but King Burghred had trapped them there. Since then King Æthelred and his brother Alfred had brought the army of Wessex north to join the Mercians.

'I pray every hour that their combined armies will destroy the pagan menace,' he said, making the sign of the cross before enquiring about conditions in the north.

It wasn't that I didn't trust him, but I was conscious that his monastery could yet be raided and he might be tortured to tell what he knew. I therefore painted a picture of a strong united Bernicia ready to repel any invader. It was, of course, very far from the truth.

It was raining again when we left the next morning and headed across country to Barwic. We reached there early in the afternoon and were glad to have somewhere to dry our sodden clothes. However, the abbot told us that Queen Osgern and her son had left with a couple of servants four days previously. She had been concerned for their safety once she had been told that the people of Loidis were aware that she was there.

Perhaps they had other concerns now, but their hatred for her husband was unabated. She decided that she and Ædwulf would be safer in Mercia and had set out to seek sanctuary with King Burghred.

Chapter Five – The Siege of Nottingham

Late Summer 867

As we crossed into Mercia I relaxed a little. It was good to have Wigestan riding by my side again too. He had suffered several wounds and had lost a lot of blood but he had more or less made a full recovery over the past six months or so. True, he walked with a limp as the cut to his thigh had permanently damaged some of his muscles and he would have to work at building up the strength in his right arm again, but he was still very lucky. When I'd last seen him I'd said goodbye, never expecting to see him again in this world.

We headed south east towards Lindocolina and spent the night in the ruins of yet another small fort before leaving the Roman road and striking due south across country. We spent another rain sodden night in a wood before we saw Nottingham ahead of us around about mid-afternoon the next day. The stronghold of its ealdorman stood on top of a steep cliff above the River Trent with the settlement sprawled on two sides of the fortress. The whole was enclosed by a tall palisade on top of rocky slopes that were lower than the plateau on which the fortress stood.

Two separate camps lay around Nottingham. One, the smaller, was sited between the river and the cliffs and the second lay wrapped around the northern side, where the three gates into the settlement lay.

As we were approaching from the north we naturally made for this camp. As we approached a score of mounted warriors rode out to intercept us.

'What are you doing here? Are you from Wessex?' the leader of the horsemen asked as soon as his men had surrounded us.

'No, from Northumbria, from Bebbanburg.'

'Northumbria, then you are enemies; toadies of the Viking horde,' he exclaimed drawing his sword.

'No, certainly not. Ecgberht killed my ealdorman. I serve his son, Ricsige, who now rules north of the River Tees.'

It was something of an exaggeration. Ricsige held Islandshire, but the rest was merely an intention at this stage.

'I ask again, what are you doing here, Northumbrian?'

He said the word as if it was something distasteful. As I was to learn, both Mercia and Wessex blamed Northumbria for the current situation. They believed that it was Ælle's fault for killing Ragnar as that had brought his sons here thirsting for revenge. Having tasted blood, they now wanted to subjugate the rest of England. I have to say that I couldn't blame them, but it wasn't Ricsige's fault, or that of his father Edmund.

'We seek Lord Ricsige's sister, Queen Osgern, and her son. Our orders are to escort them back to Bebbanburg where they will be safe.'

The Mercian spat onto the ground.

'They're certainly not welcome here. No doubt King Burghred will be very glad to see you. He's being urged to hand them over to the Vikings in exchange for some of our people they've captured, but he says that his honour won't allow him to do so.'

The man spat again to show what he thought of his king's principles.

It certainly sounded as if we'd arrived just in time. Surrounded by the Mercian horsemen we followed him to Burghred's tent, where we were disarmed before Wigestan and I were allowed inside.

Burghred was in conference with two other men. One was dressed in a red tunic and blue trousers whereas the other, younger, man wore a long blue robe similar to those worn by priests, apart from the colour.

They were discussing the problem of provisions and ignored our entrance, all except for the young man in the robe, who nodded at us and gave us half a smile. It seemed that the besiegers faced a two-fold problem: the desire of the fyrd to return home to get in the harvest and the difficulties in feeding such a large force.

Needless to say the Vikings had ejected the Mercian population, those who had survived the initial sack of Nottingham, that is. I knew little about the place but I did recall hearing that there was a cave complex under the plateau on which it stood. If these caves were full of provisions, perhaps all the Vikings had to do was wait until the Mercians and the Saxons starved.

'Desertions are increasing,' the man in the red tunic was saying. 'Last night we lost another three hundred.'

'You can't blame them,' blue robe countered. 'They are a long way from home and many hate the Mercians as much as they do the Vikings. They need to get home for the harvest and ordering them to stay won't work anymore.'

What he said had the ring of truth. Mercia and Wessex had been struggling to dominate the southern part of England for centuries. They were unlikely allies and had only come together because Æthelred of Wessex knew that, if Mercia fell, his kingdom would be next. He would rather fight on Mercian soil, than that of Wessex. The trouble was his people didn't have the vision to see that.

I coughed politely and the three men turned and glared at us.

'What do you want?' the one I took to be Burghred barked. 'Do I know you?' he asked suspiciously.

'I'm the emissary of Ricsige, Lord of Bernicia - that is Northumbria north of the River Tees, Cyning,' I said, bowing my head. 'We have been sent to escort Queen Osgern, Ricsige's sister, and her son back to Bebbanburg.'

'Oh! Good.'

The relief on the Mercian king's face was palpable.

'What's your name?' the man in the blue robe, who I guessed was probably the Ætheling Alfred of Wessex, asked me.

'Drefan, Lord Alfred.'

'You recognise me then?'

'I deduced who you are, lord.'

'Drefan,' he mused. 'Not the boy archer who brought Ragnar Lodbrok low and killed Lagertha, the Shield Maiden.'

'The same, lord,' I replied, surprised that he had heard the tale.

'You are something of a hero, Drefan. I'm honoured to meet you.'

I had the grace to blush.

'More like the architect of our misfortune. If Ragnar hadn't been killed...' Æthelred began to say.

'Yes, well. He was. We've more important things to concern us now,' Burghred snarled, rudely interrupting his fellow monarch. 'Alfred, would you get someone to show these men the way to Repton. Lady Osgern and her brat are living in the monastery with the nuns.'

Alfred glared at Burghred, irate at being treated like some lackey. Then he took a deep breath and gave me an apologetic smile.

'You can't miss it. Follow the River Trent to the west. It's about a day's ride. You can stay at our camp tonight. Ask for my chaplain, Father Swithun, and say that I sent you.'

'What a pig that Burghred is,' Wigestan remarked as we walked back to our horses.

'I agree, but probably it's not the best idea you've had to say so in the middle of his armed camp.'

We grinned at each other, collected our weapons and set off, followed by the rest of our group, to the camp near the river.

-⅄-

'Lady Osgern, I'm Drefan, one of your brother's councillors. He has asked me to escort you and your son back to Bebbanburg.'

'Ricsige? I haven't seen him since he was a small boy.'

'He's just turned sixteen, lady. He's the ealdorman now, of course.'

'What? What's happened to my father?'

My heart sank. It was obvious that no one had told her that he was dead.

'I'm sorry, lady. He died of his wounds after the Battle of Eoforwīc.'

'Both him and my husband then,' she said sadly.

I exhaled slowly. At least I wouldn't have to tell her about Ælle's death. I wondered how much of the detail she knew and prayed that she didn't ask.

'You and your men have had a long ride. How remiss of me, you must be tired. Let me talk to the abbess about food and accommodation for you.'

Repton was a dual house and five minutes later a young monk showed us where the stables and the male visitors' dormitory were. After a frugal meal in the refractory we went to bed. The next day was spent getting ready for the journey home and after the evening meal we gathered back at the dormitory.

'How are we going to get back?' Leowine asked.

'The way we came I suppose,' I replied, puzzled. 'Why?'

He and Hybald looked at each other but before they could speak Sigmund's treble voice piped up.

'Because the men of Wessex have abandoned the siege of Nottingham and are heading home. I heard the abbot and the prior discussing it. They're worried that the Mercians won't be able to contain the Vikings on their own and that they'll break out. If that happens they're concerned that they'll pillage this monastery, amongst others, of course.'

I wasn't altogether surprised. Burghred was obviously a difficult man to get along with and presumably he and Æthelred had fallen out. It must have been serious for them to have abandoned the siege though. I learned later that Alfred had tried to dissuade his brother from leaving, but the ealdormen of Wessex had sided with their king.

'If the Vikings do overwhelm the Mercians, or what's left of them, then the whole of Mercia will become unsafe,' I said, thinking out loud.

With much of the Mercian fyrd back getting in the harvest, Burghred had been left in a very exposed position. I wondered what I would have done in his position. He didn't strike me as a man who was prepared to take a risk and I was prepared to wager that he would decide to come to some sort of agreement with Ivar and his Vikings.

Time was now of the essence. I had to decide how we were going to get out of Mercia before it was too late.

-Ŋ-

We rode towards Lindocolina with caution. We had made slow progress since leaving Repton, partly due to the cart in which Osgern, the child Ædwulf and their two servants travelled and partly because of the poor condition of the road – more of a rutted, muddy track – until we met the old Roman road which approached Lindocolina from the north.

We stopped in the middle of the second day after leaving Repton Monastery whilst the three boys scouted forward. As far as I knew Lindocolina was still in Mercian hands. The ealdorman who lived in the hall beside the monastery on top of the hill could be expected to offer us shelter for the night unless, of course, the Vikings had already captured the place.

Thankfully the boys came back to report that the ealdorman's banner still flew from a watchtower beside his hall. I should have realised that he wouldn't be there; he was still at Nottingham with his warband and fyrd, or course. However, his wife and the reeve gave us a cordial reception and a bed for the night.

We were eating with the two of them and their eleven year old daughter when a messenger arrived from her husband. As I had expected, once deprived of the support of Wessex, Burghred had sued for a truce and had been allowed to retreat to his capital at Tamworth. His army dispersed once Ivar had sworn not to advance further into Mercia that year.

'Do you know what the Vikings are planning on doing next?' I asked him once he'd finished his report.

He shrugged.

'As it's September the feeling amongst our army is that they will stay at Nottingham for the winter and then attack us again in the spring, but no one knows what the bastards will do. Apologies, my lady,' he added, bowing to our host and to Osgern, who sat to her right in the place of honour.

'Attack Mercia again perhaps?'

'Perhaps not,' the messenger said thoughtfully. 'We did manage to capture a few of them earlier in the siege and they boasted that Ivar and his brothers were intent on returning to East Anglia because of the rich plunder there. Of course, they could have been trying to put us off the scent.'

'No, that makes sense to me. They will have little respect for King Edmund because of the way he gave into them last year without a fight.'

Now I was fairly confident that the Vikings would be staying at Nottingham, I thought it would be safe to take the Roman road north to the River Humber. Once we had crossed it on the ferry we would be back in Ecgberht's territory, but if we stuck to the minor tracks we should be strong enough to deal with any of his men that we encountered. I was wrong.

Chapter Six – Return to Bebbanburg

868

We crossed the Humber on the ferry, although it took half a day to get us all across with our horses and the cart. It also cost me half the silver we had taken from the tax collectors we'd killed on the way south. From now on we would be in enemy territory so I sent Sigmund and Lambert off to the side of the track and Beornric to ride point.

The weather had changed again and the rain began as a light drizzle which soon changed to a steady downpour. The cart had a leather canopy and I envied the occupants, especially Wigestan, who was driving the cart that day. He had quit his seat in the open and was kneeling just inside the front of the covered part with the reins in his hands.

'Your stay in the monastery has made you as soft as a woman,' I teased him.

He glared at me and then smiled.

'Any fool can suffer discomfort,' he replied.

I looked back at his horse, which was tethered to the rear of the cart.

'At least my saddle is dry.'

Of course his was saturated and would be very unpleasant to sit on when it came to the time for him to hand over as driver to one of the others.

The smile was soon wiped from my face however when Lambert came riding in from the right.

'There's a junction up ahead and there are a score or more of men coming down the track which joins this one,' he reported breathlessly.

'How far away from the junction are they and how far are we?'

'Both groups are about three hundred yards from the intersection.'

'Call the others in.'

Lambert put his fingers in his mouth and emitted a piercing whistle. Both the other boys came riding in at a canter, their horses slithering about on the muddy surface. It was too wet for our bows to be much good so it looked as if it would be a melee using sword, spear and shield if it came to a fight. At least we were mounted and the other group were on foot. However, five men and three boys were no match for twenty or more, even if they were on foot.

I looked about me and saw a small copse about a hundred yards from the road.

'Quick. Sigmund swop places with Wigestan and get the cart into that small wood as quickly as you can. Lambert go with him and guard the queen and her son with your lives.'

I didn't really expect the two boys to be able to defend the cart, but it achieved its object. The boys would have demanded to come with us if I hadn't given them that task. Wigestan climbed onto his horse, grimacing when his bottom met the cold, wet leather. Despite our desperate situation, I couldn't help but smirk at him. He said something unkind in return and then we set off up the track.

We reached the junction first and sat impassively on our horses blocking the way past. It might have been better to take them unawares but I wanted to try negotiation first. If these were members of the fyrd, then they probably wouldn't want to face a charge by mounted warriors if they could avoid it.

The front rank came to a halt and the rest bumped into them, earning a rebuke from a man wearing a byrnie, a red cloak and a helmet with a gold band around it. He was obviously a noble and I wondered what he was doing on foot. Then I noticed the rear of the column. I could just see from the vantage point on my stallion that there were several women and a few children at the rear of the armed warriors.

'Who are you?' the man in the red cloak demanded. 'Isn't it enough that that sheep's dropping Ecgberht ejects me from my shire without him trying to stop me leaving?'

'Lord, I am no friend of the traitor who claims to sit on the throne of Northumbria. We're from the warband of Ricsige of Bebbanburg, Ealdorman of Islandshire.'

The men breathed a sigh of relief.

'I'm Theobald, former Ealdorman of Selby. Ecgberht has ejected me from my shire and given it to a Norseman, a supposed Christian from Luncæstershire. He kindly allowed me to leave with my gesith and our families and anything we could carry on our back which, as you can see, isn't much.'

'Where are you heading now, lord?'

'To the ferry over the Humber and into Mercia.'

'We've just come from there. The Mercian king has made peace with the Vikings, so it's not the place to seek sanctuary, nor is East Anglia.' I paused. 'You were lucky to survive the defeat last year. Most ealdormen were killed, or so I heard.'

Theobald removed his helmet to reveal his face. He wasn't as old as I had thought, possibly only seventeen or eighteen.

'My father insisted I stay at home. As you say, most of the ealdormen died. I wish to God that he had taken me with him now; at least I could have killed a few of the swine.'

I smiled down at him.

'I'm glad you didn't. My lord will be pleased to see you. We need nobles north of the Tees. It's not my place to say so, but I think you might be able to remain an ealdorman, if that's what you wish. Perhaps we'll be able to exact our revenge if we bide our time.'

Osgern insisted that Theobald's mother and siblings, together with the other women and children, join her and Ædwulf in the cart. It made it rather crowded so the two servants had to ride in front of Wigestan and Leowine, not that they seemed to mind. They might be slaves, but they were young and pretty.

Beornric gave up his mare to Theobald and took over as the permanent driver of the cart and thus we progressed without further incident until we reached the old Roman cavalry fort on the banks of the River Derwent the next day. The rain had stopped at midday but our clothes were still damp and we were all looking forward to lighting fires to dry out and cook a hot meal.

Provisions were a problem now that we had so many mouths to feed. Our dried meat, lentils and flour had all but run out, but the boys had managed to come back with a few dead birds and a small deer to supplement what we had left. The venison would be as tough as leather without hanging, but that couldn't be helped. I decided that we would have to stay at the old fort the next day and forage for fresh supplies.

Theobald had a few good hunters and so I sent them with my three boys to find what game they could. The women and children went into the woods to gather firewood and collect wild fruit as well as mushrooms and beech nuts to put in that evening's stew.

Everyone had returned and we had just lit the cooking fires when Alcred and Hybald, who had been on watch to the north, came galloping in to say that a group of over thirty riders were heading down the road towards us.

We quickly threw water on the fires and took up defensive positions along what remained of the ramparts. I hoped that the riders would carry on past. As the road was a hundred yards away from the fort and the light was fading there was every chance we would remain undetected if they did so. However, I knew deep down that it was unlikely. It was the obvious place to spend the night.

As they swung off the road and walked their horses to where we lay on top of the earthen ramparts I debated what to do. Theobald, although a noble, had made it clear that he accepted me as leader of our combined forces and he was too young and inexperienced to be of much help in this situation. Of course, these riders might also be enemies of Ecgberht, but somehow I doubted it. This was no group of disposed people seeking refuge, they were a warband on patrol or on a mission somewhere.

Then Theobald hissed in my ear that he recognised the man riding at the head of the column.

'That's Bjarke, one of the Norse jarls who serves Ecgberht. He's the man who's been given my shire.'

'Time for a little revenge then,' I grinned.

I held up my hand and checked that all of our eighteen archers had their eye on me, then I dropped it.

Bjarke must have seen my raised hand because he halted his horse and yelled out a warning as he tried to pull his shield, which was hanging on his back, around to protect himself. He was too late. Sigmund's arrow smashed into his right shoulder and Lambert's went into his cheek and out of the side of his neck. The boys' bows didn't have the power of a man's but I knew how accurate they could be, even in the deepening twilight.

He was lucky that Lambert's arrow hadn't hit anything vital. He groaned in pain and pulled his horse's head round with his good arm. Perhaps he could have got away, wounded as he was, but Beornric's arrow struck his horse at the bottom of the ribcage, just above the socket at the top of its foreleg. It was a difficult spot to hit but it was where the heart was and the animal crashed to the ground, trapping Bjarke's right leg under it.

The other archers weren't nearly as good but, at thirty to forty yards, they could hardly miss and half a dozen horses and as many men were killed or wounded by that first volley.

The rest of the Norsemen milled around in panic, some trying to turn their horses and escape whilst others kicked their heels into their mounts' flanks to charge into the gap in the ramparts where the gate used to be. The second volley killed three of the braver warriors and brought down two horses. The remainder turned and joined the others in flight.

As they re-joined the road they ran into Wigestan, Leowine, Alcred and Hybald, who I'd sent out of the rear gate as soon as I'd been alerted to the party of strange riders. Normally four warriors would be no match for a dozen, but the latter had been routed and were panic stricken. Furthermore, my men had been trained since they were boys to fight on horseback; Vikings used horses for travel, not for combat.

They charged the first four Norsemen with their spears and killed them before unsheathing their swords to engage the rest. They managed to kill four more and Wigestan knocked another unconscious with a blow to his helmet, but the others got past them and sped away with the Northumbrians in pursuit.

It was now getting too dark to see much and we waited anxiously for them to return. We killed the wounded, both men and horses, but let the wounded Bjarke and the warrior who Wigestan had knocked unconscious live for now. Some of the unwounded horses ran off but we managed to round up a dozen. We stripped the dead of armour and weapons, as well as adding any silver they were carrying to my purse.

It was over an hour before we heard the sound of horses on the cobbles. Our men had managed to catch and kill every one of the Norsemen but Alcred had been wounded in the thigh. However, it wasn't serious and Sigmund quickly cleaned the wound, sewed it up and bound it with part of a tunic taken from the dead.

Theobald seemed to derive great pleasure from hanging Bjarke from a nearby tree the next morning. The Norseman asked to be given a sword to hold as he died, which showed how superficial his conversion to Christianity was. His request was denied and the man swore and cursed Theobald until the rope cut into his windpipe. He kicked and struggled for so long I though he was never going to die, but eventually he hung limp and lifeless, his body twisting slowly to and fro in the slight breeze.

The one surviving Norseman was scarcely more than a boy – sixteen years old, if that.

'Why are you keeping him alive?' Theobald asked curiously.

'To see what he can tell us about Ecgberht and what his intentions are, especially with regard to Bernicia, and to see if he knows anything about the movement of Ivar and the heathen army.'

'What would he know,' Theobald scoffed. 'He's only a boy.'

'He has ears and, in my experience, warriors know more about their leaders than the latter think they do. He will have heard his companions discussing things it would be useful for us to know. For a start, where was Bjarke going?'

'Oh, I see. How will you make him talk? Torture him?'

'I hope that's not necessary. He wet his trousers when we hanged Bjarke, if you noticed. He's scared out of his wits and all alone.'

The young Norseman, whose name was Karl, proved only too willing to talk. I thought it an inappropriate name; it meant manly and it was difficult to imagine this cowering, fearful excuse for a warrior living up to his name.

His English was as good, if not better, than my Norse so I quickly switched to the former language so that Theobald and my friends could understand what he was saying. I started by asking him where he and his companions were heading.

'To secure the ferry across some river called the Humber,' Karl responded eagerly. 'King Ecgberht intends to invade a region called Lindsey, which used to be part of Northumbria, or so Jarl Bjarke told us.'

I looked at Theobald and I could tell the same thought had crossed his mind as had occurred to me. Lindsey had been part of Mercia for centuries. If Ecgberht intended to try and capture the area it could only be because he'd been told to. Ivar might have agreed a truce with King Burghred but Ecgberht hadn't. Ivar and the other leaders of the Viking army were using the so-called King of Jorvik as their proxy.

'What do you intend to do?' Theobald asked me.

I led him away from the fire and out of earshot of the others, including Karl.

'I think we should return and burn the ferry boat,' I told him. 'Without it no one can cross directly into Lindsey. Without the ferry Ecgberht's men would have to cross the Ouse into Mercia proper and then the River Trent to reach Lindsey.

'Ivar presumably wanted him to seize Lindsey before the Mercians could do anything about it,' I continued. 'Burghred would doubtless think twice about launching a campaign to recover Lindsey with the Great Heathen Army still in Nottingham.'

'It would take Ecgberht some time to ferry enough men across,' Theobald said doubtfully.

'Not if most were on foot. In two or three days he could have several hundred south of the Humber. Lindsey is sparsely populated so that would be more than enough to defeat their small warband and the fyrd.'

Theobald nodded his agreement.

'What are you going to do with Karl?'

'He seems biddable; perhaps I'll keep him as a slave, unless you want him, lord?'

'No,' he shook his head vehemently. 'I would never trust a pagan.'

I refrained from pointing out that Karl had a crucifix hanging from a leather thong around his neck.

We left the fort before dawn and retraced our steps to the ferry. As usual I sent the twins forward to reconnoitre the hamlet around where the ferry docked and the rest of us sat down well clear of the road to eat some cheese and dried meat to break our fast.

'The ferry is over the other side of the river,' Sigmund and Lambert told me breathlessly. 'However, there are three big knarrs anchored just offshore.'

They had sauntered towards the river on foot as that would attract less attention than two boys on horses, but they had come running back, full of excitement. I just hoped that no one had spotted them. After I had told them off for being stupid, I asked them for more details.

'The knarrs are as big as the ones we use to trade with Frankia,' Lambert explained. 'Each could probably hold thirty horses and their riders or a hundred men.'

I felt a fool. Bjarke wasn't interested in the ferry; his task had been to secure the embarkation point for the knarrs. The estuary was two and half miles across at that point. With a good easterly wind it would take more than half an hour to sail across. Allowing for loading, unloading and the return journey, Ecgberht could transfer a thousand men - a hundred of them mounted - to the south bank in perhaps five or at the most six hours.

The obvious thing was to capture the knarrs but, unlike the Vikings, few of the men at my disposal could swim. It was Karl who came up with the solution, much to my surprise. He had been tied to a horse with a leading rein held by Alcred to make sure he didn't try to escape so he was close enough to hear our discussion.

'You've the armour and clothing worn by Bjarke's men. Why don't you pretend to be him?'

Few of Theobald's men could ride but we found enough, with my men, to produce a band of what looked like twenty Norsemen. We wrapped our cloaks around our faces to hide the fact that we wore moustaches, rather than the bushy beards favoured by the Norse, and rode confidently down to the jetty.

None of us could speak Norse well enough to sound genuine so I told Karl to hail the knarrs and bid them come in and moor their ships. Much to my relief the ships weighed anchor and used the few oars they carried for manoeuvring in harbour to bring them alongside.

Several ships' boys leaped ashore to secure the mooring lines as my men and I clattered onto the wooden jetty. As soon as the boys had tied the ships up we knocked them unconscious with sword pommels and spear hafts. The rest of the crew gave us no trouble and half an hour later we had boarded all three ships and secured the crews.

I was thankful that we hadn't killed the boys. We discovered that the knarrs were manned by Northumbrians, rather than Ecgberht's Norsemen. They had obeyed their new king because of fears for their families' safety. They told us that Ecgberht was extremely unpopular and revolt as in the air. However, fear of his Norse warband and the Great Heathen Army, who could return to Northumbria at any time, kept the populace subdued – for now.

We were still loading the horses onto the knarrs when Leowine and Beornric, who I'd left watching the road a mile north of the ferry point, came galloping in.

'There's an army approaching,' Leowine said in a calm voice before his young companion could say anything. Beornric was excited and the last thing I wanted was for anyone to panic.

'How many and how far away?' I asked.

'Difficult to say but there was a sizeable mounted group in front and hundreds, perhaps a thousand or more behind them. We didn't stay to estimate exact numbers.'

'You did the right thing.'

Turning to the men trying to coax the last few horses up the gangplank I told them to forget about them.

'Everyone aboard now. There's no great rush but we need to catch the tide.'

It was true that the tide was just starting to ebb, but we had several hours yet to clear the mouth of the Humber. It was my way of getting everyone to get a move on without alarming the women and children. Since we arrived the sixty inhabitants of the small settlement were fearful of what would happen to them and had elected to come with us.

I watched with amusement as Theobald went to help Osgern up the gangplank and then was equally solicitous of the servant holding Ædwulf's small hand. I would have had to be blind not to notice that the young noble's eyes seem to be drawn to the former queen whenever she was around. Although she had a four year old son I knew that Osgern was only just nineteen herself.

One of Theobald's men had to whisper in his lord's ear before he stopped staring after Osgern and rushed to escort his mother, sister and two younger brothers onto the knarr.

Thankfully the ferry had come back to our side as soon as a friend of the crew had signalled that it was safe to do so. Our last act before leaving was to set fire to the ferry boat and set it adrift.

-ᚥ-

'Two sails to the east,' the piping voice of the twelve-year-old lookout called down from the masthead as we passed the point where the coast stopped heading north and ran north-west. The ship's boys eased the sheets so that the wind from the south east now filled the sail from almost directly astern and the knarr picked up a little more speed.

The other two ships were inshore of us and so the two strange ships had probably not seen them yet.

'They're changing course,' the boy called down again. 'It looks as if they intend to intercept us.'

'Can you see what size they are; how many oars a side?'

'Not yet, but one looks bigger than the other. They're probably five miles away as yet.'

I stopped craning my neck from my position at the prow. The horizon was just over three miles away from the deck of the knarr. The lookout could see two or three miles further from his lofty position.

I was glad now that I had loaded all the horses onto one knarr and the women and children onto the other. I had all the warriors, including some twenty five archers, on my ship.

Our sail was made up of red and white stripes with no emblem to give the oncoming ships a clue as to our identity. However, we did have a black Raven banner on board used by all Ragnar's sons. Ivar had insisted that this device should also be adopted by the new Viking Kingdom of Jorvik. We hoisted this to the masthead but the longships kept heading on an interception course.

Evidently they wanted to make sure who we were; they wouldn't be on their current course for any other reason. I had my warriors and archers get ready but made sure that they stayed out of sight below the gunwale.

I called Beornric to my side and told him what I wanted him to do and he scampered away to the stern. The steersman's platform stood higher than the rest of the deck and from there the lad would have the best vantage point. The two longships were less than two miles away now and I could see that one was a drekar with thirty oars a side and the other a snekkja. They rolled more than Norse longships, which meant that they had a shallower draft, and were therefore probably Danes or Frisians.

The pattern on their sails were made up of red and white lozenges, which told me nothing. My best guess was that they intended to join the Great Heathen Army, presumably attracted by tales of the vast wealth that Ivar and his men were accumulating. I called Karl to my side and told him to be ready to reply to the inevitable challenge that would come our way once we were within hailing distance.

The boy had given me his word that he wouldn't try to escape or betray me and I believed him. He seemed to have genuinely welcomed his change in master and I got the impression that I was some sort of hero to him. I learned later that Bjarke was a cruel jarl who like to tease and beat Karl as the youngest and weakest member of his band. The boy was an orphan whose uncle had been one of Bjarke's hirdmen, but the man had never protected Karl or shown any interest in him. It wasn't altogether surprising that the lad didn't mourn his only living relative when he was killed in the fight at the Roman camp.

When the drekar got within a hundred yards of us a man in the prow called across to us, asking who we were and where we were bound. We lowered the sail and glided to a halt, bobbing up and down in the waves.

'Danish, as we thought,' Karl told me.

I had to smile at the 'we'. It made it sound as if Karl considered himself my equal.

'Tell him that we serve the King of Jorvik.'

'Is he Norse or a Dane?' the man in the prow of the drekar asked.

'Neither, but he owes allegiance to Ivar the Boneless,' Karl replied.

I had hoped that the mention of Ivar's name would satisfy the inquisitive Dane, but his ship edged closer and I began to worry that he intended to board us. Perhaps he was just a pirate who saw us as an easy prey, regardless of our ownership or connections.

'Why am I talking to a boy, is your captain a mute?'

The drakar was now less than fifty yards from us. It too had lowered its sail and the Danes were now pulling on their oars. Evidently they wanted to board us. I couldn't allow them to get any closer.

'Now,' I yelled.

Beornric was the first to get an arrow away; it struck the steersman in the chest and he toppled overboard. The steering oar, now free of his control, swung this way and that and their captain nearly lost his footing. Not that it mattered, the boy's second arrow took him in the neck. By now my other archers were sending arrow after arrow into the rowers as they tried to grab their shields to protect themselves.

Karl had raced to Beornric's side and was now frantically striking his flint into some shavings in a helmet. The shavings caught and flared up, enabling Karl to light a torch which he held nervously aloft. Fire was not a good idea aboard ship but it was essential to my plan. Beornric picked up one of the arrows he'd prepared earlier and lit the oil-soaked wool tied to the end of the shaft.

The arrow streaked away to land on the deck of the drekar, just missing the furled sail. It wasn't like the boy to miss, but he was probably nervous of the flames. His second arrow struck the sail, just as one of the Danes stamped out the fire started by the first one. A third fire arrow sealed the longship's fate.

The Danes were desperately throwing grappling hooks, trying to pull the two ships together so that they could board us. Despite the number we'd already killed and wounded, they still outnumbered us by two to one. Our arrows were more or less ineffective now as the majority of the Danes were protected by their shields.

Suddenly the sail caught and the blaze flared up. The Danes frantically tried to put out the fire with helmets filled from their water butts but, in doing so they had exposed themselves and my archers had fresh targets.

Parts of the burning sail fell onto the deck, where the pitch used to caulk the gaps between the planks burst into flame. We kept up our hail of arrows for a little longer but most of my archers were now running short. Satisfied that the fire was now beyond control, I ordered our sail hoisted and we got under way again.

I looked round for the snekkja, puzzled that it hadn't joined in the attack, but it was racing away to the south west. I looked around and saw the reason. The other two knarrs had closed on my ship and presumably the other longship thought that they too were packed with archers!

The rest of the journey was incident free and two days later we reached the fortified harbour at the mouth of the River Wansbeck. This was where the Northumbrian fleet was based, well north of the River Tees which was the de facto border with Jorvik. We spent the night there and, escorted by two of Uxfrea's longships, we sailed on north, reaching Budle Bay, under the looming shadow of Bebbanburg, as dusk approached.

Chapter Seven – Bernicia

868 to 869

It came as no surprise to anyone when Theobald married Osgern, formerly Ælle's queen, in the autumn of 868. By then he was established as the Ealdorman of Dùn Èideann in the north of Lothian. It came as more of a surprise when Sigurd Snake-in-the-Eye had married Blaeja, Ælle's daughter from his first marriage. The girl was only eleven and had been captured whilst trying to escape after the battle.

There was some speculation about this unlikely union. Ricsige thought that Sigurd was making a play for the throne of Jorvik but it was said that his ambition had been thwarted by his younger brother, Halfdan, who had similar desires. Ivar had been forced to crack the whip to stop the argument causing a rift in the heathen army, or so rumour had it.

Whatever the truth, tales of dissention within the Viking ranks was music to our ears. In early 869 Ricsige called a meeting of the ealdormen of Bernicia. Apart from Theobald, he had appointed men to the two other vacancies in Lothian: Cynefrith to rule Dùn Dè and Britric was given Selkirk. Uxfrea took over as commander of the small fleet of longships based at the mouth of the Wansbeck and Walden was made ealdorman of Durham.

Siferth, Ealdorman of Jarrow, the crucial shire which ran down the coast from the River Tyne to the River Tees, and thus bordered the new Kingdom of Jorvik to the south, had been one of the few nobles to have survived, but the ealdormen of the remaining shires had all left young sons who would take over from their fathers in time. In the meantime Ricsige appointed men from his gesith to act as regent.

That left three matters to be resolved by the Witan: the exact status of Ricsige himself, the appointment of an Ealdorman of Islandshire to replace him, and the selection of the Hereræswa of Bernicia. The latter would command the army, oversee the military training of the fyrd in the various shires and, most importantly in the current confused situation in England, be responsible for gathering information about our potential enemies, of which there were many.

We no longer had to worry about Mercia, they had enough problems of their own, but the Picts, the Strathclyde Britons, the Great Heathen Army and Ecgberht all posed a threat.

I wasn't surprised when Ricsige invited me attend the Witan in view of what he'd told me the previous evening. We met in the now fully restored King's Hall at Bebbanburg. Not only had the roof been re-thatched but the dirt floor had been replaced by timber planks. No longer did it smell of rotting animals, just the fresh rushes on the floor and smoke that hadn't managed to escape through the hole in the roof.

It was still March so fires blazed in the two hearths down the centre of the building and benches had been arranged facing the low dais on which Ricsige sat with Bishop Eardulf on one side of him and an empty chair on the other.

I sat with Wigestan, who was the advisor of the thirteen year old Ealdorman of Hexham, his young charge and the two churchmen from Hexham – the bishop and the abbot.

'Do you know what this is about?' he asked me. 'No one else seems to.'

I did but I wasn't about to say anything before Ricsige spoke so I just shrugged my shoulders.

'Thank you all for coming,' Ricsige began after Eardulf had banged his crozier on the wooden dais to stop all the chattering. 'Of course, it is not my place to invite you here, I am merely an ealdorman, or rather my father was, appointed by the last King of Northumbria. Alas there is no ruler of Northumbria anymore.'

He paused before continuing until silence settled over the hall.

'Centuries ago Northumbria was created from several diverse kingdoms: Elmet, Deira, Rheged and Bernicia. Elmet and Deira have now become Jorvik. Rheged ceased to exist a long time ago and became two shires. Now Strathclyde has conquered most of

Cumbria and Luncæstershire is divided between the Christian Norse settlers, Anglo-Saxon thegns and the pagan Vikings.

'If we are to survive and prosper we need to unite and prepare to defeat any external aggression, whether it be from north of the border, from the west or from Ecgberht and the Vikings in the south. In other words Bernicia needs to rise again.'

Applause greeted Ricsige's speech and I cheered enthusiastically along with the rest.

'I propose Ealdorman Ricsige should become our king, King of Bernicia,' cried Theobald, a suggestion that was greeted with enthusiasm, but Ricsige held up his hands.

'I thank you but that would mean acceptance that Northumbria is no more. There should be no separate Kingdom of Bernicia; that day has passed.'

'What do you propose then, Ricsige? We need a leader and the obvious person is you. You can't remain an ealdorman amongst many other ealdormen.' Siferth asked, clearly puzzled.

'No, you're right. If you wish me to lead you, then I suggest I should either be called Lord of the North or Earl of Bebbanburg. A long time ago, before there were ealdormen and shires, the kingdom was divided into regions and the governor of each region was called eorl, an old English word meaning hero. However, the title earl is now used in Wessex to denote the sub-king who rules Kent.'

It didn't take long for the Witan to reach a conclusion and Ricsige was officially elected as the earl.

'Does that mean that one day you hope to re-unite Northumbria and become its king,' Theobald asked curiously.

'If you mean do I wish to depose the traitor Ecgberht, then yes. It will be up to the Witan of all Northumbria to elect a new king.'

I smiled to myself. Ricsige was hiding his ambition for the throne well. He wanted to be King of Northumbria, of that there was no doubt in my mind, but he knew it would be a mistake to seem too eager. He went up in my estimation.

'That means, of course, that we will need a new ealdorman for Islandshire. I cannot look after the affairs of all Bernicia and govern such a large shire at the same time. I propose Drefan becomes ealdorman but, as I shall remain here, he should base himself at Alnwic.'

Of course this didn't come as a shock to me, but I had to appear as if I had been taken by surprise. I'm not sure how sincere my feigned astonishment was, but the next proposal took me completely unawares.

'I also propose that Drefan should become our Hereræswa.'

There were, of course, plenty of older warriors who were far better qualified than me to be the military commander, but my notoriety as the boy who brought down Ragnar and now the rescuer of Ricsige's sister stood me in good stead. More importantly I had an excellent relationship with Ricsige and he trusted me.

I was twenty one and the second most important man in Bernicia. My star was on the rise, but I had a horrible feeling that my perch was precarious. The great unknown was whether the Viking horde would leave us alone.

The next few months flew past in a whirl. My shire stretched from the River Twaid in the north to the River Tyne in the south and from the coast westwards into the Cheviot Hills. It was bordered by the shires of Berwic in the north, Otterburn in the west and Jarrow in the south, nearly seven hundred square miles.

Of course, part of this was wild moorland with the majority of the population living near the coast, but before the massacre at Eoforwīc there had been thirty two thegns who owned enough land for it to be classed as a vill. These varied in size, as did the number of men they could normally produce to fight. All thegns had a few warriors to help protect them, collect taxes and so on but the majority of our army were members of the fyrd. Every ceorl and villein between the ages of sixteen and thirty had to undergo military training and muster when called out by the ealdorman. The number a vill could produce varied from a dozen or so to perhaps seventy in the case of large vills like Bebbanburg.

The settlement in the shadow of the fortress had grown over the years and now numbered over six hundred, of which half were male. However, many of these were bondsmen or slaves and only one in two of the rest were the right age to be enlisted in the fyrd.

Some thegns and warriors had escaped and returned home after the battle but the great majority had been killed, or captured and sold into slavery. All of Bernicia now suffered from a shortage of manpower. Unlike ealdormen, who were officials appointed to govern their shire by the king, thegns owned their land. Not all landowners were thegns, of course. You had to own a certain amount of land to be ranked as a thegn. The rest were classed as ceorls, freemen who owned smaller plots of land. They too had to muster with the fyrd, together with any other free men who worked for them.

Many landowners, whether thegns or not, were now women or young boys. It was an unusual situation but not totally unknown. Usually the senior warrior led the vill's contingent if the thegn was not liable for military service. What was different now was the sheer scale of land ownership by women and minors. I had no more than ten thegns who were old enough to fight. That needed to change.

I decided that one way of improving the situation was to start training boys earlier than fourteen. However, that wasn't my immediate problem. I had no gesith or warband, and I needed to appoint a shire reeve to help me administer the law, collect taxes and keep my books, something I knew nothing about.

I had been worried about Beornric's mother and sister as I would have to ask them to vacate the hall but he told me that his mother had decided to become a nun and had taken his sister with her to become a novice. I felt guilty that she might have decided that she had no option but to take the veil after hearing about my appointment, but Beornric said that she had been thinking of doing so after his father's death. His departure had merely served to make her mind up and they had left a week after he had joined me.

My entourage when I set out from Bebbanburg for Alnwic two days after the meeting of the Witan was less than impressive. I had persuaded Ricsige to allow Leowine, Alcred and Hybald to form the nucleus of my gesith and I had accepted Beornric as the first member of my warband. Beornric was young to be a warrior, but he was resourceful, an excellent archer and had the makings of a leader in due course. Besides he had nowhere else to go. Karl also came with us. He had been a slave but I had given him his freedom as a reward for his help. Nevertheless he wanted to continue as my body servant and I was secretly glad that he did.

To my delight Hrothwulf had come to see me off. It seemed that the old enmity between us might have run its course. I had thought that he might have taken my elevation to the nobility badly, but it seemed that he was genuinely pleased for me.

'I'll come and visit you as soon as my duties allow,' he promised as we parted.

The weather was kind to us as we rode south west to join the Roman road that ran from Berwic to the wall built by the Emperor Hadrian. Alnwic was a small settlement that lay on the south bank of the River Aln. It was undefended, apart from the palisade around the hall, and the scene which greeted us as we splashed across the ford couldn't have been more peaceful. Women and a few men laboured in the strip fields ploughing and sowing crops whilst small children chased each other without a care in the world.

As we approached the men and older boys studied us warily whilst the children ran to clutch at their mothers' skirts, but they relaxed when they recognised Beornric and called a welcome to him. We made for the hall, which stood on its own just outside the settlement. The gate was open and we rode in without seeing anyone. I frowned. Although there was no lord in residence, the reeve should have been more alert.

At the sound of our arrival a scruffy looking urchin appeared from the stables, rubbing the sleep from his eyes. He stood there open mouthed for an instant and then ran back to the stables. I was about to send Karl to root him out to take our horses when he re-appeared with an equally scruffy groom and another boy even younger than he was.

With much bowing and muttered apologies they took our horses away, all except for the pack horse which Karl began to unload, helped by Beornric. I stomped up the steps into the hall in a foul temper. The reeve should have been outside to greet me, together with the servants and slaves who looked after the hall.

It soon became apparent why the reeve hadn't heard our arrival. He was sprawled in a drunken stupor in my bed chamber with two young girls fast asleep either side of him. All were naked.

'Take him outside and throw him in the horse trough,'

Hybald and Alcred seized the unconscious man and hauled him back through the hall. He was scarcely aware of what was happening until the cold water enveloped him. Then he screamed in outrage. I'd followed him out and waited until he had clambered out of the trough, clutching his hands over his groin in an attempt to preserve his modesty in front of the laughing groom and stable boys.

'Get out of my sight before I have you whipped,' I yelled at him as he stood there uncertain what to do.

He continued to stand there, dripping wet and bemused, and after a few minutes I took pity on him. I had no compunction in sending the wretched man packing but I allowed him to retrieve his clothes and personal possessions. He left muttering curses, which earned him a kick from Leowine's boot. I heard later that he had made his way to Lindisfarne where he'd become a monk. It must have been a somewhat abrupt change in lifestyle from rutting with slaves and drinking himself into a stupor.

It turned out that the two slave girls were the only servants left. The others had run away, so now I needed a new hall reeve and more servants in addition to a shire reeve and a warband. My straightforward life as a warrior seemed much more appealing in retrospect.

After we had settled in and the slaves had cleaned up the place, I went to visit the thegn who owned the vill of Alnwic. It turned out that he was a thirteen year old boy who lived with his mother and fifteen year old sister, Eadgifu, in a hall house in the middle of the settlement. It was no different to the other timber-built dwellings, except that it was somewhat larger.

The boy, whose name was Wardric, seemed pleasant enough, if somewhat out of his depth as thegn even though he'd had a year to get used to the idea. Most boys in his situation would have grown into the role, despite their youth; however, his mother obviously dominated him and wouldn't let him take any decisions on his own. With her around I doubted if he would ever be allowed to lead his vill.

Whilst I puzzled over the situation I kept stealing glances at Eadgifu. Wardric was a good looking lad but his sister was the most beautiful girl I'd ever seen. I'd toyed with the idea of marriage, now that I was established, but it had only been an abstract idea. Now I thought about it seriously. Not only was I attracted to Eadgifu physically, but her demeanour and what she said impressed me. She was the first girl I'd met that I could imagine being a life companion.

Of course, I'd only just met her and she'd given no sign that she was attracted to me, so I'd have to take things slowly. I turned my attention back to Wardric.

'I intend to begin training boys to be warriors at twelve instead of fourteen,' I told him. 'As thegn you will need to be able to lead your men in battle and we'll be lucky if we get two years of peace in which to complete your training.'

'He's too young,' his mother said firmly, as if it was the last word on the matter.

'Be quiet, woman. I'm talking to your thegn.'

His mother looked offended and for a moment I hoped that she'd stalk out of the hall in indignation, but unfortunately she didn't. I did notice that Eadgifu hid a smile whilst Wardric looked positively shocked that anyone could talk to his mother like that and get away with it.

'I'll send for you when I am ready to start training boys your age. You can live in my hall with the rest. You may be a thegn but you'll all be treated alike until you are ready to become warriors.'

'But, he can stay here if you're training them at Alnwic,' his mother protested.

I stared at her until she dropped her eyes.

'That would be giving him special treatment. If he's to earn the respect of the men he'll lead he needs to live with them and do everything they do.' I said in a more gentle tone.

She grunted her disapproval but said nothing further. After asking questions to learn a little more about the vill and the surrounding land I took my leave. The mother gave me a hard look as I got up but her two children followed me to the door.

'Well done. Mother has always been domineering; even father was under her thumb when he was alive,' Eadgifu said with a smile.

'May I ask if you are betrothed yet?' I asked, returning her smile.

'That's not a proper question to ask me, lord. Perhaps my brother could reply for me?'

'No, who would have her?' he replied with a grin, earning him a shove from his sister. 'To tell the truth father wanted to find a husband for her, but mother said she needed her help to run the hall.'

'Perhaps it's time your mother thought about entering a monastery? Many widows do.'

I left them with that thought, telling Wardric that I would send for him soon. I mounted my horse and rode back to my own hall thinking all the while about Eadgifu. All that day I couldn't get her out of my mind. I'd never felt like this before, but I wasn't sure how to get to know her better. In the meantime I had other matters to attend to, such as visiting all my other thegns and drawing up plans to train the fyrd and to recruit warriors for my warband.

It was early May before I returned to Alnwic bringing with me forty boys ranging from thirteen to seventeen years of age for training as warriors. Thankfully I'd found enough old warriors to train the eleven underage thegns and their fyrd. In addition to the boys, I had brought back another nine men who had survived the annihilation of the Northumbrian army a year ago. Only two of these were trained warriors, the others had been members of the fyrd, but they now thought that life as a warrior would be more exciting than farming.

The trainees would live in my hall, which in time would become the warriors' hall to house my warband. Whilst I'd been away work had started on a small stone built hall within the same compound. This would be my new hall, which I would share with those warriors chosen to join my gesith, together with my servants and, I hoped, my wife.

When I welcomed Wardric to the hall I was astonished to be taken to task by him.

'Why haven't you called upon Eadgifu again; I got the impression that you liked her. Is there someone else?'

'Is that the way to speak to your lord, boy?

I was angry, not really because of the impudent way he'd spoken, but because I realised that I had disappointed his sister. Although she had hidden it well, it sounded as if she was as interested in me as I was in her. Wardric looked hurt at the way I'd reprimanded him and, without another word, went off to find somewhere to put his gear.

The next morning I watched their training start. The men would be taught by the two warriors who had come with them and the boys would be taught by Leowine, Alcred and Hybald. Much to the boy's disappointment they were issued with wooden swords and oak shields made of planks with no central boss or metal rim. Both were heavier that the real thing. The idea was to build up their muscle and get them used to them, then their steel swords and lime wood shields would seem much easier to manipulate when the time came.

It would take two years to turn them into warriors adept at using, spear, sword, seax and bow. I also wanted them to become good riders capable of fighting on horseback. I just prayed that we wouldn't have to go to war before then.

As I watched their first clumsy attempts at fending off an attacker I saw that Eadgifu had wandered up to watch, along with several other girls. The others were quickly chased back to work by their parents, but Eadgifu stayed.

'Your brother seems to be doing well, in spite of his small size,' I said to her, not knowing how else to open a conversation with her.

'I'm pleased that he's away from our overbearing mother, but I worry that he's too young to fight.'

'He won't have to for a few years yet, or so I hope, but we must be prepared to defeat any invaders.'

'Yes, of course.'

A slightly uncomfortable silence followed whilst I struggled to find something to say.

'How's your mother?'

She laughed and gave me an amused look.

'Is that your idea of how to talk to a girl? To ask them about their mother, someone I know you dislike.'

'No, I don't,' I replied, going red in the face. 'I just think that she needs to realise that her son is now the thegn and she is no longer the thegn's wife. Otherwise it will be very difficult for her when Wardric marries in a few years' time.'

'Or it will be difficult for the poor girl he weds. She will need to be strong character to stand up to mother.'

'What about you? Wardric says that you are not betrothed, yet you are fifteen. Is that because your mother wants to keep you beside her?'

'No, it's because I have yet to meet the man I would wish to marry.'

'Oh,' I replied lamely, feeling a fool.

I had imagined that Eadgifu might be interested in me, from what her brother had said, but if she had yet to meet the man she wanted to marry, then it wasn't me.

'At least,' she added, 'I might have, but I don't know if he's interested in me.'

'Oh,' I said again, feeling hopeful that she might mean me, but she had vanished by the time I plucked up the courage to ask her who it was.

I didn't see her for a while after that and eventually I realised that I was letting the grass grow under my feet. For all I knew someone else might offer to marry her. I waited until the following Sunday when I knew she would be at church. She stood with her mother and brother in the front of the congregation on the left, as was the thegn's right, and I stood on my own at the front on the right.

The village priest was not an educated man but he knew the various offices off by heart. He rattled through mass as usual, choosing to speak briefing about the evils being done by the pagan Vikings as his homily. It was a reminder to me that I had been so intent on sorting out my shire that I had neglected my duties as hereræswa. I would go and see Ricsige this week and draw up a plan to visit each of the other ealdormen to check how the training of their new warriors and fyrd was progressing. We also needed to discuss finding more warriors to man the fleet of longships.

My mind had wandered and I realised with a start that mass was over and everyone was waiting for me to leave first. I glanced at Eadgifu as I turned to go up the aisle and saw that she was trying hard not to giggle. Wardric too appeared to be amused at my day-dreaming, but his mother was glaring at me. I frowned at them and waited outside the church for them to follow me out.

It was raining and I wrapped my cloak around me as they emerged.

'Wardric, please follow me to the hall. There is something I need to discuss with you.'

Being Sunday, there was no training and Wardric normally spent the day with his family. It was also an opportunity for him to discuss anything important with the vill's reeve.

I now had my own reeve. He was a young man called Osulf who had been educated on Lindisfarne but who didn't want to become a monk. As Osulf had a withered left arm he couldn't be a warrior, nor was he much use on his father's farm, so I'd made him my hall reeve. Without a shire reeve as yet, he also kept my accounts and advised me on the law at the monthly shire court.

Osulf was the son of a ceorl and shire reeves were normally nobly born, or at least the sons of thegns, so I had hesitated to promote him. However, the current situation meant that suitable men to be shire reeves were hard to find. Perhaps it was time that I grasped the nettle?

One further complication was Beornric. He was the son of the previous shire reeve and might have expected to succeed his father, but he was too young and inexperienced.

I used this dilemma as the reason that I had wanted to see Wardric. As one of my thegns it was sensible to consult him; I should probably talk to the other thegns as well as they were the people who the shire reeve dealt with in the main.

Wardric was growing in confidence now he was away from his mother and I was pleased that he approached the matter in a mature manner. I was impressed with some of the points that the young thegn made and I made up my mind to appoint Osulf as shire reeve once I had told the other thegns.

He re-assured me about Beornric. The boy wanted to be a warrior, not an administrator, he told me. He suggested that I promised the lad a place in my gesith when he'd finished his training.

He stood up to leave but I asked him to sit down again and beckoned one of the new servant boys over to pour us both a glass of mead. We drank for a moment in silence whilst I thought how best to broach the subject.

'I assume that Eadgifu is still not betrothed?'

'No, without a father I suppose it falls to me to seek a suitable match for her, but she is strong willed and in the past she has made it clear that she will choose her own husband.'

'How will she find one here? She can't be thinking of marrying a ceorl or a villein?'

'No, I think she knows who she wants to wed but doesn't know how to get him to ask for her hand.'

The boy gave me a meaningful look and I knew at that instant that Eadgifu wanted me as much as I wanted her.

'In that case I would like your permission to ask your sister to be my wife,'

A big grin lit up Wardric's face.

'I thought you'd never get around to it. It goes without saying that I'd be delighted to have you as my brother-in-law.'

-※-

Hrothwulf came down to perform the ceremony in early September. Ricsige attended, as did many of my thegns, other ealdormen and their families. I was amused to see Wardric deep in conversation with a pretty twelve year old, the daughter of Wearnoth, whose son was now the Thegn of Hethpool. Wardric had just turned fourteen and was too young to marry yet, but I had a feeling watching them that he might be following me down the aisle in a few years' time.

I glanced at Wardric's mother, who was frowning at her son. Suddenly I felt sorry for the girl. The old dragon would eat her alive. I needed to do something about her. It was useful to have her around whilst Wardric was still undergoing his training, but once that finished he needed her out of the way or she'd keep interfering and making life difficult for him. Still, there was another eighteen months before that problem needed to be resolved and I turned my attention back to today.

Eadgifu appeared in the doorway and her brother reluctantly left the girl's side to join her. She looked striking as she came down the aisle with Wardric at her side. I couldn't wait for us to be alone together but, of course, I had the service and then the feast to get through. Ricsige and others tried to get me drunk, of course, but I managed to remain reasonably sober until it was time to join my wife in our chamber. Suddenly I found my eagerness ebbing away, to be replaced by a feeling of nervousness.

I don't suppose that many men felt as I did on their wedding night. I had longed for this moment but, now it was here, I was terrified of disappointing Eadgifu. Unlike most, perhaps all, men my age I was still a virgin. Of course, I knew what to do, I just hadn't had any practice at it.

I needn't have worried. From our first embrace and deep kiss we seemed to flow together and, despite initial fumbling, soon discovered how to give intense pleasure to each other. After our third coupling we collapsed into a deep and blissful sleep.

I didn't want to leave Eadgifu's side the next morning but Ricsige was asking for me. He had been given Wardric's chamber for the night and that was where I went to see him. The first thing he said to me brought a smile to my face.

'How does anyone put up with that old harridan? I only hope for your sake that her daughter doesn't turn out to be like her mother.'

'She won't, lord. Thankfully Eadgifu is very different.'

'However, that's not why I wanted to see you. We need to talk about what the Viking army is up to.'

Ivar had returned to Eoforwīc to spend the previous winter and for a moment we had real concerns that he intended to head north in the spring, but he marched south instead. They had plundered their way through eastern Mercia and now seemed to be heading for East Anglia again.

'The last I heard King Edmund had decided to resist them and was mustering his army,' I reported.

'Yes, that's what I'd heard too. Do you have any idea of their numbers?'

'Well, Ivar has settled some Vikings in what he's calling the Kingdom of Jorvik but they have been more than replaced by those who've joined him in the last year or so, mainly Danes.'

'In that case I doubt that Edmund will defeat him. He's a pious and saintly man but no warrior and, although he can probably equal the pagans in raw numbers, his fyrd will be no match for the Vikings.'

'I agree. East Anglia will fall, as Deira has done. The question is, where will they strike next spring?'

'Perhaps they'll continue to attack Mercia?' I suggested.

Ricsige nodded.

'Hopefully they'll now remain in the south.'

'Possibly, provided they're not provoked.'

'What do you mean?' Ricsige said, looking at me in alarm.

'Ecgberht has already taxed the kingdom heavily and the depredations, not to mention the pillaging of winter food stores, by the Heathen Army over the past winter has driven many of the inhabitants to the brink of revolt. All they lack is a leader.'

'But if they do rebel the Vikings will return and massacre them,' he said, chewing his lower lip in agitation.

'It's a possibility. But I don't think that Ivar is really interested in Northumbria.'

'You mean Ivar and his brothers had to attack us because the pretext for his invasion was the killing of his father? Yes, I agree that was their rallying cry but they are land hungry too.'

'In that case why set up a puppet king? Why not put one of his brothers on the throne?'

I looked at the earl and wandered whether to tell him what I suspected. I decided that I had nothing to lose.

'I suspect that Ragnar's sons are less united than we tend to assume. They are all ambitious, especially for land, and each seeks to outdo the others. I'm sure that what they want is the fertile lands of the south; hopefully none of them are interested in our patch of moorland,'

'It would be nice to think so,' he muttered. 'Then perhaps they have their sights on Wessex as well as Mercia and East Anglia.'

'Wessex?'

'Yes, Æthelred isn't a strong king. He's more likely to pay the Vikings to go away than he is to fight them. That's always a mistake, of course. They'll just come back for more a year or so later.'

'What about Alfred? I was impressed when I met him.'

'I hear he is very pious, more like a monk than a warrior,' Ricsige said dismissively.

'I think you misjudge him.'

'Let's hope you are right,' he said in a way that indicated he didn't think so. 'However, this is all speculation; what I need are facts. You're my hereræswa; it's your job to find out.'

-Ẏ-

I intended to share everything with Eadgifu and so naturally I told her of my conversation with Ricsige in bed that night. She was the one who came up with the idea.

'Why don't you send Karl to spy on them?'

'Karl? But he's my body servant.'

'Yes, and devoted to you. Don't worry I'll soon find you another body servant.'

'I'll think about it,' I temporised.

'At least ask him. Who else could pass himself off as a Norse warrior?'

'But he's a Christian.'

'I'm sure he'll be willing to trade his crucifix for a Thor's hammer to please you.'

Two days later I bade farewell to Karl, wondering if I'd ever see him again. He was dressed again in what he'd been wearing when we captured him. It was a little small for him now as he'd grown somewhat over the past year or so and the blacksmith had made him a Mjolnir, as Karl told me it was called, to wear from a leather thong.

'I'll be back in time for Christmas,' he told me confidently.

He was wrong. It was well over a year before I saw him again.

Chapter Eight – Karl's Tale

870 to 872

Christmas came and went with no sign of Karl. I worried about him but when he hadn't reappeared by the time that summer arrived, I came to the reluctant conclusion that he had been found out and killed. I prayed that it had been an easy death, but I suspected not. Spies were not usually treated gently.

In the spring of 870 a new batch of twelve and thirteen year olds arrived for training as warriors. I was pleased to see that they included Sigmund and Lambert. Sigmund, the elder by ten minutes, would inherit the vill of Bebbanburg from his father in due course and I intended to invite Lambert to join my gesith when he finished his training.

By then the original contingent had finished their training on foot with sword and spear and handed their wooden practice weapons and shields to the newcomers. Now Wardric and his companions moved onto using a bow and fighting with sword and spear from horseback.

Stories proliferated about the Great Heathen Army, but all I could be certain of was that the East Anglians had been defeated in November the previous year and King Edmund had been captured. Then we heard the dreadful news that he'd been martyred by the pagans. I was told that he'd suffered the same fate as the blessed Saint Sebastian; they had filled him full of arrows.

The Vikings had spent the winter at Thetford and were now rumoured to be advancing towards Lundenwic, the settlement outside the walls of the former Roman city, ownership of which had been disputed between Mercia and Wessex for a long time. Currently it was in Mercian hands so it looked as if Ivar was still intent on subduing Mercia. I was to find out later that this was incorrect.

I spent my days visiting my own thegns and the other ealdormen to ensure that no-one had been lulled into a false sense of security. The other development of note was Eadgifu's pregnancy. In August she gave birth to a lovely little girl who we christened Agnes. I had hoped for a son to inherit my shire, assuming we survived the Viking menace, but I soon became enthralled with my little daughter.

As winter approached we held a feast to recognise that Wardric and his batch of trainees had become warriors. He was now fifteen and a strapping lad; so different from the small boy he'd been when I first met him. He returned to his own hall and the other newly fledged warriors joined my warband. I chose the best seven to join my gesith, along with Leowine, Alcred and Hybald, although they were engaged in training the new recruits most of the time. Now I had a proper escort when I rode out and my warband started patrolling the coast, something I'd been unable to do until now. I was thankful that there had been no Viking raids in the interim, but then all those who had raided us in the past now headed south to join Ivar's army.

December arrived in a flurry of snow. These turned into days of blizzards and I thought that this was the harbinger of a hard winter, but by Christmas all but a few pockets in places where the sun didn't reach had melted.

In the New Year of 871 Eadgifu delighted me with the news that I would be a father again in the early summer. Then, in early March, I had more good news.

I was in the compound watching the newest batch of boys begin their training to be warriors when I heard shouting and screaming coming from the southern end of the village. The term had only recently come into use and meant the main settlement of a vill. I walked over to the watch tower by the gate into the compound and asked the sentry what was amiss.

'I don't quite believe my eyes, lord. It's one of those heathen Vikings riding as bold as brass along the street that leads here.'

'On his own?'

'Yes, lord.'

'I suppose he must be an emissary then. Well, disarm him when he arrives and show him into my hall. Let's see what he wants.'

I was waiting at the bottom of the steps that led into my new stone hall when the man dismounted and handed his weapons to two of my gesith. A stable boy led his horse away and he walked towards me escorted by two more of my gesith.

He removed his helmet and I was startled to see that he had a big grin on his face, then I realised who he was. He had filled out a lot and grown a couple of inches, but the reason I didn't recognise him at first was because half his face was hidden behind a big, bushy beard and his long hair came a third the way down his chest.

'Karl?' I asked incredulously.

'Yes, lord. I'm sorry that I was away a little longer than I said.'

'A little,' I exploded. 'You've been absent for a year and a half.'

'Karl,' Eadgifu said as she joined me with a big smile on her face. 'Ignore Drefan, we thought you must be dead. Thank the Lord that you've returned safely.'

'Yes, welcome home, boy – though not so much of the boy now.'

Karl had to be nineteen now and was bigger than most of my adult warriors. It didn't seem possible that he was the same person as the boy we'd captured three and a half years ago.

'Go and get yourself washed and changed, then come and tell us what you've been up to. And Karl, shave off that beard. You look like a heathen.'

'Yes, lord. It's good to be home.'

-ᚥ-

When Karl reappeared he looked more like himself. Gone were the voluminous trousers with the horizontal ribbons around the calves favoured by the Vikings, together with the long tunic embroidered in runic symbols. Instead he wore gartered trousers and a shorter tunic that ended mid-thigh. Gone too was the beard; he had kept the moustache, but someone had trimmed his hair so that now it only came down to his shoulders.

He came over and joined myself and Alcred, who was now the captain of my warband, and Wardric, who I'd invited to join us. Eadgifu had wanted to be present but I thought that Karl might be inhibited by her presence and so I promised to tell her everything later.

It was still chilly and so we sat around one of the fire pits with a glass of mead in our hands to hear what Karl had to say.

'I reached Jorvik, as most people now call the city, three days after leaving here. I was challenged at the gate and said that I'd been part of a forage party and had got lost. After a few ribald comments they let me in and I found a bed for the night in a tavern, claiming that I was a messenger on my way from my jarl to Ivar.

'My story was evidently believed because the next morning two warriors came to escort me to see Ecgberht. I tried to hide my nervousness, but I was convinced that I'd been found out. Imagine my surprise when, instead of being interrogated, he gave me a leather cylinder containing a letter to Halfdan Ragnarsson and asked me to take it to him. Of course I readily agreed. Now I had a real letter to Halfdan instead of a pretend one, and I could legitimately claim to be a Norseman from Jorvik.

'My ride south was uneventful and I reached Thetford, the heathen's base for the winter, in early October. I delivered the cylinder to Halfdan and waited to see if he needed anything else.

'Had you read the contents?' I asked Karl when he paused to take a drink of mead.

He nodded, taking another drink before he continued.

'Yes, it was sealed of course, but I used a hot knife to cut the seal off and then re-sealed it the same way. If he'd bothered to examine it closely Halfdan would have seen that it had been tampered with, but he just ripped the seal off without looking at it. There was little of interest in it, just excuses why Ecgberht had failed to collect as many taxes as he'd been told to.

'Halfdan invited me to join his warband and I accepted thinking I could find out a lot more about the Heathen Army, its leaders and their intentions if I stayed for a few days. I managed to integrate myself amongst the Norsemen who followed Halfdan fairly easily.

I didn't even have to embroider the truth too much. My father and his brother had been settlers in Ireland initially and then they'd joined a jarl intent on settling in Cumbria.

'My father had married a local girl, as many Norse settlers did, but he was killed in a battle against the Strathclyde Britons when I was six. My mother died when I was eleven and my uncle took me as his servant. The rest you know, lord. The only change I made was to omit any mention that my family had converted to Christianity in order to keep their land in Cumbria.

'I soon learned that all was not well in the Viking camp. There were constant fights between Jarl Guthrum's Danes and the Norse and Swedes led by the sons of Ragnar. Ivar, Sigurd and Halfdan were always arguing too. Ivar was the elder but the youngest, Halfdan, was the better leader. Sigurd was jealous of both of them.

'The one thing that united them was the desire for plunder and for land. When Ivar heard that King Edmund of East Anglia had mustered an army to oppose them he demanded that the others put their differences to one side to defeat Edmund. The next day we began the march to Beadoriceworth. I had little option but to go along with the rest of Halfdan's men. Because I was mounted I joined the scouts sent forward to reconnoitre the enemy lines.

'The Angles were drawn up at the top of a slope in front of a line of trees. A narrow river ran along the bottom of the slope with marshy ground either side of it. It was a good defensive position, apart from one thing – the woods to their rear. The trees were widely spaced with little in the way of undergrowth. They had stripped the wood of its thorn bushes to build a three feet high obstacle in front of their position. They would have done much better to leave them where they were.

'At dawn the next day the Vikings advanced with Ivar in the middle, Halfdan on the right flank and Guthrum on the left. Being young, I was in the fifth and last rank of Halfdan's men. We were on foot, of course, Vikings don't fight on horseback. Crossing the river and the marsh took time and we lost quite a few men to the Angles' archers. I felt three arrows thump into my shield and thanked God for the stout lime wood of which it was made.

'Eventually we made it to the top of the slope. Our job was to push at the backs of the row in front and I hoped therefore that I wouldn't have to kill any Christians to maintain the pretence that I was a Viking. However, our attack was a diversion. Sigurd and Ubba had led their men around the marsh and across the river before dawn. As the Anglian army struggled against us, Sigurd and Ubba advanced through the wood behind Edmund's army and fell on the rear ranks.

'Of course, the fyrd were no match for the seasoned Danes and Frisians and they were easily routed. Many of the fyrd were cut down as they fled but King Edmund and his warband fought on, despite being surrounded and heavily outnumbered. In the end the king was wounded but captured alive.

'After celebrating the victory we went into winter quarters at Thetford. Ivar allowed Edmund to recover and then, in February a few weeks before we left, he had him brought before him in the desecrated church. The other leaders were present and I was one of the warband that had accompanied Halfdan. Ivar demanded that Edmund renounce the Christian faith and acknowledge the supremacy of Thor, Odin and the rest of the Viking gods. To my eternal shame I could do nothing to prevent what happened next.

'Edmund refused, of course, and loudly proclaimed his faith in God and His Son, Jesus Christ. This enraged Ivar and he had the king tied to one of the stone columns that supported the roof. Several of the other warriors had their bows with them and he got them to send arrow after arrow into the king's legs, arms and parts of his torso, avoiding his vital organs.

'The king started to recite the Lord's Prayer, though he must have been in agony. Ivar yelled for him to stop but he didn't, so Ivar grabbed an axe from one of the warriors and swung at his neck. It took him two blows before the head dropped onto the floor. Ivar stood there grinning and challenging the dead man to pray now. The rest of the Vikings were laughing and applauding, but I felt my gorge rising and had to creep outside, hoping my hasty departure hadn't been noticed, so that I could be sick.'

Karl broke down and wept at this point and we sat there shocked by his account of the cruel death suffered by King Edmund.

'Are you alright to continue?' I asked Karl after he had recovered a little. He nodded and took another long swig of mead.

'In early March I was once again present in the church. This time I was on guard duty when the leaders met to decide whether to complete the conquest of Mercia or to move against Wessex. Halfdan and Sigurd were in favour of the former but Guthrum and Ubba felt that Wessex was the bigger danger and furthermore offered the greater prospect of plunder.

'Ivar said nothing, which I thought was strange. There was a man standing behind his chair who I didn't recognise. I later found out that he was Olaf the White, a Norse jarl from Duibhlinn. When the debate between Halfdan and Guthrum got heated Ivar suddenly banged the table with the pommel of his dagger until everyone was quiet.

'You can do what you want,' Ivar had spat out. 'I've been offered the throne of Duibhlinn and I intend to accept.'

'As you can imagine, a stunned silence greeted this statement, but after a few moments the place erupted in uproar. Ivar looked disgusted and muttering something I couldn't hear, he stalked out followed by a smirking Olaf. The next day he and a nearly a thousand of his Norse followers left. I heard later that he had returned to the fleet and, taking twenty ships, he had sailed around the south of England to Ireland and been accepted by the Norse of Duibhlinn and the surrounding area as their king.

'A few days later Halfdan reluctantly agreed with Guthrum that the priority should be the defeat of Wessex. However, one condition of Halfdan's agreement was that we should take Lundenwic en route. By then the Mercians had repaired the old Roman walls and, abandoning their settlement, they had moved everyone inside the old city. It took several months to besiege the place, but eventually the garrison surrendered on condition that they could leave with their possessions and their families. Halfdan would have kept his word, I think, but Guthrum and Ubba attacked the Mercians once they were outside the walls, killing the men, plundering their goods and enslaving the women and children.

'They then moved their fleet round to the River Thames with the intention of making Lundenwic their base for the subjugation of Wessex. In May a new army, called the Great Summer Army, sailed into the Thames and joined the rest of the Vikings in Lundenwic. These new arrivals were all Danes led by their king, Bagsecg.'

I had heard something about this but I knew few details.

'How many ships and warriors?' I asked Karl.

'Nearly forty ships with some two thousand men, I suppose,' he replied. 'It more than made up for the departure of Ivar and the losses suffered in battle and to disease at any rate.'

My heart sank at this news. We, the Anglo-Saxons, had suffered grievous losses in manpower at the hands of the Vikings. Now it seemed that they were becoming unstoppable. If Wessex and Mercia fell, then they would inevitably turn their attention to Bernicia, the one remaining part of England outside their control.

What Karl said next merely served to increase my foreboding.

'We advanced into Wessex and eventually arrived outside Reading in the autumn. By then word had reached us that Ivar and Olaf the White had attacked the Strathclyde stronghold of Dùn Breatainn on the River Clyde. It would appear that the Britons were unwise enough to attack the Isle of Man, which was a dependency of the King of Duibhlinn. Ivar and Olaf had retaliated by besieging the fortress of King Arthgal ap Dyfnwal, capturing it after a siege of four months.

'Arthgal escaped but his people were enslaved and shipped to the slave markets of Duibhlinn. It was said that there were so many of them that Ivar's fleet had to take many of them to the Moorish markets in Spain to sell them all. Ivar destroyed the stronghold so completely that Arthgal had to move his capital to Govan much further up the Clyde estuary.

'Ivar didn't sell all his captives, however. We heard that he had fallen in love with Arthgal's daughter. Not only did he free her, but he then married her.

'By the time that Reading fell winter was approaching and Bagsecg and Halfdan decided to stay there until the spring.

'However, the Saxons had other ideas and Æthelwulf, the Ealdorman of Berkshire, advanced towards Reading at the start of January. Bagsecg, Guthrum and Ubba were in favour of advancing to attack him, but Halfdan and his brother Sigurd said that it was pointless; they preferred to stay safe within the palisade surrounding Reading until the spring.

'On the thirtieth of December the Danes marched out to meet Æthelwulf, who roundly defeated them. We couldn't see what happened but we were told later that Æthelwulf had lured them into a trap. Whilst his shield wall formed up on top of a rise, his archers and his horsemen had hidden in the trees on either side of the approach. When the Danes advanced they were attacked from the flanks, first by Æthelwulf's archers and then they were charged again and again by his mounted warriors.

'When Bagsecg was killed the Danes lost heart and began a fighting withdrawal back to Reading. Several hundreds were killed but the most serious loss was their king. He left no heir and Sigmund Snake-in-the-Eye, more like snake in the grass, managed to persuade the so-called Great Summer Army to elect him as their new king.

'Without telling his brother or Guthrum, he crept out of Reading that night with five hundred Danes and made his way back to the fleet near Lundenwic. From there he sailed back to Denmark.

'However, the other leaders didn't have much time to brood about his defection because a few days later King Æthelred and his brother Alfred arrived to reinforce Æthelwulf. They made repeated attempts to storm the walls and the gatehouse but were repulsed each time. I hate to admit it but I was forced to defend the gatehouse with the rest of Halfdan's warband, but I only killed Saxons when my own life was at stake.'

Karl broke off gloomily at this point and stared sightlessly into the fire. It was obviously difficult for him to relive those days and so I asked him if he wanted to take a break. He gratefully accepted and we agreed that he would continue with his tale the next morning.

Chapter Nine – The Battle of Æscesdūn

January to March 871

Karl walked over to the other fire pit where a boy was turning a haunch of venison on a spit for our evening meal. He cut off a few slices of the outer, cooked meat with his dagger and chewed at it as he walked over to a vacant sleeping platform near the door. He lay down to grab some well-earned sleep and, once he'd started to snore, we started discussing what he had told us.

'Do you think he's telling the truth?' Alcred asked, his scepticism evident on his face.

'Well, I do,' Wardric stated before I could reply. 'Why would he lie?'

He glared at Alcred who frowned back at the thegn.

'Think Wardric. He didn't return when he said he would and he's being living amongst the heathens for eighteen months. You saw how he looked when he arrived. He's become one of them.'

'Why would he return now, if that's the case?'

'To feed us some lie about what the heathens are up to. For all we know, they could be on their way to conquer the north.'

'I don't think so,' I intervened. 'We'd already heard about the destruction of Dùn Breatainn, though we didn't know that Ivar was responsible.'

Strathclyde was now much weaker and the balance of power between it and the Kingdom of the Picts had been destroyed. As the Norse had already conquered the islands and much of the mainland of Dalriada, the third of the old kingdoms north of the border, it had ceased to be a threat to either Strathclyde or Pictland. This development was of concern because it gave Constantín, King of the Picts, the opportunity to invade Lothian without fearing an opportunistic attack from Strathclyde.

'But we don't know if Karl's story about disagreements within the leadership of the Vikings is true. Why would two of Ragnar's sons defect?' Alcred persevered. 'We have heard nothing up here.'

'Except about the defeat and death of the blessed martyr, King Edmund,' I pointed out.

'Well, I for one believe Karl,' Wardric said.

'Let's hear the rest of his story before jumping to any conclusions,' I said, bringing the argument to an end.

The next morning the four of us broke our fast together with the rest of my gesith and the latter asked if they could stay to hear what Karl had to say, having been told the gist of the first part of his tale by Alcred and Wardric the previous evening.

Quite naturally they tended to follow the steer given them by their captain, but most were intelligent men who could make their own mind up.

Karl seemed a little wary when confronted by an audience of a dozen, rather than three, but shrugged his shoulders and joined us, sitting down at the other side of the fire pit and warming his hands before continuing.

'When Æthelwulf was killed storming the gatehouse the heart went out of the Saxons and they withdrew. I was one of the mounted scouts who monitored their retreat, but they didn't go far. They took up a strong position on the top of a ridge in the Berkshire Downs with a solitary thorn tree in the centre of their line. I don't know the name of the place but someone said it was called Æscesdūn.

'What was apparent was that King Æthelred's army had gathered reinforcements since the attack on Reading. I suppose that the Danish and Norse army now numbered two and a half thousand men but three hundred had been left to garrison Lundenwic and to guard the fleet.

'Halfdan commanded the Norse warriors whilst Guthrum and Ubba led the Danes and Frisians. This time I was in the third rank at the junction of Halfdan's wing and Guthrum's. There was a slight gap between the two forces and so I had a good view in front of the Danes as we advanced together.

112

'To my amazement the left wing of the Saxon army were still kneeling in prayer in front of a dozen priests. By this time we were only about a thousand yards from them. I felt like screaming at them to get up off their knees and form a shield wall. I had no more time to think about Æthelred and his kneeling army as our wing was hit by Prince Alfred's wing. Instead of forming a wall in a line, they had charged downhill at us in a wedge formation known as a boar's snout.

'I was told later that Alfred had placed his fyrd in the middle of the formation, which was something like a solid arrowhead with blocks of warriors in line on the flanks. He had placed three ranks of armoured warriors at the head of the snout and both flanks were again formed from warriors in the first three ranks with the fyrd behind them.

'The point, the snout, penetrated our shield wall and forced Halfdan's wing apart at the centre. Consequently I was shoved to my right, across the gap between us and the Danes, and into their ranks. As you can image chaos ensued. Some of the Danes evidently thought that we were attacking them and fought back. I had let go of my spear as useless in the confined space and used my shield to defend myself. I managed to draw my sword after a few minutes and started to jab at the Danes with it.

'I had been dreading having to fight Saxons but I set to with a will to kill the Danes. Of course, I couldn't see what was happening around me, but suddenly the pressure eased and the Danes and Frisians fell back. Apparently Æthelred had finished praying and had led his men into the fray. Their charge must have had considerable momentum behind it and their enemy were distracted by the chaos on their left flank. They were forced back and back.

'I went with them, those of us at the junction of the two wings were inextricably mixed together and, as we retreated, the bulk of Halfdan's warriors were left exposed on the right flank. I later deduced that, with the snout forcing his centre apart and with the Saxons now attacking his exposed right flank, the whole of the right hand side of his army were being compressed into a block

113

where none of the Norsemen were able to wield a sword, shield, spear or even a dagger in many cases.

'It was then that Æthelred and Alfred pulled their masterstroke. Two hundred horsemen attacked the Heathen's baggage train a mile to the rear of the battle. The Vikings had accumulated a vast hoard of treasure during their foray into Wessex and they feared that they were about to lose it. It was too much. Hundreds of men streamed away to protect the baggage train and this weakened the line further.

'I had just killed a Dane when the advancing Saxons reached me. Not wanting to fight them, I turned and shoved my way to the rear, knocking men out the way as I went. Others were doing the same and I finally found myself in the clear. I joined those running toward the baggage train.

'I had made up my mind to escape from the Heathens as soon as I could in any case and this seemed like a golden opportunity. If I could reach my horse I would join the retreat, but keep on going until I got back here. Alas, it wasn't to be. As I ran something hit me on the back of my helmet and I knew no more.'

-ᛦ-

'When I awoke my head felt as if it had been smashed with a hammer. My vision was blurred and I couldn't move at first. That was what saved me. The Saxons were walking the battlefield killing the wounded Vikings and calling over stretcher parties to collect their own injured. I learned later that the Vikings had fled all the way back to Reading, pursued by Æthelred whilst Alfred had stayed behind with his men to deal with the dead and wounded and guard the considerable amount of plunder that the Saxons had recovered.

'Slowly my vision improved but then I felt very ill and turned onto my side to vomit. As I lay there, my stomach heaving out the last of its contents, one of the Saxon fyrd noticed me and came towards me with his dagger drawn. I was too weak to even get to my knees so I called out to him, telling him that I was a Christian and a Northumbrian.

'It made no difference, even without my Norse helmet, which I must have lost when I fell. I was dressed as a Viking and the Mjolnir around my neck probably didn't help. I told him again in English that I wasn't an enemy and suddenly another voice told him to stop. He mumbled 'yes, lord' resentfully, deprived of any easy kill which he boast about to his friends, and bobbed his head towards whoever it was who had spoken.

'I couldn't see who had spoken so I turned onto my back to see a well-dressed young man in a rich, fur lined tunic worn under a polished byrnie dismount from his horse. His helmet had a gold band around it and, when he turned towards me, I saw that he was wearing a large golden crucifix studded with precious stones which hung in the middle of his chest from a gold chain.

"Before I allow this man to kill you, prove to me that you are a Christian and no Viking,' he demanded.

'I asked how I should do that and he challenged me to recite the Lord's Prayer, which I did. He then asked me what I was doing there. Unfortunately I retched again at that moment and I came close to losing consciousness again. However, he waited patiently for my response.

"I serve Drefan, Ealdorman of Islandshire. I'was sent to spy on the Vikings by Earl Ricsige of Bebbanburg, ruler of Bernicia,' I added.

"Were you now?' He looked at me speculatively then told the men with him to load me onto a cart and take me back to their camp. I spent the next few days recovering and telling Alfred what I knew of the Viking leaders and the strengths and weaknesses, as I saw it, of their tactics.

'After that he gave me one of the captured Viking horses and sent me to Reading to find out what Halfdan and Guthrum intended to do next. When I got there, I told anyone who asked that I'd been lucky. I'd been knocked out and taken for dead. I'd bided my time whilst the Viking dead were being thrown into a pit and stolen a horse. No one doubted my story until Halfdan sent for me.

'The size of the lump on the back of my head helped convince him, although he asked a lot of penetrating questions, especially about the Saxon losses. I thought it might be dangerous to lie and so I said that I thought from the bodies laid out for burial that they must have lost many hundreds. I had already learned that the Norse had lost over four hundred and the Danes nearly five hundred. Five jarls were included amongst the dead. It had been a bloody battle but it sounded as if the heathens had lost twice as many as Wessex had.

'"Are you recovered enough to ride to Lundenwic?" Halfdan asked me. I was surprised to be chosen but I suppose he thought I wasn't yet fit enough to rejoin his warband. I said I was and he handed me a sealed pouch. "Give it to Arne Bjørnsson. He is to send me all the men he can spare, including all the new arrivals."

'I asked him if I should bring the new men back with me and he nodded, saying that there should be at least three hundred of them, mainly Danes. Before I left I heard gossip that Halfdan and Guthrum had argued again. The Norse leader had wanted to wait for the reinforcements from Lundenwic but Guthrum was insistent that the Saxons wouldn't expect another attack so soon. As I left the camp early the next morning it was obvious that Guthrum had won the argument. The Vikings were preparing to march again.

'It was imperative that I reached Alfred in time to warn him so, I peeled off the road to Lundenwic and rode in a big circle to the north to avoid the Viking scouts. When I eventually found Æthelred's army they had retreated into Hampshire to recover and muster more men. Of course the King of Wessex didn't know me and it took some time to convince his warriors to let Prince Alfred know that I was here.

'It had taken time to ride around the advancing Vikings and to reach Alfred. As soon as he heard my report he cursed his own lazy scouts and went to see his brother. By the time that the alarm had been sounded it was too late. The Vikings were close to the Saxon camp and I could see that defeat for Wessex loomed.

'I was in a difficult position. I was dressed in Viking clothes and Halfdan had given me a Viking helmet to replace the one I'd lost. I was likely to be killed by the Saxons in the melee of battle and Halfdan would certainly kill me if he found me there. I decided the time had come to leave and I rode north out of the camp until I reached the top of a nearby hill.

'From there I watched the battle. The Saxons quickly formed into a shield wall but they'd been caught unawares and the terrain was flat. For a while the battle was evenly balanced. The Vikings had the most experienced warriors but the Saxons had the numerical advantage. However, the Danes on the right broke the Saxon shield wall and the men of Wessex began to give ground. It was far from a rout but in the end the Vikings drove the Saxons from the field of battle and captured their baggage train.

'The last I saw was Æthelred and Alfred making a fighting withdrawal to the west.'

Karl paused and gratefully took a flagon of mead from a servant. He quenched his thirst before speaking again.

'I decided that it was high time I returned here, lord, and so I set off on the day of the battle, the twenty second of January. I avoided settlements as far as possible, obtaining provisions from isolated farmsteads when necessary. Often the inhabitants had fled before I arrived but I always left what I thought was a fair price for what I took.'

Karl finished his tale and took another long drink of mead, smacking his lips and looking around to see if anyone had any questions. There were lots of them, of course and it was time to eat by the time he'd finished.

'As soon as we've eaten we'll leave to go and see Earl Ricsige. There is one question I have for your ears alone,' I murmured in his ear as I took him to one side. 'Did you hear anything about the heathens' intentions towards Northumbria?'

'Not much, lord. They seemed content to leave the rule of Jorvik to Ecgberht, although Halfdan did express disappointment over the amount of taxes he'd managed to send him.'

I thanked him and Eadgifu joined us for our midday meal. Unfortunately it started to snow whilst we were eating and, by the time we went outside to mount our horses, a full scale blizzard was in progress. Snow whirled around, looking like inverted cones, and piled up in heaps against the sides of huts and the palisade. It didn't look as if we were going anywhere that day.

-ᚹ-

The snow lasted until the middle of the month and so it was late March before we were able to ride up to Bebbanburg. As luck would have it, Ricsige was out hunting in the Cheviots and planned to spend the night at Yeavering. I debated whether to go and meet him there, but in the end I decided to wait for him at Bebbanburg.

He returned late the next afternoon, bringing with him six packhorses laden with dead deer, wolves, boars and even a bear. The latter were now very rare, almost extinct in England, and he was overjoyed at finding and killing one. His high spirits improved even more when he saw me.

The earl was now nineteen and I suggested quietly at the feast held that evening that he might like to think about marriage. He'd pulled a face at the suggestion.

'There's plenty of time for that sort of thing,' he replied. 'I've a brother and a nephew who are five and eight. One or other can succeed me, if that's what you're worried about. I suppose that my brother is the obvious heir, so all I have to do is live another dozen years and Egbert will be old enough.'

I thought that he was right at the time. Even if he married now, any son would be much younger than Egbert and his sister's son, Ædwulf. The latter had gone with his mother, of course, when she married Theobald. Ricsige only saw the boy when he visited Dùn Èideann, which wasn't often, and on the even rarer occasions when Theobald brought his family south to Bebbanburg. Consequently he hardly knew him.

Karl gave Ricsige an abridged account of his adventures over the past year and a half. Ricsige listened attentively, but what he was interested in wasn't the events - all but the last two battles he already knew about in any case. What he really wanted to know was what the Vikings intentions towards Northumbria were.

'What does this Guthrum want? Is it plunder before he returns to Denmark? What about the sons of Ragnar? You say that only Halfdan remains with the Great Heathen Army. Why? And what are his ambitions?'

'I can only tell you what the gossip in the camp was, lord,' Karl replied hesitantly.

'In my experience warriors normally know more than their lords anyway,' Ricsige replied with a grin.

'Very well. Guthrum has no intention of going back to his homeland. If he'd wanted to he could have seized the throne when King Bagsecg was killed. Instead he allowed Ragnar's son, Sigurd, to take it. Ubba and his mix of Danes and Frisians go where Guthrum goes and do what he tells them. Halfdan is more complex. I'm fairly certain that Ivar's driving motive was to outdo the feats of his father. He wasn't satisfied with inheriting three petty kingdoms in Norway and Sweden from Ragnar; he almost treated his inheritance with contempt from what I was told.

'Whatever his motivation, Ivar has abandoned them and Harald Fairhair has now incorporated two of them – Agder and Vestfold - into the kingdom of Norway. His brother, Bjorn, has also taken Alfheim from him and added it to his own kingdom, which covers much of Sweden. Both are too powerful now for Ivar to challenge them.

'For Halfdan this means that he won't get many Norse reinforcements from his homeland. Any Norse who are seeking new lands tend to head for the west coast, by that I mean from Orkneyjar down to Cumbria, or else for Duibhlinn on the east coast of Ireland.

'Guthrum doesn't seem to have any interest in the north of England as far as I can tell. He is ambitious, of course. His father was a mere Danish bondi who was made a jarl by Lagertha.'

Karl paused and looked at me for an instant. Evidently he'd heard the story that I'd been the one to kill Lagertha when I was a boy hiding in an oak tree with a bow.

'He wants to be a king, but over East Anglia, Mercia and Wessex I think.'

'Thank you, Karl. That was informative and I think you have the right of it. Halfdan is alone now and won't want to squabble with Guthrum over the south, especially as his numbers dwindle through death and disease and Guthrum's increase. That makes Halfdan the one who is a threat to us. What do you make of him?'

Karl thought for a moment about how to reply to Ricsige.

'He is ruthless, of course, like all Vikings. He is also clever. He will, I think, be open to negotiation to get what he wants, rather than fight for it come what may. I have to say I rather liked him and admired him, but I preferred Alfred. Alfred is religious, fair, just and honest, as well as being determined and clever. He would, I'm sure, prefer to be a priest than a warrior, but he will do what duty demands of him, and do it well.'

'I didn't ask you about Alfred, besides he's a younger brother and King Æthelred had two sons, or so I'm told.'

'Yes, Æthelwold and Æthelhelm, but they are still young boys.'

'Boys grow up quickly. Alfred is irrelevant.'

Ricsige was wrong. In June we heard that Æthelred had died suddenly on the twenty third of April at the young age of twenty four. At first it was rumoured than he'd been poisoned by Alfred, who'd succeeded him as king, but few believed that. It seemed more likely that his heart had just given out for some reason.

Worse news quickly followed. Whilst Alfred was attending his brother's funeral the Vikings attacked his army and it was defeated, fleeing to Wimborne in Dorset. King Alfred made a stand there in late May and drove the Vikings back. He pursued them, hoping to secure a decisive victory, but the Danes launched their own counter attack and managed to end the day in possession of the battlefield.

The Battle of Wilton proved to be the last conflict between the two sides that year. Both had suffered heavily, losing many men and, significantly, several Saxon ealdormen and Viking jarls. By the autumn negotiations had resulted in a truce and, in return for a payment of silver, which became known as Danegeld, Guthrum and Halfdan retreated to Lundenwic for the winter.

Chapter Ten – Return to Eoforwīc

872

'Where do you think Halfdan and Guthrum will attack next?'

Ricsige and I were sitting in my hall at Alnwic during one of his rare visits. It was a year after Karl's return; a year where little had happened of significance. The Vikings had stuck to the truce they had agreed with Alfred after the stalemate at Wilton but we now knew more details. The Danegeld paid by Wessex was enough to make every man in the Viking army wealthy but, in return, the two leaders had agreed a five year truce.

I considered the earl's question carefully before replying.

'Well, not Wessex if they abide by the terms of the treaty and they already hold East Anglia. I think it might well be Mercia. It's the biggest kingdom and Burghred isn't in a strong position. Many Mercians blame him for allowing the heathens to escape from Nottingham and he is unpopular, thanks to his uncanny knack of upsetting his nobles.'

'It would seem logical. Let's hope that you're right – although, if they capture Mercia there is little hope for Wessex, or Bernicia come to that.'

After Ricsige had left I went to find Eadgifu and my children, Agnes and the baby, Edgar, who had been born the previous July. Edgar had just started to crawl and was into everything. Agnes, who would be two in August doted on him. She was now toddling and Eadgifu said that the two of them exhausted her. Of course she had slave girls to help her look after them but she had refused to use a wet nurse and saw to their care much more than was normal for an ealdorman's wife. It was one of the many reasons I loved her.

I was still with them when a messenger arrived looking for Ricsige. I went back into the hall and asked for the man to be shown in. He was covered in mud and looked exhausted.

'Who sent you and what is your message?' I asked after inviting him to sit.

'It's for the ears of Earl Ricsige only,' he replied with a hint of defiance.

'I'm his hereræswa and chief counsellor, you can tell me.'

He hesitated and then shrugged his shoulders.

'The people of Eoforwīc have risen in revolt. They've killed most of the traitor Ecgberht's Norsemen and driven him and the archbishop out of the city. The rumour is that they've fled into Mercia.'

I sat there stunned. What have they done I asked myself silently. The use of the old English name for Yorvik was a criminal offence under the code of law introduced by the Vikings. There was no way that they wouldn't punish them for this, and punish them severely. When I'd recovered from the shock I looked at the messenger again and got the distinct impression that there was something he wasn't telling me.

'What else?' I barked at him.

'It's for the ears of Earl Ricsige alone,' he stuttered.

'Tell me or I'll have my gesith beat it out of you.'

He refused to look me in the eye but mumbled something which I didn't catch.

'Speak up, and stop looking so shifty.'

He looked up from studying the rushes on the floor and took a deep breath.

'The Witan of Deira have elected Ricsige as King of Northumbria.'

'What will you do?' I asked Ricsige when I caught up with him.

He gnawed his lower lip and hung his head in thought.

'I don't know. I'll have to think. As you know, the last thing I ever wanted to be was king of anywhere. I strongly suspect that the mere fact that the Deiran Witan have elected me has condemned me to death at the hands of the Vikings, whatever I do.'

I rode back to Bebbanburg with him in silence and stayed the night there. The next morning I awoke to the sound of the wind howling around the hall and when I went outside to relieve myself horizontal rain lashed my face and other areas of exposed skin. I wouldn't be travelling back to Alnwic that day.

Ricsige wanted to send out messengers to summon a meeting of the Bernician Witan but sensibly decided that would have to wait until after the storm had abated. He decided to hold the meeting at Berwic so I stayed on for a week and then rode north with him.

During that time we discussed the options endlessly. If Ricsige ignored his election to be king he felt that he would be betraying those who had chosen him. However, if he accepted, then he would need to prepare for war.

'Won't you have to fight the Vikings anyway?' I asked.

'I'm not sure. From what Karl said I don't think Guthrum or Ubba have any interest in fighting in Northumbria, it's Halfdan who will want to launch a campaign here. I'd be willing to wager a chest or two of silver that the other two would rather invade Mercia again.'

'They won't like the fact that their authority up here has been flouted and their puppet king ousted. They depend to a large extent on fear to keep those that they've subdued quiescent. After all, they can't have more than three or four thousand warriors in total. If all of England was mobilised we could probably muster twenty five or thirty thousand men. Admittedly all but a few thousand would be in the fyrd but, nevertheless, we could drive them out of England. The problem is we're divided and lack a leader to unify the whole of Anglo-Saxon England.'

'I'm sure you're right,' Ricsige said, 'but throughout our history we have always been too busy fighting each other; Saxons distrust Angles and Mercians distrust both the West Saxons and the Northumbrians. Even now, I'm hoping that the pagans will invade Mercia and not the North.'

'Our other problem is the Picts,' I reminded him. 'Theobald is constantly having to deal with raids across the Forth and from the west. I'm sure that Constantín has a firm grip on his people, and on the Britons of Strathclyde now, so these are probing attacks to see how strong we are. We can't deal with a war on two fronts.'

'No, I'm not sure we can deal with a war on one front at the moment,' he said dispiritedly.

The Witan was enthusiastic about the prospect of reunifying Northumbria under one king once more. Most seem to think that the only reason we had lost Deira in the first place was because the kingdom had been weakened by the civil war between Ælle and Osbehrt, both of whom were unpopular. In contrast, Ricsige was well liked and respected.

In the end we all travelled down to Eoforwīc – the name Yorvik having been ditched along with Ecgberht – for Ricsige's crowning by Bishop Eardulf. However he had chosen to call himself King of the North Saxons, rather than King of Northumbria. Normally the archbishop, Wulfhere, would have officiated at the coronation but he was still in Mercia somewhere. In any case, he was still despised for accepting Ecgberht as king to save his own skin.

Two days after Ricsige's enthronement, whilst we were still celebrating, we got word that the Great Heathen Army had left Lundenwic and were heading north along the old Roman road called Ermine Street. There was no doubt about it; they were headed for Eoforwīc.

I sat in the trees with my hundred horsemen watching the long column wind its way along the track below us. The Viking horde had reached the valley of the River Wharfe ten miles south west of Eoforwīc. Ricsige had ordered the population to evacuate the area and they had driven their livestock into the fenland around the city and up into the high moorland to the north east.

The remains of the crops from last year had been burned and this year's wouldn't be ready for harvesting for another couple of months. It meant that our people would go hungry for a while but that was preferable to becoming slaves of the heathens.

The Heathen Army were therefore starving. They had run out of the supplies they had brought with them and were now dependent on foraging. My task was to harry their forage parties and prevent them from hunting, gathering wild fruit or digging up root vegetables.

As we watched, the enemy prepared to make camp for the night and several groups of horsemen rode out to see what food they could find. One of the largest groups – some fifty mounted warriors – headed north-west straight towards us. I signalled silently to my men and they peeled off to take up their positions. This wasn't the first time that we'd ambushed groups of mounted Vikings; far from it, and everyone knew what to do.

I was about to turn away when Karl gripped my arm. He was no longer my body servant – that was a young lad called Bran, a Pict who'd been captured by Theobald during a raid into his shire and given to me as a gift. Karl was now a member of my gesith.

'Look, lord. The riders who headed north have turned to the west. It looks as if they are heading to intercept the group we're planning to ambush,' he told me.

'No, not intercept. They are getting to know our tactics it seems. My guess is that they will follow the other group, intending to come to their aid as soon as we attack the first lot. Well spotted. Ride and tell Alcred to let the first group pass through the ambush and then attack the second. Leowine is to take a dozen archers to the west of the killing ground to prevent the first group from interfering until it's too late.'

Once I got close to the site we'd picked for the killing ground I dismounted and left my horse with Bran. I cautiously edged forward, making as little noise as possible, until I reach Alcred's side. The last of the first group were just riding past about thirty yards away as I got there.

We didn't have long to wait until the second group arrived. There were some forty riders who I thought were probably Norsemen, rather than Danes, and therefore Halfdan's men. They rode like sacks of grain; they weren't experienced riders, just warriors who sat on a horse to get from one place to another quickly.

Alcred put his fingers in his mouth and emitted a piercing whistle. Immediately fifty arrows sped out of the undergrowth, hitting men and horses. Chaos ensued, made worse as a second volley cut more men and their mounts down. Then I led my men out of the woods onto the track and we started to kill the bewildered Norsemen.

Within five minutes it was all over and in the relative silence than followed I could hear shouts and screams coming from a hundred yards further up the track. I waved to Alcred; this time he whistled twice and we melted back into the trees.

Leowine's archers came running back down the track pursued by the first group of Vikings. When the latter reached the scene of carnage they pulled their mounts to a sudden halt. They weren't fools and, before we could do much damage to them with our bows, they wheeled around and rode back up the track.

Alcred and I looked at each other and grinned. We knew what their next move was likely to be. Sure enough, the Vikings advanced on foot through the trees and scrub in line, their shields held in front of them. They assumed that we were lightly armed archers who would be easy prey for armoured warriors. There were about thirty five of them left and so were heavily outnumbered by my warband.

They were two ranks deep so we met them with a shield wall four deep. Even so we overlapped the end of their line. To make matters even worse for them half a dozen of my youngest and most agile archers had climbed into the trees so that they could pick off the Vikings from above.

Seeing a few of their men fall with arrows in their backs unnerved them even further and then we charged. I held my spear over the top of my shield as I fixed the eyes of a bearded warrior with mine. He expected me to try and stab him in the narrow gap between the top of his shield and the rim of his helmet, but I dropped the point at the last moment. As I deflected his spear with my shield, I dropped my own spear and thrust it into his knee. His leg gave way as I pulled the point out and I thrust again into his neck.

The warrior behind him was little more than a boy. He had no beard and his eyes betrayed his fear. I took pity on him – usually fatal in a fight – and rammed my shield into him with sufficient force to knock him onto his arse. He hadn't secured his helmet on his head tightly enough and it fell off. I brought the base of my spear haft down sharply on the boy's temple. Either he was unconscious, as I'd intended, or the blow had killed him.

I looked around for another opponent but it was all over. A few Vikings had escaped on foot but the majority were dead or badly wounded. We killed the wounded, both men and horses, and rounded up the other mounts.

It was only then that I remembered the young Viking. Evidently he'd been left for dead when the other survivors were slain, but now he was conscious again. I found him lying on his side vomiting and feeling very sorry for himself. I called Karl over and told him to ask the boy his name and age.

'He's called Fiske and he's fourteen. His father is one of Halfdan's jarls,' Karl told me after a brief exchange.

'He seems very eager to talk,' I remarked.

'I told him that I too was Norse but that life was much better as an Englishman. At first he didn't believe me but I managed to convince him that he should join us.

Suddenly Karl paled.

'I hope that's what you intended, lord?' he stuttered.

I smiled reassuringly.

'Why not, provided he's prepared to be baptised.'

The boy nodded eagerly when Karl put this to him and so I acquired my second Norseman.

-ᚹ-

The return of less than a dozen of the ninety riders who'd set out must have enraged Halfdan because two hundred more mounted Vikings set out to find us. However, it was a foolish errand as dusk was almost upon us. We evaded them with ease and headed for Loidis to spend the night.

Like Eoforwīc some twenty odd miles to the north east, Loidis has been abandoned. Of course, a few stupid people ignored the king's order to leave but that was their choice. The next morning we checked that there were no provisions left in the place that the Vikings could plunder and then headed towards Eoforwīc. After seven miles, two of the scouts I had thrown out as a screen came galloping back to report that a thousand Vikings were moving down the old Roman road towards us.

We left the road and headed into low hills to the north. Once out of sight I walked up to the nearest summit and watched as the small army below me moved along the road. Evidently they had been sent to capture Loidis and I wished them joy of their hollow victory. Without food they would be forced to abandon it.

We rode across country and reached the monastery at Ripon by nightfall. Once my men had set up camp outside the palisade I washed the dust from my face, took off my byrnie and went into the monastery in search of Ricsige. I found him ensconced with the abbot in the latter's hall.

'Drefan,' he said getting up with a smile and embracing me. 'I'm glad to see you safe and sound. What's your news?'

After I told him all that had happened since I'd last seen him he clapped me on the shoulder and congratulated me.

'When they get to Eoforwīc they'll find it just as deserted as Loidis. They can call the place Yorvik again for all I care; they won't be able to stay there without food.'

'What about resupply by sea, Cyning? There's plenty of food in East Anglia that they can bring up using their fleet.'

'That's true,' he said glumly. 'Uxfrea is at sea with our fleet but I don't know what he can do when he's so heavily outnumbered by the damned Vikings.'

'They may have sixty or seventy longships but they must have brought nearly all their men north on land. How are they going to crew them?' I reasoned after thinking about it. 'And how long will it take a messenger to summon them north and then for them to load the ships they are able to man with provisions?'

Ricsige laughed.

'You're right. Not before they are forced to either retreat from Eoforwīc or starve,' he said with a wide grin.

We stayed at Ripon with the main Northumbrian army just in case the Vikings decided to penetrate further into the kingdom. They sent out patrols but whenever possible we ambushed these and they stopped. By now it was harvest time and the fyrd were agitating to go home. They didn't seem to understand that, if they got the crops in all they would be doing in effect was feeding our enemies.

In late August things were getting desperate. If harvesting wasn't started soon there would be no wheat, barley or oats to see everyone through the winter. Of course livestock such as goats, sheep, chickens, pigs and cows had been taken up into the hills for safety but meat wasn't a feature of most people's diets, except on special occasions. In any case, once they started to eat them, the supply of domesticated animals would soon run out.

In the end Ricsige allowed the fyrds from shires to the north of Ripon to return home but that still left the harvest in all of Deira to be collected. Of course, Vikings were farmers too and one of our worries was that they would start to cut the wheat, barley and oats themselves. In some cases they did but my mounted warriors and I did our best to hinder this.

A few ships got through with supplies but Uxfrea had managed to intercept a fleet of fifteen ships, mainly knarrs, off the mouth of the Humber and had sunk seven of them for the loss of two of our own longships. The rest of the resupply ships had fled back south.

In early September we began to wonder whether the Vikings were going to remain in Eoforwīc for the winter. They had been there for over a month and had achieved little and so it was difficult to know what they were planning. That's when I remembered my two Norsemen. Karl could no longer serve as a spy; he was too old to pass as a beardless Viking, and in any case he was known to too many of the enemy. Fiske, on the other hand, could say that he'd managed to escape from us.

Of course, he could betray us once he was back with his own kind, but he'd been baptised by the Abbot of Ripon and seemed to have become a good Christian. I gathered that he and his father were far from close; he was a younger son and his father didn't think much of him as a warrior. It was worth the risk anyway.

We kept a close eye on the city after Fiske had left, just in case my faith was misplaced and the heathens decided to march on Ripon, but nothing unusual seemed to be going on.

Then, five nights after he'd left us Fiske was found making his way east on foot.

'They're leaving,' he said when he was brought before me.

'Where are they heading?' Ricsige asked as he came into the small hut I was using, having been told of the boy's return.

'Back south of the Humber, Cyning. The rumour is that they plan to overwinter somewhere in Lindsey, which is part of Mercia I think?'

Ricsige nodded and sat down next to me and Bran offered the king a tankard full of beer.

'Fiske, you better sit down too,' I told him. 'Bran, give him some beer as well; he looks as if he needs it.'

'Right, now start at the beginning,' Ricsige said. 'What happened when you left here?'

'I rode up to the gates,' the boy began nervously, 'and fortunately they recognised the name of my father. I was disarmed and taken to him. Far from being glad to see me he seemed to think that I was a coward for having allowed myself to be captured. I told him, as we'd agreed, that I'd been put to work looking after the horses in the camp here at Ripon, mucking out, grooming and feeding them oats to supplement the grass from the pasture.

'However, he didn't believe that we had so much food to spare that we could give oats to the horses. They were, of course, very short of cereal crops themselves and had to make do with a thin gruel made of root vegetables, cabbage, fungi and a little meat from wild animals and rats.

'I asked him why I would lie and eventually he believed me. He took me to see Halfdan, Guthrum and Ubba who were arguing about what they should do next. Halfdan wanted to advance further into Northumbria but the other two were adamant that they should return south to conquer Mercia.

'They questioned me closely about the Northumbrian army and I told them it was five thousand strong. I lied about the location as well, saying you were in a valley five miles to the west of here. Your supposed strength strengthened the argument to retire south of the Humber before winter set in and Halfdan reluctantly agreed.

'He obviously didn't trust me, though, and insisted that I guided a patrol to where you were so that he could verify the truth of what I'd said about your strength for himself. I had little option but to agree. However, their horses are in a bad way now and they've started to eat them so Guthrum was reluctant to lose any. In the end we set out on foot just after dark two days ago. Thirty Vikings accompanied me and they kept a close eye on me, so I was beginning to panic about escaping from them.

'I was lucky. When we were about ten miles from your supposed location we came across a deserted village. The place had several bee houses and the production of mead was obviously the main activity. The store next to the thegn's hall contained several full barrels. God had answered my prayers. I waited until the middle of the night when they were all fast asleep in a drunken stupor. I crept out of the hall and ran east. Just before dawn I ran into your sentries and the rest you know.'

Neither Ricsige nor I doubted Fiske's story but I took a large mounted patrol out just to make sure. The boy led us to the village and, although it was mid-morning by then the Vikings were still fast asleep. My men disarmed them and herded them into the middle of the village.

'What do you want to do with them, lord?' Hybald asked me and, in truth I didn't know.

The easy answer was to kill them, but I was getting tired of slaughter in cold blood. As I debated what to do with them, they caught sight of Fiske. His obvious betrayal of them infuriated them and they surged towards him, yelling and cursing. My men reacted and, once they had started to cut the unarmed Vikings down, there was no controlling them. I shouted at them to stop, of course, and a few obeyed me but, such was their hatred of the pagans who were trying to take our land from us, they mostly ignored me.

By the time that I had restored order only five were left alive, and they were all wounded. We stripped them of their armour and clothes and left them to make their way back to the city, if they could. They were naked, without food or weapons and, lacking Fiske as a guide, no doubt lost. It would probably have been kinder to have killed them.

A week later I sat beside Ricsige on a hill to the west of Eoforwīc as the Great Heathen Army marched south. It was a cloudless day with scarcely a breath of wind, so the plumes of black and grey smoke from the burning city rose straight up towards the heavens. Eoforwīc was no longer the seat of the Kings of Northumbria. Bebbanburg would once more become a royal stronghold.

Chapter Eleven – The Raid on Whitby

873 to 874

Life returned to normal after the departure of the Vikings. I learned later that they had spent the winter at a place called Torksey in Lindsey and then spent the next year conquering and settling in north east Mercia.

Despite evacuating Deira before the advance of the Viking army, the people there suffered during the winter. The heathens had stripped the land bare of crops like cabbages, and of fruit. The yield from the fields of wheat, barley and oats was poor, thanks to the late harvest, and the wild animals such as deer had been decimated.

The people of Loidis returned, as did the population of Eoforwīc, but the latter was a charred ruin. Ricsige did his best to help the inhabitants to build some huts but there were never going to be enough and a lot of people moved elsewhere. They blamed Ricsige for abandoning the capital and his grip on Deira weakened as a result.

I was happy to be back with my family and spent my time administering my shire, training more boys to be warriors and hunting. One of my concerns now was money. Keeping a large warband wasn't cheap and building my new stone hall had been expensive. I decide to follow the example of the lords of Bebbanburg and started to build two knarrs to trade abroad and a longship to escort them. Ricsige lent me a master shipwright and a few experienced carpenters and they started to both construct the ships and to train some of my men to help them.

These included Fiske and Karl. I suppose that the sea was in their blood and it solved the problem of what to do with Fiske. Beornric also showed interest and I sent him to Uxfrea to be trained as a sea warrior and a helmsman. As the son of the previous shire reeve I wanted him to have a command of his own and I had it in mind to make him captain of my longship when he was ready.

So life went on. We heard few tidings of the war in Mercia, only that King Burghred was having little success in holding back the Viking advance into his kingdom. He lost three battles in succession and the Mercians seemed to give up hope of keeping the heathens out of the eastern half of their kingdom. Burghred retreated to Nottingham and the Vikings pillaged the monastery at Repton before building a fortified camp there for the winter.

Some of the monks had managed to escape from the monastery and made their way north. They were found by one of the Deiran patrols along the border and escorted to Eoforwīc where work to rebuild the monastery and the church had started. One of the monks turned out to be Wulfhere, the archbishop who had fled into Mercia when Ecgberht was deposed.

'I want you to go down to Eoforwīc and speak to Wulfhere. He may know more about the Vikings' plans,' Ricsige told me when I arrived at Bebbanburg for one of our regular meetings.

It was now late November and hardly a good time to travel. Thankfully for most of the way we could follow the old Roman roads but it would be a cold, wet and miserable journey. Furthermore, because there were only nine hours of daylight at best at this time of year, we would be lucky to cover thirty miles a day. We would therefore be in the saddle for four or five days.

Ship building had finished for the year so I decided to take Beornric, Karl, Fiske, Lambert, Leowine and Hybald with me as my escort. My servant, Bran and a stable boy named Tancred completed our small group. We could stop the night with the ealdormen of Jarrow and Catteric and at the monastery at Ripon for three of the nights but we would have to impose on one of the thegns in the shire of Durham. We only took one packhorse but I had included a quantity of dried meat and bags of flour in its paniers as gifts for our hosts; no one would welcome having to feed extra mouths so close to the onset of winter.

The night before we left Alnwic was clear and cold so the rutted track that led to the Devil's Causeway was frozen hard. We reached the Roman road without incident but dark clouds were scudding in from the east and I feared that we were in for a soaking. Lambert and Beornric were now officially warriors but they chattered away excitedly like boys half their age. Unsurprisingly, Karl and Fiske had become close friends and, although they joined in the banter with the others, often they rode side by side talking in Norse.

Leowine and Hybald were suspicious - their view was the only good Norseman was a dead one – but I knew enough Norse to know that their chatter was innocuous. In fact, the two weeks we spent together was useful in dispelling the misgivings of Leowine and Hybald and bringing us all closer together.

By early afternoon the clouds were black and freezing rain started to fall. My brother had told me that there was a scroll on Lindisfarne which he had copied dating from the time when Rome ruled Britannia. Apparently there had been a stone bridge called the Pons Aelius across the River Tyne, linking the Devil's Causeway to the road south. It had fallen into ruin long ago so we had to leave the road and head for the nearest ford upstream over the Tyne.

It was a long diversion and the track was fetlock deep in slippery mud. Our speed was halved and I began to worry about reaching Jarrow before dusk. The freezing rain was unpleasant but when it changed to hail our misery doubled. The little pellets of ice stung our faces and made the horses skittish. We had to dismount and lead them until the hail ceased.

When we reached the ford it was to discover that the river was higher than usual and we had to mount again to get across. Even then, the water came up to the horses' bellies. At least it washed most of the mud from our leather boots. I smiled grimly to myself at the thought that Bran and Tancred would have to spend the evening drying our footwear and making them supple again, and that was in addition to caring for the horses and getting the rust off our byrnies and helmets.

We followed the south bank of the Tyne eastwards to Jarrow and I passed the spot where Ragnar Lodbrok had been thrown into a pit of snakes. The bleached bones of the Vikings who had fallen in battle over a decade earlier still lay scattered around, picked clean by wolves and other carnivorous animals.

The place had an atmosphere of gloom and despondency hanging over it and we were all glad when we left it behind us. We reached Jarrow an hour or so later and were given a warm welcome by its young ealdorman. The abbot and his prior joined us for the evening meal and I hoped that they might have had more news about the Vikings. However, they knew no more than I already did.

The dark clouds had disappeared the next morning but everywhere smelled dank. The sky remained grey and gloomy all the next day and our mood was sombre when we reached a village ten miles south of Durham. The local thegn was both honoured and flustered by our arrival. His hall was little more than a hovel and scarcely large enough for us all to sleep in, in addition to his own half a dozen warriors and his family.

In fact his family outnumbered his warriors. Apart from his wife and wizened old crone of a mother, he had nine children ranging in age from two to fourteen. Unsurprisingly his wife looked old before her time and his mother did little but cackle inanely when one least expected it.

I handed him a leg of smoked ham and a bag of flour to thank him for his enforced hospitality and he seemed suitably grateful. However, the meal that evening was a broth of cabbage, turnips, wild mushrooms and barley. It was filling, if not exactly tasty.

The floor of the tiny hall was bare earth with puddles of muddy water dotted all over it where the rushes of the roof had let in water. There were gaps between the upright timbers of the walls where the old daub had fallen out, letting the wind whistle in and waft the smoke from the central hearth around inside the hall. Little of it seemed to find the hole in the roof as a consequence. I heard Tancred, the stable boy, muttering to Bran that his bed in the stables back in Alnwic was like a king's hall by comparison.

We all had a thoroughly miserable night, especially as the family had no separate chamber and one or other of the thegn's innumerable children seemed to have to go outside to pee every few minutes.

I forced myself to smile when I thanked our host for his hospitality the next morning.

'We look forward to seeing you on your return,' he said as we left, no doubt looking forward to another ham and bag of flour.

'Over my dead body,' Hybald muttered as he rode out of the village at my side.

Our night at Ripon Monastery was luxurious by comparison, even though it was a saint's day with only baked carp, coarse bread and water for a meal. We reached the burnt out shell of Eoforwīc the next afternoon, only to discover that the archbishop was at Whitby. It appeared that Wulfhere had taken one look at the hut he'd been offered whilst his hall was being rebuilt and decided to stay at the monastery fifty miles to the north-east until the work was completed.

-ᚹ-

We reached Whitby two days later. Had I known where Wulfhere was in the first place, we could have saved ourselves three days of riding. We were all seasoned horsemen but saddle-sore didn't adequately describe how we felt by the time we'd run the archbishop to earth.

On the last day the weather had deteriorated markedly. It had got bitterly cold and the rain that started around midday had turned to sleet initially and then to snow for the last hour of our journey. Fortunately the ground underfoot was quite wet and so it hadn't started to settle by the time we arrived. It continued to snow all through the night and we awoke to a white landscape.

Unfortunately it wasn't the only thing we awoke to. I was sitting in the abbot's hall with Wulfhere discussing what he knew about Guthrum and Halfdan and their plans when Lambert came barging in unannounced. I was about to reprimand him when what he had to say had me running for the door instead.

'Come quickly lord. There's a Viking fleet heading this way.'

At first I didn't believe him. No one in their right mind would be out in this weather, let alone be at sea. However, I supposed the Vikings might have been caught out by the snow storm. I rushed to the watch tower beside the one and only gate into the monastery on the headland above the village of Whitby.

The boy was right. There were five longships of various sizes making for the entrance to the River Esk. Although the snow had ceased falling, the wind was still gale force and the ships appeared to be in trouble. Two of them had lost their masts and, whilst the others had all managed to lower their sails and secure the yardarms to the upright gaffs either side of the mast, the rowers were having trouble keeping the longships from broaching in the turbulent sea.

As we watched one of the ships swung around broadside on to the wind, despite the rowers desperate efforts to bring her round so that the wind was directly aft. The next big wave rolled her onto her side. She righted herself after it had passed but there must have been a lot a lot of water in the bilges as she was riding a lot lower in the water than she had been.

The next wave crashed into her side and a lot more water ended up in the hull. She was now settling in the water and the crew started to abandon her. Most Vikings were good swimmers and these men were sensibly not wearing byrnies. However, they were being tossed around by the huge waves and none of the other four ships were in a position to save them.

The next wave swamped the ship and it started to sink. Meanwhile rowers in two of the other ships were pulling desperately to save their ships from being dashed onto the rocks below the monastery. They were doomed to failure and they were broken into pieces as the mountainous waves drove them to disaster. One or two of their crews may have managed to survive, but nearly all of them were either drowned or smashed to pulp on the rocks.

The other two longships – a drekar and snekkja – made it into the safety of the estuary where the waters were relatively calm, even if the wind was still blowing strongly. The longships made for the jetty and when they reached there I saw no movement, apart from the ships boys climbing ashore to tie the vessels up, as the exhausted crews tried to recover.

I hadn't been idle whilst this drama was unfolding, sending a messenger to the local thegn to warn him what was happening and advising him to arm his fyrd and get everyone up to the monastery. By the time the ships had moored there was a long stream of people struggling up the steep path towards us.

It took the Vikings some time, but eventually about eighty warriors started to climb up the path towards us. I had my half a dozen warriors and the Thegn of Whitby had another eight, making sixteen in all. We also had forty two members of the fyrd. We were therefore outnumbered by the Vikings and all of them would be trained killers.

'Open the gates and we'll let you go with your miserable lives intact. You have five minutes. If the gates are still closed after that time, then you will all die,' the man in front of the Vikings shouted in Norse when they reached the open space in front of the monastery.

The archbishop and Beornric had joined me in the watch tower. The abbot had tried to climb up but there was no room.

'Do as he says,' the archbishop yelped in panic.

'Shut up. May I remind you that I'm the hereræswa? Now you are taking up valuable space Wulfhere; I'd be grateful if you would leave this to the warriors.'

When the man made no attempt to leave I bundled him to the hatchway and told him he could either climb down or I'd push him out of the way. I'd made an enemy for life but, just at that moment, I couldn't care less.

'Can you put an arrow though their leader's neck?' I asked Beornric once Wulfhere had disappeared, shouting insults and threatening to excommunicate me.

'Yes, I think so. The wind is the problem. It's gusting so I'll have to time it right.'

The Viking leader was standing with his hands on his hips about seventy feet from the gates evidently expecting the monks to surrender without a fight. If it had been up to that fool Wulfhere they would have done so, and paid the price.

There was a sudden lull in the gale and Beornric stood up, pulled his bowstring to his ear, aimed and released the arrow all in less time than it took to take a breath. It didn't take the arrow long to reach its target, but to me it seemed like forever. If the Norseman saw it coming, he must have been so surprised that he was rooted to the spot.

It struck him at the base of his neck where it joined his torso, barely an inch above the top of his byrnie. It may have been a fluke, but then Beornric always was a lucky archer. The man collapsed with blood spurting out the wound.

There was a boy standing next to him who was no more than twelve, or thirteen at most. He was dressed in a highly polished byrnie and a gleaming steel helmet embellished in gold. His cloak was a deep blue with a wolf skin sewn to it. I was sure that he was the leader's son, especially when he sobbed with rage and cradled the dying man to him.

I was loathe to kill him, though Beornric suggested it; not just because of his age but because he was hot-headed and inexperienced. I signalled for the other archers on the parapet and seconds later a ragged volley of war and hunting arrows sped towards the massed Vikings. We managed to kill or wound perhaps eight or ten before the enemy had the sense to swing their shields off their backs and shelter behind them.

Because we were shooting down at them, there was little exposed skin visible and any further shots would be wasting arrows so I ordered everyone to cease shooting. As soon as I did that the young firebrand ordered his men to charge the gate and batter it down with their axes.

The gates were made of stout oak studded with steel bolts attached to bracing on the inside. Given time they might have been able to get through them, but it would have taken hours using battle-axes. They didn't have hours though. Although those close to the gates were out of sight of those on the walls, the watch tower jutted out about four feet. I climbed down to make room for Lambert and he and Beornric started to pick off the axemen at an almost leisurely pace.

Of course, the Vikings had some archers of their own but they hadn't bothered to bring their bows with them from the ships. By the time they'd retrieved them Lambert and Beornric had killed ten more men at the gate and the rest had hurriedly retreated.

The boy Viking was screaming at his men to attack again until one of the older warriors back handed him across the face and told him to shut up. His father might have been their Hersir or Jarl but that didn't mean that his son would inherit his mantle. I knew that their Thing – the equivalent of a Witan except that every free man could vote – would choose their next leader in due course, and it was unlikely to be a boy.

We waited to see what the Vikings would do next. Nothing happened for an hour or more and then men appeared from the village carrying a pitcher of fish oil. I knew what that meant; they were about to use fire arrows to set the monastery ablaze. That might put their prospective plunder at risk, but I had a feeling that it was now more a question of honour and revenge.

I climbed back up the ladder and whispered in Beornric's ear.

'Can I try too?' Lambert asked eagerly.

'Yes, no harm in that, but don't release until Beornric has.'

Their archers took up position over a hundred yards away from the palisade. They must have thought that they'd be safe at that range. What they planned to do was light the oil soaked wadding and then run forward and fire at a high trajectory over the wall and into the thatch of the nearby huts. It would still be damp from the snow but the strong wind might well have dried out the top layer.

When the first archer dipped his arrow in the oil and another man lit it Beornric let fly. It wasn't a perfect shot and it was at maximum range. It lodged in the man's thigh and he dropped the flaming arrow. As luck would have it, it fell into the open pitcher of fish oil, which went up with a whoosh. He and two other Vikings standing nearby were splashed with burning oil and screamed as their clothes ignited.

The Vikings were now furious and eager to kill us, no matter what the cost, but someone evidently had a cool head. They did what they should have done at the beginning. They went and found every ladder they could in the village and prepared to make an assault on the walls. Our numbers were roughly equal by this stage but it wasn't just a question of numbers; the enemy had the better fighters in the main, but we had the defensive palisade. I had a feeling that it would be a close run thing.

The Vikings had found ten ladders but not all were long enough to reach the top of the palisade. They had overcome this problem by making platforms from the walls of some of the huts on which to place the short ladders. As they ran forward carrying the ladders and three platforms the raiders ran into a hail of arrows which caused half a dozen casualties, despite the shields the leading men held in front of them.

Once the ladders were in place the Vikings started to swarm up them. Lambert and Beornric killed another five men on the nearer two scaling ladders from their vantage point and the fyrd managed to use pitchforks to push two of the ladders away from the walls. A few more were killed as they tried to climb over the top of the palisade but over forty Vikings managed to get a foothold.

My men retreated leaving them in possession of the parapet to the left of the gate. They started to celebrate thinking they'd taken the monastery but then the four archers I'd sent up onto the roof of the church started to pepper them with arrows. The church was a mere thirty yards from the perimeter so they could hardly miss.

It wasn't long before the Vikings scrambled back down their ladders and left us in possession of the monastery. Of course, we too had our casualties, but at the cost of eight dead and nine wounded we'd managed to halve the Vikings' numbers.

In the middle of the afternoon their two ships cast off but evidently they didn't have enough men to man both of them. They sunk the snekkja in the middle of the estuary and the drakar sailed away to the south. The storm had blown itself out and they hoisted the sail to catch the light breeze. There was still quite a swell running though and, as I watched the longship, it would appear on the crest of a wave and then disappear completely in the trough.

The abbot was full of gratitude for the salvation of his monastery but the archbishop just scowled at me and muttered that I'd been lucky.

'You think that this is over do you?' I asked them.

'Yes, of course. They've sailed away with their tails between their legs,' Wulfhere replied scornfully.

'Karl, Fiske; come here. Do you think we've seen the last of the Vikings?'

Both shook their heads.

'No, lord. They are Norsemen. They won't give up that easily.'

'Pah, what do these boys know about anything,' Wulfhere asked scornfully.

'Both of them are Norse. They may be Christians, but they know how their fellow Norsemen think.'

The archbishop said something in reply but I was no longer listening.

'Go and get your horses' I told the boys, and take Leowine with you. I want you to find where they've landed.'

I turned to the abbot.

'Where is the nearest place where they could beach their ship to the south of here?'

'Just around the next headland,' he asked, evidently surprised by my question. 'Why? Do you think they'll return, Drefan?'

'I'm certain of it. They'll come back at night thinking that we'll be busy celebrating our victory. One or two will climb over the walls silently and open the gates for the rest.'

Wulfhere had gone pale whilst I was speaking but the abbot was looking tranquil.

'You have a plan?'

'Of course,' I replied.

-ᚢ-

144

'We soon found them, lord,' Leowine told me a few hours later. 'They had beached the drekar in the big curving bay where you told us it would be. The waves were crashing onto the sand so they pulled the ship as far as they could up the beach.'

'The tide has washed part of the beach clear of snow and they've set up camp near the high water mark, gathered firewood and cooked a meal of some sort; we couldn't see what,' Lambert put in, eager to add his bit.

Leowine gave him an irritated look before continuing.

'We waited until they gathered up their weapons and started up the path through the dunes and then rode back here.'

'How far is this bay from here?' I asked.

'About three quarters of a mile.'

'The snow will slow them down a bit but I should think that we can expect them in about half an hour or so. Right, you know what to do; off you go.'

I went back up the watch tower. The night was overcast but the snow reflected what light there was. It was enough to see perhaps fifty yards once your eyes were accustomed to the dark.

As I waited it was eerily quiet at first. Then I heard the rustle of the monks' habits as they made their way quietly towards the church for the last service of the day. After the door of the church had closed I heard nothing further until the crunch of a foot in the snow alerted me to the presence of someone outside the palisade.

I touched Leowine on the shoulder and he struck a flint a few times until the collection of shavings in a metal pot caught. Once a few twigs and then small pieces of wood were added, the fire in the pot had caught sufficiently for him to light a torch soaked in oil. Once it was well alight Leowine threw it high in the air.

It turned lazily end over end as it sailed through the air before landing forty yards from the palisade. There was a whoosh as the oil soaked grass caught light and then the flickering flames spread outwards like the ripples on a still pond do when a stone is thrown into it. The fire not only illuminated the Vikings creeping towards the monastery, but it set light to half a dozen of those in the immediate area.

The archers, who had been waiting crouched below the palisade, leaped to their feet and sent arrow after arrow towards the figures silhouetted by fire below them. The Vikings lucky enough to still be in the shadows turned tail and fled, but they didn't get very far.

They encountered the thegn's warriors, backed up by his fyrd, as they ran back through the snow to the beach and the men of Whitby weren't inclined to be merciful. They took no prisoners.

Meanwhile Tancred and Bran came running up to the gatehouse with our horses and my warriors and I rode out of the gates and along the path taken by the fleeing Vikings. I had impressed on everyone the importance of keeping one eye shut when the fire trap was sprung so we didn't lose our night vision. We passed the scene of the thegn's ambush and he called out that all but a few who had escaped inland were dead. I thanked him and we rode on towards the bay where the longship lay.

When we got there six boys and two older warriors were still sitting around one of the fires. Doubtless they thought that we were their men returning until they realised that we were mounted. There was no possibility of so few pushing the longship back off the beach so they bravely grabbed their weapons and prepared to make a fight of it.

'Surrender and you shall live,' Karl called out to them in Norse. 'Refuse and you will die like the rest of your crew.'

One of the old warriors replied that it was time he went to join his comrades in Valhalla but asked us to spare the boys. Then he and the other man ran at us and we cut them down. The ship's boys sullenly threw down their spears and daggers and it was all over.

-Ɏ-

'So did you manage to get any useful information out of that fat fool Wulfhere?' Ricsige asked me after I'd ridden up to Bebbanburg to report.

'Not much. He'd fled Ripon as soon as the Heathen Army appeared. He did say that Halfdan and Guthrum detested each other and that, when he looked back after they'd reached the safety of the hills, he saw that they'd established two separate camps outside the monastery. It's an indication that the army has split.'

'That's a good thing, isn't it?'

'Yes, for Mercia as they will be facing fewer Vikings next year, I suppose. Not so good for us if Halfdan comes back our way.'

'But he'll have far fewer men if he parts company from Guthrum and Ubba surely?'

'Yes, that's true. Perhaps we can risk facing him on the battlefield if that's the case.'

He nodded his head and then surprised me by saying 'tell me about Whitby.'

I'd mentioned that there had been an attack on the monastery whilst I was there and that we'd beaten it off but hadn't given him any details. It had seemed irrelevant.

As he'd asked, I gave him a brief account.

'I suspect that you are being far too modest. What did you do with the ships' boys? Did you bring them back to turn them into more Christian Norsemen for your warband?'

'No, I didn't,' I said with a smile. 'I suspect that Karl and Fiske are rather special cases. I left them there to become slaves and work in the fields.'

I returned to Alnwic for the winter but in the middle of March I sent Hybald and Karl back towards Ripon to try and find out if my supposition about the army splitting was true. They returned in early April to say that it was as I suspected, but Halfdan wasn't heading for Deira, or even Bernicia; he was making for Cumbria.

Chapter Twelve – In Ivar's Footsteps

874 to 875

'Why Cumbria?' Ricsige asked as he paced the floor of my hall at Alnwic. It was May and he was making his annual visit to each of his ealdormen.

'Well, according to the reports we've received, only just over a thousand warriors chose him as their leader when the army split up at Repton. Most of those were Norse and there are a lot of Norse settlers in Cumbria. Perhaps he's seeking to recruit some of them?'

'Why would they join him? They are already settled on their own farms with families for the most part. What can he offer?'

Karl coughed politely from the door where he was on guard duty.

'If I may speak, Cyning?'

Ricsige waved his hand in assent and Karl cleared his throat.

'Whilst Norsemen, like the Danes and Swedes, want to own land they can call home, they are essentially raiders. It's a lot easier to take what you want with the sword than to have to work hard on the land in order to produce food that barely sustains you and your family.'

'Thank you, Karl. So where does he plan to raid? Northumbria?'

'Perhaps, although I've heard a rumour that he covets the throne of Duibhlinn which his brother Ivar held for three years before he was killed,' Ricsige said thoughtfully.

'Karl? What do you think?' I asked him.

'When I was with the heathen army it was generally believed that Halfdan was jealous of Ivar. He was the youngest of the four and Ivar the eldest. Perhaps it's not surprising that Halfdan is always seeking to outdo him.'

'Let's hope that he turns westwards towards Ireland then, and not eastwards into Northumbria,' Ricsige said in conclusion.

We heard nothing more for a while then rumours began to reach my ears that Halfdan was besieging Caer Luel, the former seat of the Ealdorman of Cumbria before the shire fell to the Strathclyde Britons a decade or more ago.

Cumbria, together with Luncæstershire, had once formed the Kingdom of Rheged, populated by the Britons – the same people who inhabited Strathclyde. However, when King Oswiu had married the heiress to the throne centuries ago he had incorporated it into Northumbria and Angles and Saxons began to settle there. Now these people were fleeing eastwards into what was left of Northumbria.

Their individual stories differed, of course, and often conflicted with one another, but gradually I began to piece together what was happening. Halfdan had been joined by the Norse settlers along the coast of Cumbria and by five hundred more from Ireland. The new King of Strathclyde, Rhun ab Arthgal, son of the man defeated by Ivar the Boneless, was in no position to reinforce Cumbria and, when Caer Luel fell, the remaining Britons fled north across the River Lynne, which had been the traditional border.

Halfdan had settled more of his Norsemen in Cumbria but the bulk of his forces had accompanied him and the Irish Norse across the sea. From what I could gather Eysteinn Óláfsson, son of Olaf the White who had helped Ivar to seize the throne in 870, was embroiled in a dynastic struggle with the supporters of Barith, Ivar's four year old son. I don't suppose for a moment it was as simple as that. The jarls who claimed to support Barith were no doubt struggling for power amongst themselves and using the young boy as a figurehead.

If the stories were true it seemed that Ivar had sired two more sons with his Strathclyde princess before he was killed - twin boys called Sigfrøðr and Sigtryggr Ívarrsson. I was surprised that Halfdan wanted to get involved in such a complex struggle for power until I remembered the smouldering jealousy between him and Ivar. Perhaps it extended to his nephews as well?

I heard nothing more until a monk from Iona visited Lindisfarne. Ricsige sent me a message to let me know that Halfdan had prevailed and had now been enthroned by the Irish Norsemen as King of Duibhlinn. I made the mistake of thinking that he would now stay across the sea. I was wrong. In March 876 he landed back in Cumbria with an army two thousand strong. That could only mean one thing: he was intent on invading Northumbria once more.

-ᛉ-

Ricsige and I stood on the parapet of the stronghold known as Dùn Èideann with Theobald, the ealdorman of the shire that stretched along the south bank of the Firth of Forth. Below us lay the village of the same name, now deserted by its inhabitants and occupied by the invading Norse. Halfdan had marched north from Caer Luel through the hills, pillaging Selkirkshire on his way north. He had learned his lesson from the failed incursion of 874. We had little or no warning and this time he seized livestock and grain stores as he went.

We didn't even have time to muster the complete strength of Northumbria to oppose Halfdan. It was doubtful if the ealdormen of Deira would have responded in any case. They were nervous about Guthrum and Ubba, who were still in Mercia to their south, although the latest reports said that they were advancing towards Cambridge where King Burghred had mustered his army to oppose them. Furthermore, they had suffered the most from Ricsige's scorched earth campaign two years previously and resented his transfer of the capital back to Bebbanburg. Consequently he was unpopular in the south of the kingdom.

We had five hundred trained warriors and another two thousand men of the Bernicia fyrd inside the fortress. Food stocks would only last for about a month as four hundred women and children from the settlement of Dùn Èideann had also taken refuge with us. We stood little chance of winning an engagement in the open. Our only hope was to stay bottled up in the impregnable fortress and hope that the rest of Northumbria would come to our rescue before it was too late. It wasn't much of a hope.

I was also worried about Eadgifu and my children, Agnes and Edgar. They were still at Alnwic and I wished now that I had told them to take refuge at Bebbanburg.

'I don't want to just sit here,' Ricsige told me two nights later. 'Our one hope is the Picts.'

'The Picts?' I queried incredulously. 'They have always been our enemies. There is nothing more they would like than to see us driven out of Lothian.'

'I am well aware of that,' the king replied, annoyed at my statement of the obvious. 'However, they may well be more concerned about Halfdan's Norsemen. They have driven Strathclyde out of Cumbria and now they are camped on the southern border of Pictland. Their Danish counterparts are in the process of conquering all of southern England. Who would you fear most if you were Constantín?'

Constantín mac Cináeda had been King of Pictland since 862 and four years later he'd been trapped at a place called Dùn Dè on the east coast by a raiding party of Norsemen some four hundred strong. According to rumour he paid five chests of silver as the ransom for his release. He was hardly likely to be well disposed towards the Norse.

'Perhaps you are right,' I conceded. 'How do we find out if he would be prepared to ally himself to us?'

'Someone needs to go and see him,' he replied looking me in the eye.

'You mean me? But I don't speak their language.'

'No but your body servant does.'

'Bran? Yes, of course, but Constantín might disapprove of a Pictish slave.'

'Then free him. Of course, Constantín may speak Latin. He's a Christian, like most Picts, and an educated man, so I'm told.'

'Very well. But how on earth do I get there? Do we even know where he is?'

'No, but the most likely place is Dunkeld where his senior bishop lives.'

'Dunkeld? Do we know where that is?'

I turned to Theobald as he had more contact with the Picts than we did.

'I don't know exactly where it is, but I believe it's a day's ride inland from Dùn Dè, which is on the coast of the Firth of Tay; the next estuary north of the Forth.'

I went back to the small chamber I'd been allocated and which I shared with Alcred and Bran to think about the impossible task that Ricsige had set me.

-Ẋ-

The Vikings had arrived overland, presumably leaving their fleet at Caer Luel, but there were several knarrs docked two miles north of Dùn Èideann alongside a wooden jetty. There were also a few storage huts there but little else. However, the initial problem was how I could escape from the besieged fortress with enough men to man a knarr.

The fortress only had one entrance, at the eastern end of the rock on which it stood. The rest of the perimeter lay along the top of sheer sided cliffs. The besieging army had occupied the settlement and surrounding land beyond the entrance gates, but they didn't bother to invest the inaccessible sides.

'As I see it we have two options for me and those men I need to take with me: either you sally forth and launch a lightening attack on the enemy camp so that we can sneak away in the confusion, or we construct a rope ladder that my group can climb down.'

'How many do you plan to take with you?'

'I'll need a captain, helmsman and four ship's boys to sail the knarr and six warriors to man the oars so we can get out to sea and to protect us. I'll also take Bran as he speaks their language.'

'Fourteen in total? It'll take you some time to climb down a rope ladder. You might be seen by one of their patrols before you can all reach the bottom. I think the diversionary attack might be the best option.'

Ricsige decided that a sudden charge into the enemy camp by fifty riders followed by an immediate withdrawal back into the fortress should give us sufficient time to slip out on foot and make our way on foot into the trees below the southern ramparts.

We waited for a moonless night and when it came the conditions were perfect for what we had to do. A light mist permeated the atmosphere so that most Norsemen had taken shelter in the huts of the settlement or their tents. Only those guarding the gate were outside and they were clustered around a few campfires that spluttered and smoked in the damp air.

The gates were open and the horsemen were upon them before they had a chance to gather their wits and pick up spears and shields. Our mounted warriors speared and cut down the sentries before heading for the tented camp to the north of the settlement. Several carried lit torches and they threw these inside the tents before turning round and heading for the gates again.

By this time scores of Vikings had erupted from the huts and the tents, but they were confused and panic stricken, thinking that the whole Northumbrian army was attacking them. By the time they had formed themselves into a fighting force our mounted warriors were nearly back at the gate.

They had hacked down several Norsemen as they withdrew and now the rest rushed forward eager to trap them before they could regain the safety of the fortress. However, our men threw down lit torches to illuminate them and the archers sent a volley of arrows into their packed ranks.

Because of the damp, the bows didn't have their normal power or range but they still managed to cause fifty or more casualties before the Vikings hastily withdrew out of range. The gates clanged shut and, apart from two who had been killed, all those who had sallied forth were safely back in the fortress.

153

Meanwhile my group had slipped away as soon as the horsemen rode down the sentries and ran for the cover afforded by the trees and shrubs at the base of the southern rock face. I breathed a sigh of relief as soon as I was certain that no one had seen us and we moved off together towards the coast of the Firth of Forth.

An hour or so later we crawled forward to the top of a slight rise that overlooked the small port. The hubbub caused by the mounted sortie had died down but we could faintly hear the exchange of insults between the besiegers and the besieged in the still night air.

The damp mist had soaked everything we were wearing but it also meant that, if we were successful in stealing a knarr, we could quickly disappear into the murk, making pursuit less of a problem.

By this stage dawn was less than an hour away so we had to get a move on. We crept through the storage huts without encountering anyone. I peered inside one but could see little. I felt around and discovered that it was empty, as were all the other huts. Evidently the Viking forage parties had stripped them bare.

There were three knarrs moored to the jetty but there was no sign of life on them. Either the watch was asleep or their crews were all ashore. I had no idea whether the knarrs belonged to the Norse, Danes, Northumbrians or Picts. They might even be Frisians or Franks, however the latter seemed unlikely. My guess is that they were recent arrivals who had been surprised to find Halfdan's army besieging the stronghold. However, where the crews were now was a bit of a mystery.

It was a puzzle that I didn't plan to stay around long enough to solve. We chose the largest knarr and I was delighted to find that the hold was full of animal skins, presumably awaiting export: sheep fleeces, goat skins, tanned leather and even a few wolf and bear pelts. I knew that bears had all but disappeared from the south of England, but up in the North they could still be found up on the wild moors and in the forests remote from settlements. The furs would make an excellent gift for Constantín.

An hour later, just as the impenetrable murk began to grow lighter, we cast off. We rowed slowly to the east with two of the ship's boys in the bows looking for rocks and another up the mast to look for any breaking water that would indicate that we were too close to the shoreline or to the four islands at the entrance to the firth. Visibility, even when it became day, was a hundred yards at best, so we proceeded at no more than two miles an hour – not that a knarr propelled by just six oars could go a great deal faster anyway.

After about an hour the sun began to burn off the mist and a light breeze came from aft. We hoisted the sail, but kept it reefed until the visibility improved further. I was confident now that we had avoided the south shore where it bulged northwards and the three inshore islands, but the Isle of May lay more or less in our path.

'There, dead ahead, lord,' the lookout called down.

'How far?'

'Not far, not far at all. Perhaps two hundred yards?' he called down trying to keep the panic out of his voice.

'Bear away,' the captain roared before I could say anymore.

The steersman leaned on his oar and the prow swung round to the right. Now the wind was still behind us but, instead of being on our port quarter it was now on the larboard quarter. As the bows came round the other ship's boys ran to trim the sheets attached to the bottom corners of the mainsail for the new course.

The captain looked at me as the Isle of May slipped past us on the left and I nodded.

'Shake out the reef,' he called and once again the boys ran to obey.

The mist was burning off all the time, helped by the strengthening breeze, and shortly after leaving the island behind us, we turned onto a new tack heading north, or as close to it as we could get close hauled.

The entrance to the Firth of Tay lay fifteen miles to the north west of us. The problem with a knarr was that it could only really go where the wind took it. Although there were six oars, three a side, they were only intended for manoeuvring in port. Consequently we would have to sail well north of the entrance and then head south west close hauled to enter the mouth of the Tay.

Once in the firth we would probably have to row the last eight or nine miles to Dùn Dè on the north bank. However, we were in luck. The breeze died away just after midday and we lay becalmed as it backed from west to south and finally to east. At the time we were just north of the Firth of Tay and so we were able to run into it and head for the jetty.

Being a knarr we didn't attract too much excitement until I sent Bran ashore to ask if the king was there. He came back bringing with him the port master and three wild looking men with spears and shields that I presumed were his escort.

The port master barked something at me in his barbaric tongue and Bran explained that he wanted to know our business in his port so that he could work out what dues were payable.

'Tell him that I haven't come to trade; my business is with his king.'

At this the port master's eyes lit up.

'He says that if you have an expensive gift for Constantín, you will still have to pay him five per cent of its value in order to land it,' Bran said after a further exchange.

'Tell him that the only gift he will get from me is my sword in his fat belly. Now ask him again if Constantín is here; if not, where can I find him.'

When Bran repeated my threat the man's eyes widened and he looked behind him to assure himself that his men were there to protect him. However, they had taken one look at my own warriors, who had now donned their armour and were carrying their shields and spears, and were busy backing away. The port master gave a startled yelp and scuttled after his fast disappearing escort.

I heard laughter coming from the jetty and turned to see that everyone was enjoying the discomfiture of the unpopular port master. However, all of this was hardly helping my mission.

'Does anyone know if the King of the Picts is here?' I called and Bran translated.

'No, he's not. I hear that he's at Arbroath, some thirty miles from here, further up the coast,' one of the men on the jetty replied in passable English.

'Thank you, friend.'

I gave Bran a silver coin to give to the man who nodded his head in thanks. Ten minutes later we had cast off and were pulling hard at the oars and seemed to be making little progress into the wind; however, Dùn Dè was disappearing behind us and I realised that we'd caught the ebb tide. As the place faded from view I could just make out the fat port master shaking his fist at us as he stood at the end of the jetty with a dozen warriors behind him.

-ᛉ-

'What is your name and what message has Ricsige got for me?' Constantín asked me in Latin once he'd been told that I was emissary from the King of the North Saxons.

It had been easier to get an audience that I'd anticipated. There was nowhere to land near the settlement itself so we beached the knarr in a cove where there were a few fishing boats and half a dozen huts. At first the inhabitants had run away from us but Bran had called out that we came in peace and had a gift for their head man.

The toothless greybeard had been greatly impressed with the wolf skin I gave him and had readily allowed us to make use of the cart and pony that they used to cart their catch into Arbroath for sale. We had loaded the rest of the furs and hides onto the cart and I prayed that they would lose the smell of fish in time.

We were challenged at the gateway into the local chieftain's hall, where the king was apparently staying, and we had to leave our weapons there before we were allowed to proceed. A priest came to fetch us after a wait of scarcely half an hour and I followed him into the dim interior of the hall with Bran behind me. The others waited outside.

I was relieved that the king spoke such good Latin; it saved Bran from having to translate and it meant that communication between us was on a more personal level than it would have been through a third party.

'I'm Drefan, Ealdorman of Islandshire in Northumbria.'

I was about to go on and say that I was also the Heræswa. Picts were impressed by status and boasting of ancestry, importance and heroic deeds were usually part of an introduction. However, I was struggling for the right words for army commander in Latin until I remembered the title used in the late Roman Empire.

'I am King Ricsige's Magister Militum,' I concluded.

'Yes, I know who you are Lord Drefan. I suspect that you are also the archer who wounded the infamous Ragnar Lodbrok when you were a boy, and so facilitated his capture.'

'You are well informed, Domine.'

'Now that we have got the introductions out of the way, what do you want with me? You are brave to come here, are you also foolhardy?'

'I hope not,' I said with a smile. 'I'm sure you know about the capture of Caer Luel by Halfdan and his Norsemen and his victory over the Britons of Strathclyde.'

Constantín didn't reply but merely nodded.

'Now he lays siege to Dùn Èideann and most of the Northumbrian army. If it falls he will have gained, not just Lothian but all of Northumbria. Given that Guthrum and his Danes are rapidly overrunning Mercia, you will find yourself with the Vikings as your neighbours. Is that what you want?'

'No, of course not. But what makes you think that Halfdan wants to invade my kingdom?'

'He has defeated your vassal, Rhun ab Arthgal. The man's ambitions know no bounds. His driving force is to surpass the reputation of Ivar the Boneless. He has already taken the throne of Duibhlinn. Ivar captured much of Northumbria as well as defeating Rhun's father and driving him out of the strongest fortress in Strathclyde. If Halfdan is allowed to overrun Bernicia

158

he will only have equalled Ivar's success. He needs to do more. He can't invade Mercia or Wessex without coming into conflict with Guthrum. So where else can he turn?'

'North, into my kingdom; that's what you are saying?'

'It must be a possibility.'

'Perhaps, although I can't see why he would want to.'

'Have you no monasteries that he can plunder? Are your mormaers and chieftains so poor that they have no wealth to seize?'

'You may have a point, though I am far from convinced. But you didn't come here to warn me out of the goodness of your heart. What do you want from me?'

'An alliance, Domine. Let us fight the heathens together.'

At this the priest by his side got animated and spoke urgently in the king's ear. I didn't have a clue what they were saying and looked to Bran for help.

'The bishop is urging the king to agree,' he whispered. 'I think your mention of pillaging monasteries and fighting heathens got him on our side.'

The phrase *our side* told me that, whatever his birth, Bran now considered himself a Northumbrian and I was glad I'd freed him.

'Very well, but I expect something more than a few skins reeking of fish for my help. I could just leave you and your king to your fate and then slaughter the pagans when and if they are foolish enough to invade us.'

'King Ricsige is prepared to recompense you for your trouble and expense in mustering your army, Domine.'

'To what extent?'

'We will share the plunder we recapture from the Norse pagans equally.'

'Equally? I can bring over six thousand men to attack Halfdan. How many men do you have?'

'Don't forget that much of their treasure has been looted from Northumbrian homes and the monastery at Hexham. That will have to be returned out of our share.'

'One third to you and two thirds to me. That is my final offer.'

I appeared reluctant but finally agreed. Ricsige would be pleased. He had authorised me to agree to a split of one quarter to him and three quarters to the Picts. After all, without them Northumbria would be finished.

Chapter Thirteen – Halfdan's Campaign in the North

Autumn 875

'You've heard about King Burghred I assume?' Constantín asked as we rode south west towards Stirling where his army was mustering.

Burghred had been ousted by Guthrum the previous year after the Danes had captured his capital of Tamworth and forced him to flee. He had disappeared and no one knew where he was. We had hoped that he was mustering another army in secret and would recommence the struggle against the Danes. In the meantime Guthrum and Ubba had put a thegn named Ceolwulf on the throne as their puppet.

'Is he mustering another army in western Mercia,' I asked.

'No, I fear that there is no chance of that. I gather than he has managed to reach Rome and the Pope has given him sanctuary there.'

We rode on in silence. I knew that the Danes had overwintered in Cambridge but I had received little news of them this year. Unfortunately Constantín didn't know much more, only that Guthrum had spent most of the year so far consolidating his hold over Mercia. It meant that now only Wessex stood against the Danes and, unless we could defeat Halfdan, the Vikings would rule Northumbria as well.

The interior of Bernicia was sparsely populated but here the hills, after we left the wide valley known as Strathmore, seemed deserted. The only people we saw were shepherds high up on the hillside. However, once we turned south out of Strathallan we came across several settlements, the southernmost of which was Stirling with its impressive stronghold high on a cliff overlooking the plain to the west.

Stirling lay just to the south of the River Forth and was near the meeting point of three kingdoms: Pictland to the north-east, Strathclyde to the west and Northumbria to the south. Stirling used to belong to Strathclyde but when its king became Constantín's vassal, the Picts took it over.

We crossed over the wooden bridge to the south bank of the river and rode towards the camp which had been established in the shadow of the stronghold. There were already a thousand Picts there when we arrived and they cheered Constantín as he rode through the camp to find a spot for himself and his entourage upstream from the rest.

Over the next few days further contingents arrived, including fifteen hundred from Strathclyde. The weather had been fine, if a little chilly at night, but the day we set out it started to rain; not the type which was useful for watering crops, but the tiny droplets of water that seems to fill the air and permeate every stitch of clothing.

The drizzle continued all morning but it didn't seem to dampen the spirits of Constantín's army. They chattered away excitedly as if they were boys going on their first hunt. They radiated confidence, and no doubt they thought that they would have any easy victory over the Vikings as they outnumbered them by over three to one. However, I wasn't so confident. Halfdan might only have two and half thousand men, but they were all hardened warriors who had been taught to fight since they were boys – and all of them had been blooded in battle.

The Picts and their allies were poorly armed and inexperienced. Few had a byrnie or even a leather jerkin and no more than a third had a helmet. They carried a motley assortment of spears, axes and long daggers they called dirks. Most had a shield of some sort but few were the large circular lime wood type we used; some were made of wicker and others were small round wooden shields called targes. Often the latter would have a six inch long spike instead of a boss at the centre which made them useful in close quarter fighting, but they did little to protect the body of the owner.

Many Picts were barefoot; they must have had soles like leather not to feel pain as they walked. Most wore a long piece of woollen cloth, often saffron in colour, which was wrapped around the waist and held in place by a belt or a piece of rope. The rest was thrown across the chest and over one shoulder. This appeared to be their garb in summer and winter alike and I admired their hardiness.

Only two hundred or so were mounted. They were the mormaors – we would call them earls I suppose as they were sub-kings of the seven regions that made up Pictland – chieftains, their sons, their bodyguards and, of course, the two kings – Constantín and Rhun of Strathclyde.

Their steeds were small mountain ponies, rather than the horses my small group and I were used to. I felt rather a fool sitting on a pony with my feet barely more than a foot off the ground. I formed the impression that riding was little more than a status symbol; certainly you could never fight whilst mounted on them, or so I thought.

I had never seen the Picts fight but I'd been told that they didn't form a shield wall; in fact they were totally ill-disciplined. They charged in waves, each man trying to outstrip his fellow in the rush to reach the enemy first. Then they fought as individuals.

There were a few archers but I gathered that they weren't used en bloc as we did. Each bowman picked a target to shoot at as and when he felt like it.

'Isn't there a danger that they will shoot their own men,' I said in surprise when Constantín had told me this.

'Oh yes, and they often do. I've tried to organise them into a group and to control them. It worked for a short while but they soon split up, each seeking their own target as if they were on a hunt.'

It didn't give me great confidence.

-Ẅ-

I soon learned that the bigger the army the slower it moves. It took four days to get within striking distance of the Vikings and by then they knew we were on the way. Halfdan was faced with a difficult problem. Did he abandon the siege and march to meet the Picts, or did he take up a defensive position and hope to beat our combined forces. If he chose the former course he would have to worry about Ricsige's army to his rear.

He did neither. When Constantín sent out his scouts the next morning they came back with the news that the besiegers camp was deserted. I, like everyone else, jumped to the conclusion that Halfdan had given up the siege and was now heading south to recapture Eoforwīc, pillaging and raping his way through Northumbria as he went.

Then reports came in that he had done no such thing. He'd skirted to the south of us and had headed for the bridge at Stirling. By the time that Constantín realised what was happening Halfdan was laying waste to the land between the Ochil Hills and the north coast of the Firth of Forth. He wasn't after plunder - although the Norsemen naturally took what they could find - he was intent on teaching the Picts a lesson.

I said goodbye to Constantín and rode on to meet Ricsige.

'Well, it seems you managed to solve our little problem without spilling a drop of Northumbrian blood,' he said with a grim smile after I'd told him what had happened. 'Well done.'

We were far from certain that the danger was past, of course. Halfdan seemed intent on regaining Eoforwīc and so we fully expected him to cross back into Northumbria at Stirling and make his way south from there. Thankfully - at least as far as we were concerned - we were wrong.

It was March the following year before I heard what had happened in Pictland and it was my brother who brought me the news. He came down on a visit and we greeted each other warmly, all signs of our past estrangement forgotten. I was glad that whatever animosity had existed between us was now in the past and we got drunk together, much to Eadgifu's annoyance.

Before he got too inebriated Hrothwulf told us what he knew of the battle between the Vikings and the Picts. Constantín had caught up with Halfdan near a settlement called Dol Ar on the

River Devon on the southern edge of the Ochils. Both armies were on the north bank but the Vikings had taken up a defensive position on the steep slopes of a mountain called the King's Seat.

Constantín had been surprised that Halfdan only seemed to have fielded half the number of men he was expecting, but he assumed that the rest were away raiding elsewhere. The Picts were eager to attack the Vikings and their king was unable to keep control of them. Some three thousand young hotheads broke away from the main army and charged uphill at their enemies. By the time they reached the shield wall they were exhausted and no match for the experienced Vikings. The Picts came reeling back to the base of the mountain having lost nearly a thousand men.

Constantín had berated his men and this time he managed to get them organised in three waves who advanced slowly and surely up the slope. When the first wave had exhausted itself, the second moved forward to take their place. When the first wave withdrew they left a fresh mound of dead bodies behind, but they had managed to kill or wound hundreds of the Norsemen as well.

Just as the second wave engaged the enemy and the remnants of the first wave were recovering Constantín heard yelling to his left. The other half of Halfdan's men appeared out of a re-entrant on the Pict's flank. He sent his third wave to meet the new arrivals but they were disorganised and the Vikings advanced inexorably through their ranks using the formation known as the boar's snout.

It didn't take the second half of the Viking army long to cleave their way through the mass of Picts, killing as they went. The Picts in the third wave were routed and the rest panicked. The advancing Vikings were over a thousand strong and looked invincible. Although the Picts in the first wave still outnumbered their enemy by two to one, they joined the third wave and fled the battlefield.

Constantín was beside himself with fury, but there was nothing he could do. The second wave were still fighting the Viking shield wall on the slopes above them when the second half of the Norse army attacked them in the rear. They were trapped and doomed to die or be taken captive. Weeping, the King of the Picts allowed himself to be led away to the east and safety.

Constantín had lost nearly three thousand men – nearly half his army – killed or taken captive. The Vikings had then continued to rampage their way eastwards until they reached the coast at a place called Kilrymont, where they moved into winter quarters.

Constantín had suffered a severe blow to his reputation and, though he had tried to raise another army, few had answered his summons. In early March Halfdan's fleet had arrived from Caer Luel, having sailed around the top of the country via Orkeyjar, where they had recruited more young Norsemen looking for adventure and plunder. Halfdan had then sailed on southwards with the majority of his men, leaving a few hundred behind to keep a foothold at Kilrymont. A messenger had brought a letter asking Ricsige to bring his army north so that they could move against these Vikings together. However, Ricsige was more concerned about where Halfdan and the majority of his army were now headed.

Chapter Fourteen – The Last Raid on Lindisfarne

Summer 875

Ricsige wasn't the only one worried about the Vikings. The monastery on Lindisfarne had been sacked numerous times since the first raid in 793. Bishop Eardulf and his processors had always been determined to re-build and to remain on the Isle of Saint Aidan and Saint Cuthbert, but in the spring of 875 the prior died and Brother Aldred had been elected to replace him.

Aldred had many admirable qualities. He was devout, scholarly, pious and a good administrator. The one thing he wasn't was brave. The mere mention of the heathen Vikings made him pale and shake in fear. To put it bluntly, he was a coward.

As soon as he became prior he started to whisper in the abbot's ear. The abbot wasn't a man of strong character and before long Aldred's constant drip of poison had its effect and he went to see Eardulf to urge him to move the monastery to somewhere safer inland.

Eardulf was made of stronger stuff but the speculation about Halfdan's next move worried everyone. Eventually Eardulf had had enough and he called a meeting of the whole community so he could address them.

'The land on which this monastery stands was given to us by Saint Oswald, the martyred King of Northumbria slain by the pagan Penda of Mercia. It is the monastery of Saint Aidan and Saint Cuthbert; they would be ashamed at your cowardly talk of abandoning this sacred site. Yes, we have been raided by the Vikings on several occasions, but we have survived. To leave now would not just be cowardice, it would be a betrayal of our faith and of those who founded the monastery here.

'This is not called the Holy Island of Lindisfarne for nothing. Pilgrims visit us to pray at the shrine of Saint Cuthbert. What would he say if we deserted him because we feared for our worthless lives?'

Silence greeted the bishop's speech until Aldred broke it.

'We could always take the coffin of Saint Cuthbert with us to our new monastery, lord bishop. We can build a new shrine to him there.'

The suggestion was greeted with enthusiasm by the less stalwart members of the community.

'And where exactly do you propose to locate your new monastery, Brother Prior? Do you have a gift of land you are able to donate to the Church and money to build it?'

Aldred was silent for a few moments before he suggested that King Ricsige might be asked to grant the land.

'Do you think so? And what excuse will you give for leaving here? Will you confess your fear and lack of backbone?' Eardulf asked contemptuously.

'I am not being fearful, lord bishop, merely prudent,' the affronted prior replied, going red in the face.

'Well, it doesn't seem like prudence to me. No, the monastery has been here for two hundred and forty years; as far as I'm concerned it will remain here for another two centuries and hopefully longer.'

-ᚹ-

My brother told me about the situation at the monastery and I went to discuss it with Ricsige. He was already aware of the dissent that Aldred had fostered, but he regarded the matter as closed after the bishop had vetoed the proposal to leave. I wasn't so sanguine. However, the matter seemed to have been resolved and so I said nothing.

It was most unfortunate that a lone Danish longship, presumably seeking to join Guthrum's army, was driven off course and was wrecked on the north shore of Lindisfarne shortly after this. There were only twenty survivors out of a crew of seventy but that was enough.

I was told the story later by the thegn who owned the vill on Lindisfarne.

'The first I knew of the Vikings' landing was when a shepherd boy came running into the settlement saying that there was a dragon ship wrecked on the point and lots of Vikings had landed. When I managed to get the lad to calm down I learned that what he had seen was lots of bodies on the beach and on the rocks. A score of men were collecting them and putting them on a pyre they'd built of driftwood. However, that wasn't what the boy was stressed about; they had killed one of his ewes and were cooking it on a fire on the beach.

'I only had five warriors of my own but I sent the boy to tell the men in the fields that I was calling out the fyrd. That would give me nearly another thirty men. I sent another lad to warn the monks and to ask for the warriors guarding the monastery to join mine here at my hall.'

I nodded. Ricsige had kept to his father's policy of stationing ten or a dozen of his warband to guard the monastery on rotation.

'However, the abbot refused, saying that he needed the men to protect the monastery. He didn't seem to realise that by dividing our forces he was playing into the Vikings' hands.'

I recalled that Eardulf was away visiting Lothian at the time. With no other bishop in Bernicia he had a vast diocese to look after. It was a pity as his presence would undoubtedly have avoided what followed.

'I led my men towards the point near where the Vikings had been shipwrecked, according to the shepherd boy but, by the time we got there they had disappeared. A fire was burning on the beach and the stench of burnt meat wafted towards us on the wind. The pagans had obviously lit the fire to cremate their dead and, realising that the smoke would be seen, had then left the beach in haste.

'One of my men suddenly said the monastery was under attack and I led my men there as fast as I could. The Vikings were

169

assaulting the palisade around the monastery; two men lifted a third up so that he could grasp the top of the timbers and then haul himself over the top. The boy had said that there were a score of the heathen warriors but it looked to me more like forty.

'A few had already managed to get a foothold on the parapet and were trying to hold King Ricsige's men back to allow more of their fellows to join them. At that moment some of the Vikings had obviously reached the gates and unbarred them. They swung open and the rest of the heathens poured through them.

'All I could do was follow them inside with my men and attack them in the rear. It was a hard fought battle but eventually the last dozen or so fled out of the monastery. We followed them and hunted them down. It was a victory, but a hollow one. I had lost two of my warriors and the fyrd had fifteen casualties. Those not already dead were likely to die in time.

'I blame myself for not preventing the Vikings from entering the monastery as the abbot and seventeen of his monks had died trying to keep the heathens out of the church.'

Of course, I knew the gist of what had happened, but the detail explained why it was so easy for the remaining monks to defy the orders of the bishop when he returned and insist on leaving Lindisfarne.

On a grey day in September a procession of twenty three monks and seven novices left Lindisfarne, led by Bishop Eardulf and Prior Aldred. At least Eardulf had refused to recognise Aldred as the next abbot, saying that an abbot had to have a monastery and Aldred had abandoned his. They took several carts with them including one in which lay the coffin of Saint Cuthbert.

Ricsige, my brother and I had ridden to the end of the causeway to bid the monks farewell. When the king asked Eardulf where he was bound, he replied that God was leading them and they would wander until God showed them where he wanted them to establish their new monastery.

Later I asked Ricsige why he hadn't offered Eardulf land for his new monastery somewhere inland. He replied that he'd be damned if he would reward the monks for forsaking Lindisfarne.

As it turned out they were destined to wander the North of England for seven years before they established a new monastery at Conganis, an old fort on the Roman road which ran from Eoforwīc north into Pictland.

Chapter Fifteen – The Meeting at the Tyne

May 876

It was a glorious day in early May when we set out to ride from Alnwic to Bebbanburg. Eadgifu rode a beautiful grey mare on one side of me and my daughter Agnes sat proudly on her pony at my other side, much to the annoyance of my son Edgar who had to make do with sitting in front of me. He'd been badgering me for a pony of his own but, at just five, he was too young.

Six members of my gesith accompanied us as escort and Bran brought up the rear with Edagifu's maid, both leading a packhorse. As it was only a day's ride, I wouldn't have bothered with anything I couldn't fit into a couple of panniers, but both my womenfolk insisted on bringing several changes of clothing.

We passed an orchard of fruit trees in blossom and I reflected that such a scene of pastoral tranquillity belied what was happening elsewhere in Northumbria. Eoforwīc had thrown open its gates to welcome Halfdan, largely at the insistence of Archbishop Wulfhere, or so it was said. At least that had saved the city from being sacked.

The last son of Ragnar still in England had been enthroned as King of Jorvik and Wulfhere had blessed him, although the man remained a pagan. The extent of his realm remained unclear but, with two kings in Northumbria now - although neither of them claimed the actual title of King of Northumbria - Ricsige had called a meeting of the Witan at Bebbanburg to discuss the situation.

War clouds loomed, especially as Halfdan was in the process of displacing the Anglo-Saxon thegns and distributing their land to his followers. Many thegns, their warriors and dispossessed ceorls had fled north across the Tees. Their ealdormen had either accepted Halfdan's rule or had been killed and replaced by Norse jarls.

So far he hadn't ventured north of the River Tees but he was rumoured to be mustering an army again.

The Witan met two days later but the attendance was disappointingly small. No replacement for the Bishop of Hexham had yet been made since the murder of the last one by Halfdan's Norsemen when the pillaged the place the previous year. With the departure of Eardulf from Lindisfarne the only churchmen present were the abbots of Melrose and Jarrow and the Abbess of Coldingham. The Lothian ealdormen and those from Jarrow, Otterburn and Durham were the only others present, apart from myself.

'What do we know of Halfdan's intentions,' Ricsige asked me after he had formally opened the meeting.

'From what I can gather he is either mustering his forces to march north against us or he is being forced to return to Duibhlinn to deal with a revolt there,' I replied.

'Well, he can't do both,' Ricsige said, obviously irritated by my lack of reliable knowledge.

'Perhaps he can, Cyning,' the Abbot of Melrose said somewhat diffidently. 'If he can secure his position here, he would be free to return to Ireland.'

'Secure his position?' Ricsige queried.

The abbot looked uncomfortable and paused before replying.

'I've heard from the archbishop, Cyning. He says that Halfdan seeks a treaty with you so that he can leave for Ireland leaving Northumbria at peace.'

'You are in communication with that traitor?' Ricsige almost bellowed.

'May I remind you that he is still my superior in the Church? He has every right to write to me, as I have to him. I'm not involved in his politics, but I thought that what he'd told me might be of use to you. I apologise if I was wrong.'

Ricsige sat chewing his lip for a moment before making up his mind.

'We'll discuss this later, but you'd better tell me what you know.'

The abbot looked a little affronted that Ricsige evidently wanted to pursue the matter of communication between him and the archbishop further, but he told the king the gist of what he'd learned.

'Wulfhere believes that Halfdan will advance as far as the Tyne where he will seek to negotiate with you. He doesn't want to have to spend time and manpower invading Bernicia unless he can't reach an agreement with you. If he can, then he'll leave part of his army at Yorvik and return to Ireland.'

'And once he's done that, what's to stop him returning here and invading Bernicia?'

'Guthrum has abided by the oath he gave to King Alfred not to invade Wessex for five years – so far at any rate.'

'Only because he's been too busy subduing most of Mercia.'

'Don't forget that Halfdan has men scattered all over the place, from Pictland to Ireland and now southern Northumbria. He'll overstretch himself if he's not careful,' I pointed out.

'That's all very well,' he replied, 'but how many can he bring against us and how many can we muster?'

'As we no longer need to worry overmuch about the Picts in the north, we can probably raise six to seven hundred trained warriors from the warbands of ealdormen and thegns and a further three thousand from the fyrd. Of course many of them are still young and inexperienced. In addition there is your own warband and the crews of the fleet; that's another five hundred.'

'And Halfdan?'

'That's more problematical. The latest estimates are that he has just under two thousand Norsemen but we don't know how many of the fyrd of Deira and southern Bernicia might join him, whether coerced or not.'

'Why would they support an invader?'

'Because they want to protect their families, Cyning. Not all thegns and ealdormen have been replaced by the pagans, far from it. However, if they don't cooperate they risk being disposed or even seeing their families killed. They may not want to support Halfdan, but what alternative do they have?'

'Well, I suppose it can't do any harm to meet this pagan leader, but we will do so from a position of strength. Drefan, you need to mobilise the fyrd.'

-Ⱳ-

A chill wind had sprung up out of the east as we rode south to meet Halfdan at the agreed place on the River Tyne. It was a place I knew well – the ford at Wylam. It was where Ricsige's father, Edmund, had waited for Ragnar Lodbrok behind defensive works, only to be outwitted. Now their two sons were about to meet for the first time.

The local thegn was flustered by the king's arrival. He had inherited his vill from his father as a boy. Like many another his father had been killed ten years ago in the trap that Ivar the Boneless had set inside the walls of Eoforwīc. He was now a young man of twenty two who nevertheless gawped like an eight year old at the host that had descended on him.

He had, of course, been summoned to join the king's army but had then been told to stay where he was, which no doubt had puzzled him. He had only been alerted to Ricsige's arrival an hour before when a dozen scouts had informed him. They then headed south though the river using the ford. It had been created by building a roadway under the water, but the heavy rains of three days ago had increased the depth of water. The horses were over knee deep by the time that they got to the middle of the river and a man on foot would have been in danger of being swept away.

The thegn had rushed to get his servants to clean his hall ready for Ricsige's arrival but the king had disappointed him by electing to pitch his tent to the north of the settlement in the ruins of an ancient Roman fort lying on the wall built by the Emperor Hadrian centuries before. The place had been called Vindovala, or so I was told by my brother, who had an interest in all things Roman.

The wall at this point had been built along a low ridge and the army set up camp to the north of the wall on either side of the fort.

If the meeting went badly at least we occupied a good defensive position.

The scouts came back the next morning with the news that Halfdan was five miles away. He had a mounted contingent about five hundred strong, a further twelve hundred or so Norse warriors on foot and about two thousand Anglo-Saxons. The latter were mostly members of the fyrd, but there were two hundred well-armed men with them, presumably the Deiran thegns and their warbands.

Chapter Sixteen – The Empty Throne

May 877

The next day didn't start well. Heavy rain began to fall and in a few days, when the water from the hills had reached the ford, the river would become impassable. Ricsige and I rode down to the ford with a small escort but there was no sign of anyone coming to meet us. Instead we got catcalls and disparaging comments about our ancestry from the Norsemen who had gathered on the opposite side of the ford.

Not surprisingly, Ricsige got angrier and angrier until he abruptly yanked his horse's head around and cantered back up to the wall. We followed, pursued by laughter and more derogatory comments.

Just after midday, when Ricsige was considering packing up and leaving, a group of horsemen rode into the Viking's camp from the south. As one of the riders was carrying a red banner on which I could just make out a stylised depiction of a raven with its wings outspread as it flapped in the breeze, I realised that this must be Halfdan himself and went to inform Ricsige.

'The bloody man should have been here earlier to control his unruly mob of pagans,' the king muttered as he donned his helmet and yelled for someone to bring him his horse.

Once more we rode down to the ford. In addition to Ricsige and me, there was Hrothwulf, Theobald, Karl and four members of his gesith in our party. One of the latter carried the king's banner of a black wolf's head on a field of yellow.

We waited on our side of the ford and this time there were no insults thrown at us by the pack of heathens. Instead they watched us in baleful silence.

A few minutes later a group of Norsemen rode to the far side of the crossing. The man in the ornate helmet which covered his eyes and nose, leaving only his bearded chin exposed, was presumably Halfdan.

'Meet me in the middle of the ford,' Halfdan called across in Norse. 'Bring only one man.'

'What's he saying?' Ricsige asked.

'He wants to meet in the middle of the ford and says to bring only one man,' Karl replied.

'Tell him I'm bringing an interpreter as well as evidently he doesn't speak English. The likelihood of him speaking Latin is non-existent I suppose.'

'My king says that I need to accompany him to translate in addition to the,' he paused trying to think of the Norse for hereræswa. 'Leader of his warband,' he concluded.

'Very well, but your interpreter leaves his weapons behind.'

Karl pulled his sword from its scabbard and his dagger from its sheath and handed them to Bran. The boy hefted the sword as if checking its balance and I laughed. Ricsige, however, wasn't in a laughing mood and he kicked his horse forward into the river.

Karl and I urged our nervous horses into the river behind the king and came up either side of him. The ford was quite wide but I wasn't sure how close to the edge of the submerged stone roadway I was.

Halfdan and a giant of a Viking who made his stallion look like a small pony approached the centre from the far bank. They came to a halt three yards from us and for a moment no one said anything. The only sounds were the rippling water rushing past and the fluttering of the banners on the two banks. Somewhere a bird squawked and another replied. Both armies were silent as the grave, striving to hear what was being said.

Halfdan eventually broke the uncomfortable silence by introducing his companion, a jarl called Harald Scarface. I was intrigued by his nickname as I couldn't see a scar, but then I noticed a grey line running through his long, blond beard from his ear to his chin.

'This is Drefan, my hereræswa and chief counsellor and my interpreter...'

'Is a renegade Norse traitor,' Halfdan finished for him. 'I have a score to settle with Drefan, if he is the same person who killed Lagertha and brought down my father with arrows whilst hiding up a tree. It was the act of a coward.'

'I was fifteen and they were raiding my homeland,' I protested.

The Viking leader ignored me and addressed his next remarks to Ricsige in passable English.

'You will abdicate as so-called king and cede to me all the territory south of this river,' he demanded.

'I never sought the throne and, as you hold what used to be called Deira and you call Yorvik, I agree to abdicate as king, a title I never sought in the first place, and not to contest your rule south of the River Tees.'

Evidently much of Ricsige's reply had tested his understanding of English too much and he gestured for Karl to translate, something which obviously irked him. After Karl had complied Halfdan scowled at Ricsige.

'The Tyne, not the Tees.'

'Then we seem to have reached an impasse. The land between the two rivers is historically part of Bernicia. You are welcome to what you already rule - I never much liked the Deirans anyway – but we will fight for anything else that you claim.'

Halfdan chewed his lip and Scarface whispered in his ear, apparently urging him to attack us.

Suddenly there was a commotion on the south side of the river as armed men appeared out of the trees to the west.

'Treachery,' Harald Scarface yelled and drew his sword.

'No,' Halfdan shouted in alarm. 'They're Norsemen from Cumbria.'

But he was too late. Harald had brought his sword down on Ricsige's helmet. His blow was so powerful that it snapped his sword in two, but by then it had cut deeply into Ricsige's helmet and into his skull. My friend and lord was dead before he toppled out of his saddle into the swirling waters of the Tyne.

I was consumed by blind range and wasn't aware of what I was doing. Karl told me later that I was like a man possessed. I drew my own sword and thrust it into the giant Norseman's chest. My blow was so hard that I dislocated my wrist but the point severed several chain mail links, cut through the padded tunic underneath his byrnie as if it was made of paper, and broke several ribs before it entered his heart. He too crashed into the river with a tremendous splash.

Halfdan knocked my sword up and, because of my injured wrist, I lost my grip and it went spinning away into the water. Ignoring Halfdan and the commotion on both banks, I dismounted and groped around to find Ricsige's body, but the river had immediately washed both corpses downstream.

The Vikings had begun to wade across the ford and Karl pulled me away, helping me to mount before we were both hacked to pieces. Halfdan didn't do anything to stop us. He just sat there on his horse, obviously stunned by what had just happened. Then he turned and called on his men to stop, but they were in no mood to listen to him. They streamed past him intent on killing us.

As we reached the far bank our archers sent volley after volley into the packed ranks of the Vikings as they slowly made their way after us. In their rage at Harald Scarface's death they didn't even have the common sense to pull their shields around from off their backs to protect themselves. Hundreds must have died in that insane attempt to cross the ford before Halfdan's repeated orders to withdraw permeated their minds and they withdrew.

I organised the army to defend the ford in case there was a more organised attempt to cross it but neither Halfdan nor I was eager for a full scale battle. His Cumbrian reinforcements, whose sudden appearance had caused the tragedy, numbered no more than two hundred and didn't much affect our relative strengths. With the river as our first line of defence and the ruins of the wall as our second, I was certain that the odds were in our favour in any case.

The two armies sat staring at each other for some time. It wasn't until then that what had happened really sank in. Ricsige had been my friend and, although not a perfect lord – he was too hot-tempered for a start – he had ruled Bernicia well and kept it independent.

I mourned his loss but I didn't allow my grief to unman me; I had other things I needed to think about. For a start it looked as if I would have to command the army in battle and, even if we won, I didn't know who would succeed Ricsige as Lord of Bebbanburg and Earl of Bernicia. I was realistic enough to know that, whoever his successor was, he was most unlikely to be King of the North Saxons. Those days had passed.

In the middle of the afternoon the patrol I'd sent downstream returned with two bodies draped across two pack horses: Ricsige and Harald Scarface. Hrothwulf blessed the body of Ricsige and had it sewn into a length of leather ready for the journey back to Bebbanburg.

'It's fitting that he's buried on Lindisfarne,' my brother whispered in my ear and I nodded.

I looked down at the bloated corpse of the giant Harald, then an idea occurred to me. A little while later I rode down to the river bank with Kurt and Bran, the latter leading a horse on which Harald's body had been placed. We waded out to midstream and waited.

We weren't kept there for long. Halfdan rode out to meet us accompanied by a young boy.

'Thank you for returning Jarl Harald; at least, I presume that's what you intend?'

I nodded after Karl had translated, looking at the six year old sitting on a pony by his side.

'This is my nephew, Ivar's son, Bárðr,' he added with a dismissive wave of his hand.

I acknowledged the boy with a nod; he didn't reply but continued to stare at me, which I found slightly unnerving. This then was the eldest of the three children that the Princess of Strathclyde had born Ivar the Boneless before the latter was killed three years ago.

'I will reluctantly agree that the border between us should be the Tees,' Halfdan continued. 'I'll allow whoever succeeds the unfortunate Ricsige to rule the north for me, provided that he keeps the Picts in place.'

I shook my head.

'No, that's not acceptable. Ricsige's heir will keep the peace with you and respect the border on the Tees, but he won't be your vassal. You want a buffer state between Yorvik and the Picts; I understand that. But it can be agreed without any pledges of subservience.'

The Viking was silent for a moment.

'Who will succeed Ricsige? You?' he asked eventually.

'No, he has a brother, Egbert. I will propose him to the Witan but the choice is theirs.'

'Then make sure that Egbert understands the terms under which I'll allow him to rule Bernicia. He doesn't have to swear allegiance to me, if that's a problem, but he'd better be my friend or I'll sweep him, you and that rabble behind you from the face of the earth.'

I didn't add that the boy was only eleven and so the Witan might very well not elect him.

'I hear you, Halfdan. You'll leave us alone and we won't trouble you or your Vikings in Yorvik.'

He held out his arm and I clasped it near the elbow; he returned my grip and nodded. Satisfied, he and his nephew rode back to the south bank. As they left the boy turned and gave me a cheeky grin. Had the occasion not been so sombre I would have laughed. I couldn't remember Egbert being so insolent when he was younger. I was sad when I heard that the boy had been killed in a dynastic squabble in Ireland some five years later.

-ᚢ-

The rest of the army dispersed back to their homes a few days later, once I'd satisfied myself that Halfdan had kept his word and had withdrawn south of the Tees. I set off with the warriors of my warband and that of the late Ricsige's for Alnwic taking his corpse with us in a cart. For the moment I supposed that I was in charge of Bernicia until a new earl could be appointed. I had said that Egbert would succeed, but I was far from certain that the nobles and senior churchmen would agree. Underage boys were far from ideal rulers, however well advised they were.

Perhaps Ædwulf, the son of King Ælle and Ricsige's sister, Orgern, might be a contender, but he was only a few months older than his uncle, Egbert. I needed to sound out Theobald as Ædwulf's stepfather. The last thing I wanted was a rift between the southern part of Bernicia and Lothian as to who should be earl.

We buried Ricsige on a sunny day in early June in the cemetery on Lindisfarne. The holy island was bucolic, the deserted monastery seeming to add to the peace and quiet. Birds flew overhead, the only discordant note coming from the cawing of the gulls. The waves lapped the shore lazily and the few clouds that marred the bright blue sky meandered slowly above our heads. It was difficult to imagine the raids that the place had suffered in the past.

My brother took the service. I wondered what he would do now that he was no longer Ricsige's chaplain. I looked over at Egbert standing on the other side of the grave with his mother. He should be going to the monastery soon to improve his Latin and to study the Christian faith, but that wouldn't be possible if he became the earl. Perhaps Hrothwulf could become his tutor at Bebbanburg?

Egbert was a slim boy, slightly taller than most boys his age, but he needed to build up some muscle if he was to become a good warrior. I would need to find someone to train him to fight as well.

My gaze switched to Ædwulf standing with Theobald and Osgern standing next to Egbert and his mother. Although they were nearly the same age, Ædwulf had a stockier build but was shorter than his uncle. I realised that I didn't really know the boy at all. I had probably met him two or three times but, apart from a formal greeting, I hadn't spoken to him. I needed to rectify that.

I was brought back from my daydreaming with a start as Hrothwulf finished the funeral service and looked at me expectantly. I had asked to say a few words, but I hadn't prepared anything. I wanted to speak from the heart.

'I first got to know Earl Ricsige when he was around the same age as Egbert and Ædwulf are now. As most of you know, I was his military tutor and he was a good pupil. He turned out to be a good man too. Oh, he wasn't perfect, but then which of us are. I seem to recall something in the Bible about he who is without sin casting the first stone.

'He could be impetuous and he sometimes lost his temper too easily, but he saw Bernicia through the most difficult years of its existence. Only our part of England and part of Wessex remain free of the Viking menace and all credit for keeping out homes safe must go to Ricsige. He will be sorely missed. Whoever is elected as Earl in his place will have big boots to fill.'

Lindisfarne monastery was not the place to hold the funeral feast in memory of Ricsige and so we returned to Bebbanburg. We celebrated Ricsige's life in style and I had a very sore head the next day.

'You're getting old, brother, if you can't take your drink anymore,' Hrothwulf said cheerfully, giving me a friendly slap on the back as he made his way to the fortress's small church.

My family and I followed, my son giving me a knowing grin. Edgar was now six and knew too much of the world for such a young boy. I blamed my gesith. He was a favourite of theirs and they indulged him. They also told him things a six year old was better off not knowing. Eadgifu blamed me, of course.

After mass the Witan met in the king's hall. It was still called that, though its correct name was now the earls' hall. Ricsige had never wanted to be King of Northumbria; he'd have been content just ruling Bernicia. He always said that very few kings died in their beds, unless it was as monks after being forced to abdicate. In his case it had proved to be only too true. He was only twenty four when he was killed.

As I suspected the Witan recognised two candidates to succeed Ricsige; one was his brother and the other his nephew. Then some fool nominated me.

'I am deeply honoured by the trust that some of you appear to place in me,' I replied with a smile. 'But I am not of the House of Catinus. The lord of Bebbanburg has always been a member of that family ever since Bernicia and Deira united to become Northumbria. I don't believe that need change.'

What I had said wasn't quite true. There had been times when the first lord of Bebbanburg had been ousted, including Ricsige's father, Edmund. However, the stronghold had always returned to the family.

Theobald proposed his stepson, Ædwulf, as expected and I nominated Egbert. Ædwulf was invited to present his case first by the Ealdorman of Berwic, who I'd asked to preside as I was hardly impartial.

'Ealdorman Edmund was my grandfather and, although my uncle Egbert is his son, I am the son of the last King of Northumbria. I mean no disrespect to my uncle Ricsige but he never ruled over the whole of Northumbria as my father did. I know I'm young but Egbert is even younger than I am.'

'By three months,' someone called out and one or two nobles laughed.

The boy flushed with annoyance but he continued unperturbed.

'I realise that I cannot rule by myself for at least another three years so I propose that my stepfather, Ealdorman Theobald, and the Hereræswa, Drefan, be appointed as co-regents.'

As he sat down I thought it was a clever move. He sought to unite the most prominent noble in Lothian and the senior ealdorman behind him. It wasn't his idea of course; it was Theobald's, as had been the whole speech.

Egbert got up and glanced nervously at me. I had helped him decide on what to say but I didn't write it for him. Most of the ideas were his and the words certainly were.

'My brother was a great man. As Ealdorman Drefan said at his funeral, he held Bernicia together and today, when we are weakened by his untimely death, we are at peace with the Vikings to our south and to the west in Cumbria, and the Picts are weakened by the war with Halfdan and by the death of Constantín mac Cináeda at Kilrymont last month.'

This last statement drew a gasp of surprise from the members of the Witan. I had only just heard the news that the King of the Picts had been killed when he tried to oust the Norse garrison from Kilrymont just over a month ago. I had kept the news to myself but suggested to Egbert that he might like to include it whilst presenting his case.

'This means that we should be able to look forward to a relatively peaceful few years whilst I learn the art of government and complete my training to be a warrior. I mean no disrespect to my nephew but it is not the Anglo-Saxon way that inheritance follows the female line; we leave that to the Picts.'

That produced a laugh or two. In the past the Picts had followed a matriarchal line of succession, though that practice had died out now.

'I am Ealdorman Edmund's son and Earl Ricsige's brother. Unless you find some defect in me that bars me from leading you when I'm ready, I believe that you should elect me to be your earl. In the meantime I don't believe a dual regency is the best way of uniting our people and I would ask you to appoint Drefan as sole regent.'

He sat down to applause; the result was a foregone conclusion. I tried to hide my pleasure when I caught the eyes of Theobald and Ædwulf. From their expressions I had a nasty feeling that unity was an unlikely outcome.

I was sitting eating in the ealdorman's hall at Bebbanburg with my family and my gesith when the messenger arrived. Egbert and his mother had joined us, as was normal for the main meal of the day, although they lived with their servants and a few boys chosen to be the earl's companions and training partners. Hrothwulf, as the boy's tutor and chaplain lived there as well but Beornric – the young man I had chosen as military tutor to the boys – lived in my hall with the rest of my gesith.

The messenger was a monk sent by Archbishop Wulfhere, which came as something of a surprise. The archbishop knew full well the low opinion in which I held him. The monk didn't reply to my questions except to say that everything was in the letter, which he then handed to me.

My beloved Drefan,

I am writing to you as the regent of Earl Egbert as you both need to be aware of what had transpired recently, both in Ireland and subsequently here in Yorvik.

I had to smile as the thought that I was beloved by Wulfhere; he couldn't stand me any more than I could stand him. However, ever since Erdulf had started his wanderings with Saint Cuthbert's coffin, he was the only bishop left in Northumbria – a sorry state of affairs. I turned back to the letter.

When King Halfdan arrived back in Duibhlinn he found that one group of jarls had ousted him as their king and placed the boy Bárðr, the son of the barbarian Ivar the Boneless, on the throne as their puppet.

Halfdan gathered forces loyal to him and met the rebels at a place called Strangford Lough. I understand that Halfdan was killed during the battle and Bárðr was wounded, though not badly.

What happens far off across the sea is, of course, of little interest to us, but it has left Yorvik without a king. The jarls who remained here met here a few weeks ago to discuss who should succeed Halfdan, but they couldn't agree amongst themselves. No further meetings have taken place and it seems that none are planned. Each jarl appears to be content to rule his own territory with no central authority. It seems a strange state of affairs and it may be one from which we Anglo-Saxons can profit.

The letter concluded with the usual flowery phrases and, importantly, the archbishop's signature and seal.

The death of the two sons of Ragnar who had initiated the invasion of England should have been an occasion for rejoicing but I, for one, didn't feel like celebrating. Of course, it was good news for us that Halfdan had been killed but it left us in a parlous state as far as I could see.

Áed mac Cináeda had succeeded his brother as King of the Picts but he was unpredictable and unpopular. No one had any idea how he viewed his southern neighbours or what his intentions towards us might be. With the death of Halfdan the truce between us was fragile, or even might be non-existent. Certainly with no central government we could expect raids across the border.

As Christmas approached I waited apprehensively to see what the new year would bring.

Chapter Seventeen – The Perilous Path to Peace

878

In March 878 a merchant ship arrived with news of the war in Wessex. Alfred had fought several battles against Guthrum and Ubba and, although Alfred had won some engagements, Guthrum had managed to advance into Dorsetshire and had captured Wareham. Alfred had besieged the Danes there but had been unable to retake it.

It was rumoured that the Danes were running short of food and so Alfred had negotiated peace with Guthrum. They had exchanged hostages to guarantee the truce and Guthrum had sworn on a ring said to be sacred to Thor to keep the peace and to withdraw to Mercia.

The faithless Guthrum had killed the hostages and the Vikings had taken Exeter instead of withdrawing into Mercia. However, it was rumoured than it was Ubba who had murdered the Saxon hostages, forcing Guthrum to break the truce.

Some of this I'd heard already, but I wasn't aware of what had followed. Alfred had besieged Guthrum and his Danes in Exeter but learned that Ubba hadn't accompanied Guthrum. Apparently he had taken a third of their army and sailed along the south coast and before landing in Devon. The plan was to trap Alfred between the two forces.

The merchant, who was a Christian, told me that God had intervened and had sent a great storm to wreck the Viking fleet. Twelve ships had been lost and Ubba made it to shore with barely half of the number he'd set out with.

Odda, Ealdorman of Devonshire, was despatched with his warband and fyrd to forestall the Dane's plan to trap him in a pincer movement and he met Ubba and what remained of his army at a place called Arx Cynuit. Ubba was killed and Guthrum's strategy was left in tatters. He negotiated another truce with

Alfred, though why the King of Wessex trusted him after the last time was a mystery to me. At any rate this time he and his army were escorted across the border into Mercia, where they stayed for the winter – or at least part of it.

At the beginning of January Guthrum learned that Alfred was still at Chippenham, where he'd gone to celebrate Christmas. He marched south and attacked Chippenham, catching Alfred unawares. The king only had his personal gesith with him and he was forced to flee as the Danes sacked the place.

No one was certain what had happened to him after that, though there were rumours that he had taken refuge with his family and a few followers in the marshes of the Somerset Levels.

I thanked the merchant and gave him a pouch of silver. It was grim tidings indeed. If Wessex had fallen then only Bernicia remained in English hands.

The lack of central leadership in what had been Deira led to increasing raids into the territory between the River Tees and the Tyne. The Ealdormen of Hexham and Durham appealed to Earl Egbert for help in dealing with the raiders in June. It was not an appeal that he and I could ignore. There were only seven shires in Bernicia north of the Tees and Durham, in particular, was one of the most densely populated.

We mustered the fyrd and, unpopular as this was at a time when sheep were usually shorn for their wool and everyone was needed to harvest the early crops, we managed to muster over two thousand members of the fyrd. The other ealdormen and thegns kept a total of four hundred trained warriors in their warbands and the earl and I maintained another hundred.

The fleet, still commanded by Uxfrea, was a pale shadow of what it had been in Northumbria's past. Now we could only afford to man two longships, and they were away with their crews of one hundred and forty escorting our knarrs. As most of those men were trained warriors we could have done with them.

Theobald was unhappy at bringing most of his fighting men south but he accepted that an invasion by the Picts in his absence was unlikely. Their new king, Áed mac Cináeda, had lasted less than a year before he was assassinated by his own council. No one knew why exactly. He was unpopular but many kings were and their reigns weren't normally so short. However, various rumours circulated about his taste in bed partners and being accused of sodomy was probably enough reason for his untimely removal.

He'd been succeeded by his nephew, Gregory, but his right to the throne was contested by his distant cousin Eochaid, the King of Strathclyde. Whilst the two struggled for the crown there was little risk of trouble in Lothian from the Picts.

It was the end of May when we reached the Tees at Darlington, where there was a ford. Obviously the Norsemen of Yorvik knew of our advance towards their territory and had assembled an army to oppose us. As dark fell we made camp on the north bank and dug defensive works on our side of the ford.

The next day dawned bright and clear, if a little chilly until the sun warmed up the air. I rode down to the ford with Egbert and the ealdormen of Durham and Hexham, Dunstan and Badda – both in their early twenties, and Karl as interpreter. Egbert had just turned twelve and, at thirty one, I felt quite elderly by comparison.

The jarls who rode down from their camp to meet us were much older though. There were seven of them ranging in age from mid-thirties to early fifties. I was surprised to see Archbishop Wulfhere with them but realised that they had probably brought him as their interpreter. We rode into the water and met them in the middle of the ford.

'Greetings Earl Egbert, ealdormen, why do you come here threatening war? Do you intend to deliberately break the peace agreed with King Halfdan?' the archbishop began.

I realised then that Wulfhere wasn't just an interpreter, he was one of the leaders of their army.

'Why are you with these pagans, archbishop? Are you an apostate who has abandoned your faith?'

'No certainly not!' he spat back. 'However, after the unfortunate death of King Halfdan, the Thing of Jorvik, the equivalent of our Witan, asked me to administer the kingdom until they can agree on a successor.'

'The Thing is, I think, a meeting of all freemen, so not like a Witan which is a council of nobles and senior clerics. I rather think that the jarls are using you in the same way as they did that puppet king, Ecgberht. Tell me, Wulfhere, does your administration include collecting taxes for them?'

The archbishop had the grace to blush before he began to bluster.

'You are splitting hairs. You haven't said why you intend to invade Jorvik; on what pretext have you come here to threaten these peaceful Norse settlers?'

'Peaceful settlers? They have got you dancing to their tune, haven't they Wulfhere; or have you forgotten the thousands of Northumbrians who have died defending their land from these heathens? Do you condone the cruel murder of Saint Edmund of East Anglia as part of their peaceful settlement too?'

'No, of course not. However, that is all in the past. All the Norsemen want now is to be allowed to live the lives of peaceful farmers.'

'If that is so, why then do they raid across the Tees and pillage south Hexhamshire and Durhamshire?'

'That maybe a few young hotheads, but it is not with the permission of these jarls.'

By now the said jarls were beginning to mutter amongst themselves, no doubt wondering what Wulfhere and I were discussing. One of them barked a question at Wulfhere and Karl whispered to me that he was asking whether I had agreed to surrender all the land south of the Tyne yet. I nodded my thanks.

'So Wulfhere, these peaceful jarls have come here intending to cross the Tees and take the sires of Hexham and Durham by force. Is that the act of the peaceful farmers you portray them as?

Enough talk. If they think that they can defeat us I invite them to try.'

As we trotted back Egbert asked me brusquely what was going on and why I hadn't consulted him during the negotiations. He was evidently irate at being left out of the discussion.

'Because there was no negotiation, lord,' I said trying to soothe his hurt pride. 'They have come here to move the border up to the Tyne and we have to stop them; it's as simple as that.'

'Wouldn't it be better to give them what they want? I don't want to risk losing everything.'

'No it wouldn't,' I said, rather too impatiently. 'Show weakness to these people and they will just demand more. They have broken the agreement we reached with Halfdan and the only argument that they will understand now is force.'

I rode back to our camp in a foul mood. I had enough to worry about without trying to placate a twelve year old who thought he knew enough to make all the decisions. What he didn't appreciate was that to the Vikings we were no more than a useful buffer between them and the Picts. With the latter bickering amongst themselves for now, it seemed we were no longer useful to them. It was short sighted of them, of course. Sooner or later the Picts would unite behind one leader, and if that leader was Eochaid, then Strathclyde and Pictland unified as the Kingdom of Alba would pose a real threat to us all.

-ᛈ-

I was awoken in the middle of the night by shouting and the clash of arms. The Vikings had crept across the ford in the darkness and taken our less than alert sentries by surprise. A fierce fight for the defensive works we had built on our side of the ford was in progress but as more and more of our warriors rushed to counterattack, the Norsemen were pushed back into those seeking to follow them across the ford.

They were fighting on too narrow a front to win, however many men they threw against us, and eventually they withdrew, taking their dead and wounded with them.

Egbert was incensed at what he saw as the Viking's underhand tactics and refused to listen when I, supported by others, tried to explain that a night attack was a perfectly legitimate way of conducting a battle. It was our sentries who were to blame for not being alert.

Unfortunately there were other hotheads who were prepared to follow him and attack the Viking camp. An argument developed between the young earl and his supporters and the ealdormen who counselled against a reprisal raid. In the end Egbert ignored me and his other nobles and gathered together a force which he then led across the ford.

Of course, the Vikings weren't about to be taken by surprise, especially as they must have heard the commotion in our camp and then the splashing of men crossing the river. Egbert made no attempt to try and cross silently but rushed at it like a crazed bull.

The outcome was inevitable. There was a brief skirmish on the far bank and then our men were driven back. Egbert had only just started his military training and was evidently no match for the Viking he fought with as he tried to exit the river. The man cut him down with his first blow and his body was washed downstream. When we recovered it we saw that his head had been half severed from his torso.

I was in despair. Once again Bernicia was without a ruler and we were faced by a Viking army intent on eroding what little territory we Anglo-Saxons had left. The next morning I rode down to the ford once again accompanied by Dunstan, Badda and Karl.

The enemy were, of course, elated at having killed our earl but soon realised that his removal had only served to unite us. Negotiations were inconclusive but I least I managed to extract a promise from them that they wouldn't try to force the crossing that night. We parted agreeing to meet again the next day.

However, we received information that evening which strengthened our hand. A rider came galloping in from

Bebbanburg with tidings from Wessex. Alfred was no longer skulking in the marshes of the Somerset Levels. He had sent out messengers as soon as winter was over for the ealdormen of Somerset, Devon and Hampshire to meet him with their warbands and fyrds at a place known as Egbert's Stone near Selwood in early May.

Alfred had won a decisive victory in the ensuing Battle of Edington. He then chased the Danes back to their stronghold at Chippenham and starved them into submission. It was a great victory and Alfred had insisted that one of the non-negotiable terms of the surrender was that Guthrum convert to Christianity. The Danish leader and thirty of his jarls were baptised with Alfred sponsoring Guthrum as his godson.

Guthrum agreed to quit Wessex and in return Alfred recognised the Dane as King of East Anglia. The fate of Mercia remained unresolved but the two kings agreed that they would meet again the following year to partition it between them.

It was tremendous news. It meant that Wessex had been saved and, furthermore, peace had been agreed between the West Saxons and the Danes. The Norse of Yorvik would be on their own if they continued to pursue a war of conquest.

'You have heard what has happened in the rest of England, I presume,' I asked Wulfhere when we met again.

This time the weather wasn't so kind to us and we met in a rainstorm which quickly drenched everyone. The sensation of cold water trickling down the back of my neck made me determined to keep the meeting short.

'Yes, I'm surprised the news of the treaty between Alfred and King Guthrum has reached you so quickly,' he replied.

'We aren't quite as isolated up here as you might think. Now, your friends have two alternatives. They can try and force the ford or they can agree to leave the border between us on the Tees and promise not to raid into Bernicia. Which is it to be?'

'You are without your earl and so leaderless after his foolish attack last night.'

'That wasn't my idea and, until the Witan elect a new earl, I am in command as the Hereræswa. At least we have an experienced leader. Who commands your rabble? You, Wulfhere? Or are you led by a council of jarls. That is hardly a sensible way to fight a war.'

The archbishop turned to the jarls behind him and they conferred in Norse for some time, the discussion getting more heated as the time dragged on. I was fed up with sitting in the downpour, which showed no sign of easing up. Eventually I'd had enough.

'This is pointless. I'm going back to get dry. I suggest that you do the same, Wulfhere. When you have agreed what you want to do, you know where I am.'

With that we turned our horses around and went back to our camp.

I heard nothing further that day but Theobald came to see me in the afternoon.

'I assume that you are happy to accept Ædwulf as earl now that fool Egbert is dead?' he stated without preamble.

From the way he said it he evidently expected an argument.

'Yes, he is the last survivor of the House of Bebbanburg and the son of the last king of all Northumbria. I just hope that he isn't as pig-headed and stupid as his cousin was.'

Theobald smiled.

'No, I consider him to be a thoughtful, diligent and sensible lad. He is undoubtedly clever and if he has a fault, it's that he is too serious for a boy of his age.'

'Hmm, he didn't come across like that when he spoke at the last meeting of the Witan.'

'That was because I coached him in what to say.'

'Very well. As all the ealdormen are present, even if the abbots aren't, I suggest that we convene here in an hour's time to confirm his election. We can then write to the abbots asking them to confirm their agreement.'

'It'll be too late if they don't,' Theobald pointed out.

'Yes, it's just a courtesy so they don't feel ignored.'

This time it was the Norsemen who were waiting for us at the ford. The sky was overcast but, so far at least, the rain had held off. The wind was strong enough to cause ripples on the river, but it wasn't cold.

'If you pull back your forces we'll do the same,' Wulfhere said without preamble.

Then he noticed thirteen year old Ædwulf sitting on his mare beside me.

'I see you've got another boy to rule you. Do you have a thing for young boys?' he continued with a leer.

'No, I leave that to priests and monks,' I replied with a grin. 'Forgive me. I didn't have a chance to introduce you. This is Earl Ædwulf, the son of King Ælle.'

The mention of the hated Ælle's name caused a stir amongst the jarls with Wulfhere and they began firing questions at him in Norse. He held up his hand for quiet and they withdrew to the far bank to confer.

'Can you hear what they're saying?' I asked Karl quietly.

'It's difficult to hear everything over the sound of the river but I caught Ælle's name quite a lot.'

He listened intently and then leaned over to whisper in my ear.

'They are determined to kill Ædwulf. I am fairly certain they plan to withdraw and then double back and cross here tomorrow, follow us and catch us unprepared.'

'Well done Karl; I suspected as much.'

'That's why you mentioned King Ælle's name, wasn't it.'

I merely smiled but said nothing. I wasn't happy for both sides to tamely withdraw, even if the Norse jarls hadn't planned to attack us. The question of the shires of Durham and Hexham south of the Tyne had to be resolved one way or the other before our army was allowed to disperse. Now they had played into my hands and we could ambush the duplicitous Vikings and send them back home with a bloody nose. Perhaps that would teach them a lesson.

The archbishop and the jarls came back to where we were waiting.

'Very well, we will both withdraw immediately and be clear of the area by the time the sun is at its zenith.'

'If you mean midday, why don't you say so,' snapped Ædwulf before I could reply. 'How do I know I can trust you? Even if you swear on a bible that doesn't bind those heathens behind you.'

At first I was annoyed that Ædwulf had suddenly taken over the negotiations, but as he spoke it seemed that he and I thought along the same lines and I was intrigued to see to how he would handle things.

'We are men of honour, even these pagan jarls. If they swear on something sacred to their gods I assure you that you can trust them.'

'I seem to recall that Guthrum once swore on an arm ring sacred to some mythical being called Thor to seal a truce with King Alfred. However, it didn't stop him killing his hostages and breaking the truce as soon as Alfred's back was turned.'

'He's a Dane,' Wulfhere said contemptuously. 'These men are Norse; quite different.'

'Not so very different if they believe in the same gods. It was Ivar and Halfdan who gave my father the blood eagle, or so I'm told. Were they dishonourable Danes then?'

'Your father killed theirs. They were entitled to their revenge.'

'You have been living with the heathens too long, archbishop.' Ædwulf's lip curled in contempt. 'You are more like them than you are your own kind if you can say such a thing. I would challenge you, were we not meeting during a truce.'

Wulfhere backed his horse away in fright and at the rage in the young earl's eyes.

'I think we are done here, Wulfhere. Take your pack of mangy curs back to Yorvik or whatever you are calling Eoforwīc now. Come north of the Tees and we will kill you, archbishop or not.'

'Well done, Ædwulf, you will make a fine earl,' told him, biting my tongue to stop myself adding when you are older. It would sound patronising.

'What happens now? Do we just go home?' he asked.

I glanced behind me to make sure we were not overheard.

'Far from it. Between us we said enough to goad them. They intend to cross after we leave and attack us whilst we are unprepared in any case. Now they will be thirsting for our blood. But it's not us who will be taken unawares; instead we'll be the ambushers.'

-Ⅴ-

The weather had changed for the better when I awoke the next day. We had travelled a mere five miles along the valley of the River Skerne that first day before we made camp but I had put a screen of scouts behind us to watch for the Norsemen. Sure enough they waited until we had disappeared and then they had crossed behind us. It had taken the rest of that day and they'd camped where we had on the north bank.

We moved ten miles north on the second day and camped on open ground enclosed on three sides by a bend in the river like an ox bow. One of the party of scouts came in at dusk to say that five hundred mounted Vikings had bypassed us to the west and were waiting to bar our path five or so miles to the north. The main body on foot were still a few miles behind us. Obviously they planned to trap us in a pincer movement.

No doubt they counted on the fyrd - the least experienced fighters and the poorest armed - being at the rear. When attacked by seasoned Viking warriors they could be expected to panic and be routed fairly easily. It would have been a good plan had we not guessed what they planned to do.

Instead of continuing our march north the next day we went away from the river and into the large wood to the west of the open space where we'd camped the night before. There we waited, our nerves on edge. What if I'd misjudged what the Vikings were up to? What if their scouts had spotted our ambush and had gone back to tell their jarls? They could be advancing through the wood to take us unawares.

It was all foolishness, of course. Had they done that we'd have heard them coming from a mile off. I had nearly given up hope by midday when it was still deathly quiet, but then their first mounted scouts appeared on the track.

I was worried that they would check the woods but they just continued along the track, not talking, but their focus was straight ahead and they were in column instead of being spread out. Doubtless they were looking out for stragglers from our army. That would tell them that they were getting close.

I let the scouts pass and everyone tensed, ready for action. It was a good quarter of an hour before the main body of Vikings appeared. Their vanguard moved across the open ground to our front, leaving the river bank to follow the track which led directly to the end of the curve in the river.

I'd hoped that the rear of the column would have entered the ambush zone before the vanguard moved out of sight, but they were spread out and only some twelve hundred had appeared by the time that the head of the column passed out of sight.

I had a choice. I could wait for the rear-guard or attack before the vanguard got too far away. I chose the former but sent my hundred horsemen to bypass the vanguard, get ahead of them and block their advance. I was confident that their own horsemen were too far away to be aware of what was happening, especially as the trees to the north would deaden the sound of battle.

Once I calculated that my horsemen had enough time to get into position I sprang the ambush. Three hundred of my men had bows and they opened the attack, running clear of the trees and firing volley after volley into the column of Vikings; some aiming directly at those in the left hand file and others sending their arrows up at high trajectory to strike those in the centre and far side of the column.

The Norsemen were caught completely by surprise. All had their shields slung on their backs and many were carrying their helmets. Three volleys struck home before they reacted and formed themselves into a shield wall. By then my archers had killed or wounded over two hundred of them.

However, that still left a thousand and they were after blood! Their shield wall five men deep advanced towards us. These weren't young novices, they were veterans in the main and they didn't make the mistake of rushing us. They kept the line straight and ensured that their shields stayed overlapping one another. After one last volley at high trajectory into the middle and rear ranks, my archers ran back, unstrung their bows – placing them on the ground at the rear – and ran back to their places in our line, either in the fyrd or amongst the first two ranks of warriors.

We had more men and therefore the benefit of greater weight when it came to shoving shield against shield. Of course, we attempted to stab our adversaries as we heaved against the enemy wall and every so often a man would fall. As soon as he did another man stepped forward to take his place. For this work our short seaxes were ideal. Swords were too long and unwieldy and spears were even worse at such close quarters.

My first opponent was an axeman, but as soon as he raised his weapon to bring it down on me I stabbed him in the armpit. He howled in pain and rage, but he was bleeding copiously and rapidly losing strength. He was quickly pulled to the rear, still yelling and swearing, by those behind him. The next man tried to step back to bring his sword into play, but I followed him into the gap and stuck my seax into his neck. In doing so my left side was covered by my shield but my right was exposed.

The Viking on that side tried to stab me with his spear but Hybald chopped off the point with his seax. The man dropped the useless haft and took a step back to give himself room to draw his sword. He never got the chance. I grabbed the top of his shield with my right hand, letting go of my seax so that it dangled from the leather strap around my wrist. I butted him in the face with my helmeted head and his own nose guard crushed his nose to a pulp and broke several teeth. He reeled backwards and I flicked my wrist, catching the hilt of my seax as it flew upwards. Before he could recover I thrust the point upwards into his mouth and into the base of his brain.

There was no more time for killing. The rear ranks made a concerted effort to push us forward and I found myself trying to keep my feet as we advanced over prone bodies and blood slicked grass.

As we advanced, pushing the Vikings before us, they were forced back into the spit of land formed by the curve in the river. I was almost crushed by the pressure behind me and in front of me and I struggled to breathe, but we were gradually gaining ground. At one point I thought my left arm might break and, in desperation, I managed to free my right arm sufficiently to thrust the point of my seax into the thigh of the man opposite me.

He howled in pain and I must have severed something important because his right leg collapsed under him. He tried to thrust his sword into my groin as I stepped over him but I kicked it aside. I bent my knees and shoved the point of my seax into his throat, then I was pushed onwards and I stumbled, nearly falling to the ground. I managed to stand and once more the pressure behind me forced me onwards.

From where I was in the thick of things I had no idea what was going on elsewhere, of course, but I later learned that the leading Norsemen had turned around when they heard the sound of battle behind them and charged into our left flank. They had nearly succeeded in routing them when our horsemen appeared somewhat belatedly and charged into the rear of the enemy vanguard, throwing their spears before cutting them down like stalks of wheat before a scythe.

Our horsemen withdrew before they could be surrounded and pulled off their mounts and then they charged again. The Vikings weren't used to fighting this way and tried to get out of the way of the oncoming horses. Had they formed a shield wall and used their spears to resemble a hedgehog they could have withstood our attacks, but they didn't.

From where I was I thought I could hear faint splashing sounds above the din of battle. We had forced the Norsemen back to the river bank; now some of them were either being pushed into the water or were trying to make their escape across the river. It wasn't a formidable obstacle, not like the Tyne for example, as it was only six yards across at the narrowest point, but it was quite deep in the middle and fast flowing. Some men were swept away whilst those in chainmail sank. Most Vikings were good swimmers but not good enough once they were sucked into the current.

By this time men on both sides were nearing exhaustion and I gave the order for my army to pull back a little. It took time for the order to reach everyone, but slowly our shield wall edged back ten paces or so and stood facing the Vikings warily, waiting for them to attack.

Theobald, who I'd put in command of the horsemen, came riding up with a grin to tell me that the vanguard had been routed and were fleeing with his men in pursuit. I smiled back, albeit a trifle wearily, and congratulated him.

It was difficult to estimate numbers, but I thought that there couldn't be more than seven hundred Vikings left between us and the river. No doubt we had suffered a lot of casualties too, but looking along our line I estimated that we now outnumbered the enemy by more than two to one.

One of their jarls stepped forward from their line and looked left and then right. Three more jarls went and joined him. I assumed that the others had fallen. Unsurprisingly, there was no sign of the archbishop.

I too stepped forward and Ædwulf came and joined me. I had placed him in command of the rear ranks of the fyrd to keep him safe, but I noted that his byrnie, arms and face were covered in blood – thankfully not his. I was told later that he had pushed his way to the front rank and had managed to kill two men before someone realised that he was there. Two members of my gesith had unceremoniously pulled him back to the rear and kept him there, much to his fury.

Karl appeared at my other side and faced the four jarls.

'You invaded my land after you swore not to,' Ædwulf said angrily.

When Karl translated the four jarls looked at one another but no one replied to the accusation.

'What are your terms for allowing us to collect our dead and wounded and return south of the Tees?' one of them asked.

'What do you think, lord?' I asked Ædwulf.

The angry look faded from his eyes and he looked pleased that I had consulted him.

'If we let them go, what's to say they won't just come back some other time?'

'We could take hostages, I suppose. They have lost a lot of men today and achieved nothing. I'm not sure that they'll think it worth it to cross the Tees again in the near future. They will try again, of course, but not for a while.'

He nodded.

'I can't think of any other options,' he admitted.

'Karl, explain that we will pick twenty hostages at random to guarantee a truce for five years. If they break the truce, or any of their men do, then the hostages will be hung and their bodies left to rot; and we'll invade Jorvik. They will hand over their weapons and we will return them once we reach the far side of the Tees. If they agree to our conditions we will escort them to make sure no one gets, er, lost.'

Once Karl had explained the terms the jarls withdrew and there was a heated discussion. Evidently the youngest one was in favour of fighting on rather than submitting. I decided that he would be one of the hostages. Eventually they came back to say that they accepted our terms.

-ᛉ-

We took Egbert's body back to bury it next to his brother in the deserted monastery on Lindisfarne, but we had to bury the rest of our dead near where they had fallen. We had lost just over three hundred, including six thegns. Another hundred were seriously wounded and we'd probably lose over half of those.

The Norsemen had suffered far worse though. We calculated that they must have suffered between five and six hundred killed and some two hundred of their wounded were unlikely to survive the journey back south. In total they had lost a third of their army.

It was a heavy price to pay for peace – on both sides – but at least we had secure borders now; or as secure as they could be in these troubled times.

As I rode back to Bebbanburg beside Ædwulf I couldn't help thinking that perhaps the most significant thing to come out of this campaign wasn't the defeat of the Vikings, but the exchange of a petulant boy for a promising young man as the Earl of Bernicia.

Epilogue

Summer 927

King Æthelstan sat under a specially constructed awning outside the gates of the city of Jorvik as Godfraid, a grandson of Ivar the Boneless, rode towards him accompanied by his jarls and a collection of Irish chieftains. Godfraid had seized the throne of Jorvik after the death of his brother, Sitric, killing Sitric's sons, his nephews, in the process. Ever since 902, when the Norsemen of Duibhlinn had invaded and captured Jorvik, a descendant of Ivar's had ruled the city and the surrounding territory, but no more.

The struggle between the Anglo-Saxons under Alfred and then his son Edward and grandson Æthelstan, had continues sporadically for half a century. For decades England had been partitioned between the Danelaw in the north and Wessex in the south with the Earls of Bebbanburg maintaining their independence north of the Tyne. The struggle for the disputed territory between the Tees and the Tyne having finally been won by the Norsemen.

Several of Æthelstan's senior ealdormen sat with him for the negotiations with Godfraid but at his right hand sat Ealdred of Bebbanburg, Ædwulf's eldest son and the earl for the past fourteen years.

The past fifty years hadn't been easy ones for Bernicia. The kingdoms north of the border had been united into one called Alba by Constantine, the son of Áed mac Cináeda, and his desire to extend his southern border down to the Twaid was no secret. Lothian had resisted up to now but Alba was growing increasingly powerful.

Behind Ealdred stood his brother, Uhtred, Ealdorman of Islandshire. Drefan had died peacefully in his bed in 899, the same year as King Alfred. His son Edgar had succeeded him but his son had died childless. However, Edgar's daughter had married

Uhtred. Drefan's male line may have come to an end, but his grandson would one day sit in his chair in the hall at Alnwic.

The negotiations were protracted but in the end Godfraid agreed to return to Duibhlinn with his Norse and Irish followers. Æthelstan could at last call himself King of the English.

One of the first things the king did was to reunite Northumbria and make Ealdred its first earl. No longer did it include the shires west of the Pennines – Cumbria was part of the sub-kingdom of Strathclyde along with the northern half of Luncæstershire; the area around Chester now being incorporated into the Earldom of Mercia. Nevertheless Deira and Bernicia were now one again.

'Will you make Jorvik your capital now Ealdred?' Æthelstan had asked before he returned to Winchester.

'I think not, Cyning. Godfraid may have left with his heathens and, although Jorvik is now a mainly Christian city and the seat of the archbishop, it still reeks of its Viking past. No, I shall return to Bebbanburg and make Archbishop Hrotheweard governor here.'

The king nodded before asking another question.

'What about Lindisfarne? Now that the Viking menace has gone, will you encourage Bishop Wigred to move from Conganis back there?'

'I suspect he wouldn't want to, even if I asked him to. I believe that he's more inclined to relocate his cathedra in Durham.'

'It is more central to his diocese I suppose.'

'What about you, Cyning, now that England is unified and pacified?'

'Pacified maybe, for the moment, but far from united. My half-brother Edwin thinks he should sit on my throne and he has his supporters. Constantine is too powerful as King of Alba for my peace of mind too. You and your predecessors have done well to keep Lothian part of Bernicia. Make sure you keep it that way. Northumbria has other enemies too across the Pennines. You'll need to keep your wits about you if you want to hang on to your earldom.'

-Ⅴ-

As Ealdred rode back to Bebbanburg a month later his people were harvesting the crops and the sun shone out of a clear, azure sky. Even the German Ocean looked a deep inviting blue instead of its normal steel grey colour. Birds tweeted and twittered in the trees and it all looked like an idyllic pastoral scene.

'What are you thinking about?' Uhtred asked as he rode beside him, noting the happy smile on his brother's face.

'About how lucky we are to live here. Now all we have to do is hang onto it.'

The smile faded, to be replaced by a look of grim determination.

'That might not be as easy as we thought, if Æthelstan is right.'

'Why? What's he said to you?'

'We've always known that Constantine has his greedy eyes on Lothian. Now he has had word from his agents in Alba that Constantine is making preparations to invade.'

Uhtred sighed.

'Well then, we had better train the next batch of boys to be warriors then, hadn't we?'

THE END

AUTHOR'S NOTE

This the last book in the series and so I have included a very brief synopsis of the history of Northumbria after the year 900 as well as an explanatory note about the period covered in this novel.

865 to 900

Ragnar's Sons

The main events following the invasion by the Great Heathen Army are fairly well documented; those affecting Northumbria, particularly Bernicia, less well so. The main events as depicted in this novel are based on what is recorded though, as is often the case for this period, there are conflicting accounts and not all records use the same names for what appear to be the same person. For example Halfdan may be the same person as Hvitserk, which means white shirt, so this may have been a nickname.

Ivar's own nickname, the Boneless, may be a mistranslation. Exosus could easily have been interpreted by someone whose Latin was imperfect as ex (without) os (bones), thus the Boneless. The actual meaning of exosus is the hated. He disappears from accounts of the Great Heathen Army in England in 870 when Halfdan takes over command. Some sources think he is identical to Ímar (Old Norse Ivar) in the Irish annals but this man may not have been a son of Ragnar. I have assumed that they are one and the same and that Ivar died in Ireland in 873.

Ubba is another enigma. A monk writing in the twelfth century states that he was a son of Ragnar but a contemporary source describes Ubba as a dux of the Frisians, dux being Latin for leader or chieftain. Although not recorded by name it seems possible that he was commander of the fleet sent to land in Devon to trap the Saxons, acting in conjunction with Guthrum's army, in a pincer movement.

We do know that the Viking commander of this fleet was killed in a battle at Arx Cynuit. The exact location is unknown but it may have been Countisbury in North Devon. The Saxon commander was Odda, the Ealdorman of Devonshire, but the name of the leader of the Vikings is not recorded. However, there is a burial mound in Devon called Ubba's Barrow. Ubba may therefore have been the leader of the defeated Vikings at Arx Cynuit. Other sources state that Ubba was killed in Yorkshire.

It is unclear whether Ivar or Halfdan was the leader of the force that captured and destroyed the fortress of Dumbarton (Dùn Breatainn) after a siege of many months. Ivar married a princess of Strathclyde and had a son, Sigtrygg, by her. However, this was all supposed to have happened during 870 when the Viking army was in Wessex. If it's true, Ivar must have left the army whilst it was in East Anglia over the winter of 869/870.

After the fall of Mercia in 874 the Great Heathen Army split into two; the Danes under Guthrum headed back to Wessex and the Norse under Halfdan headed north. Some accounts say that he captured Caer Luel (Carlisle) and Hexham before laying waste to Bernicia. He may have also fought against the Picts. Other sources say that he didn't venture north of the Tyne.

In 875 Halfdan was apparently in Ireland trying to regain the throne which had been held by his brother Ivar before he was killed two years previously. In 876 he returned to Yorvik (York) to be crowned king there before returning the Ireland where he was killed in battle the following year.

The Tales of Ragnar's Sons record that Sigurd inherited Zealand, Scania, Halland, the Danish islands, and Viken from his father, Ragnar and that he later succeeded his brother Halfdan as King of Denmark after he was killed in 877. Sigurd married Blaeja, the daughter of king Ælle of Northumbria and they had four children. The records of Danish Monarchs of this period are unclear. Bagsecg is listed as dying in 871 and this is consistent with his recorded death at the Battle of Ashdown in 871. However, one list of Danish kings includes Halfdan from 871 to 877, but at this time he was in England and Ireland.

Sigurd is variously recorded as king from 877 after Halfdan's death but is also shown as king earlier than this. If Halfdan was king he seems to have been an absentee one and I have assumed that Sigurd left the Viking army after the defeat at Ashdown to take the vacant throne.

Even less is known about Björn Ironside. According to the Hervarar Saga, *the sons of Björn Ironside were Eric and Refil. The latter was a warrior-prince and sea-king. King Eric ruled the Swedish realm after his father and lived but a short time. Then Eric the son of Refil (i.e. Björn's grandson) succeeded to the kingdom.* This would tend to confirm that Björn was King of Sweden, or at least much of it, and didn't take part in the invasion of England by the Great Heathen Army.

The House of Bebbanburg

According to Symeon of Durham *in 876 the pagan king Halfdene divided between himself and his followers the country of the Northumbrians. Ricsige, King of the Northumbrians, died, and Egbert the Second reigned over the Northumbrians beyond the river Tyne.*

It's not clear if Ricsige was king of all Northumbria between 872, when Ecgberht was deposed, and 876 when Halfdan Ragnarsson took the throne for himself. There seems to have been an interregnum between Halfdan's death in 877 and the accession of Guthred in 883 to the kingdom of Jorvik, so it's quite possible there was also one between 872 and 876 as well but I have assumed that Ricsige ruled over what was left of Northumbria for those four years.

There is no reliable record of how Ricsige died. Roger of Wendover, an English chronicler in the 13th century, reports that Ricsige died of a broken heart after the partition (of the Kingdom of Northumbria), but that first happened in 866 and Roger was writing over three hundred years later.

Ricsige was succeeded by Ecgberht II as ruler (called king, high reeve of Bamburgh and earl in various sources) of Bernicia in 876 and he died in either 878 or 883. I have used a simplified version of his name, Egbert, to try and avoid confusion with King Ecgberht, the Viking vassal.

Egbert was followed by Eadulf, possibly a grandson of King Ælle. I have also changed his name slightly - to Ædulf - again to avoid possible confusion as so many names of this period began with an 'E'.

After 900

England

After the death of Alfred the Great on the twenty sixth of October 899, the conflict between the Danes and the Anglo-Saxons of Wessex, Mercia and East Anglia continued. During the lifetime of his son, Edward (899 to 924), that part of Mercia outside the Danelaw was merged with Wessex and Edward called himself King of the Anglo-Saxons. However, the first to call himself King of the English was Edward's son, Æthelstan (924 to 939). By then England was more or less unified.

A period of relative peace followed until the invasion of Sweyn Forkbeard, King of Denmark, in 1013. He defeated Æthelred (often called incorrectly the Unready, the correct translation being 'the ill-advised') and drove him into exile. Æthelred returned in 1014 after Sweyn's death.

When he died two years later his son Edmund Ironside succeeded him briefly until Cnut (or Canute) arrived to claim the throne. After a number of battles a truce was agreed but Edmund died shortly afterwards. Cnut became King of England and he was followed by two more Danish kings.

When the last one – Harthacnut - died in 1042, Edward the Confessor, a Saxon brought up in Normandy, became the last king of the House of Wessex. The story of his death in January 1066, the election of Harold Godwinson to the throne and his subsequent defeat and death at the hands of William the Conqueror are too well known to require repetition here.

Northumbria and Bebbanburg (Bamburgh)

Eadulf (or Ædulf) ruled until 913 and was followed by his son, Ealdred. Some records imply that Ealdred only ruled part of Bernicia. Possibly the Picts had encroached into Lothian by that stage. In 933 Æthelstan, King of the English, is listed as the overlord of all Northumbria and so it's probable that Ealdred was the last earl (or king?) of an independent Bernicia. In 934 Æthelstan invaded Scotland so this would tend to confirm his mastery over Bernicia by that stage.

When Æthelstan conquered the Danes in the south of Northumbria and became King of the English, Ealdred – the king's half-brother - was appointed Earl of Northumbria. Initially he faced some opposition from the Danes, but in 954 Northumbria officially became part of the Kingdom of England. However, the earldom seems to have reverted to Ealdred's family at some stage.

Meanwhile at Bebbanburg, Ealdred's grandson, Osulf, had two sons who succeeded him in turn – Eadwulf the Evil Child (today we would probably say 'bad boy'), who was earl from 963 to 993 and Waltheof (994 to 1006).

The latter's son, Uhtred the Bold, was killed at the Battle of Carham in 1016 or 1018 (the year is disputed and even the exact location is unknown) when Malcolm II, King of Scots and Owen the Bald, King of Strathclyde, defeated the combined forces of Earl Uhtred and the Archbishop of York.

Lothian had been disputed between Scotland and Northumbria for much of the tenth century. After Carham it remained permanently part of Scotland, with only Berwick upon Tweed changing hands between Scotland and England thereafter.

Berwick finally came under English rule for the last time in 1482 when Richard of Gloucester (later Richard III) captured it during the Wars of the Roses.

The records of the period after Uhtred are incomplete as far as the lord of Bebbanburg (at some stage the name changed to Bamburgh) is concerned but the list is thought to be as follows:

- Eadwulf II 'Cudel' of Bamburgh (died 1019), son of Waltheof of Bamburgh
- Ealdred II of Bamburgh (died 1038), son of Uhtred the Bold
- Eadwulf III of Bamburgh (died 1041), son of Uhtred the Bold
- No recorded earl during the period 1041–65
- Osulf II of Bamburgh (1065–67), son of Eadwulf III of Bamburgh

After 1067 Bamburgh was probably held, albeit briefly, by Gospatrick, Earl of Northumbria. In 1068 he fled north of the border to escape the Normans and became Earl of Lothian. Bamburgh became a royal castle and it remained so until 1610 when it was abandoned as a stronghold, its defensive role having ceased after the Union of the Crowns of England and Scotland.

The last Earl of Northumbria was Robert de Mowbray, a Norman, who was in post from 1086 until 1095 when he was deposed for rebelling against King William Rufus. Prince Henry of Scotland and then his son, King William the Lion, held the title in the twelfth century but they regarded the earldom as part of Scotland. King William was the last Earl of Northumbria.

After a long gap Henry Percy became the first Earl of Northumberland (a shire, as distinct from the region of Northumbria) in 1381. His seat was at Alnwick where the present Duke of Northumberland still lives.

Bamburgh Castle (Bebbanburg) had a chequered history after 1610 until it was bought and restored by the industrialist, Lord Armstrong, in 1894. If you visit, even though the coastline has changed a little over the centuries, it's not difficult to imagine the Anglo-Saxon lords of Bebbanburg standing on the ramparts and looking across the bay to the monastery of Lindisfarne.

NOVELS IN THE KINGS OF NORTHUMBRIA SERIES

Whiteblade
616 to 634 AD

Warriors of the North
634 to 642 AD

Bretwalda
642 to 656 AD

The Power and the Glory
656 to 670 AD

The Fall of the House of Æthelfrith
670 to 730 AD

Treasons, Stratagems and Spoils
737 to 796 AD

The Wolf and the Raven
821 to 862 AD

The Sons of the Raven
865 to 927 AD

27105830R00124

Printed in Great Britain
by Amazon